I0687544

The Paris Notebook

by

Cynthia Harrison

The Paris Notebook

Cover Art by *Angela Anderson*

The Wild Rose Press, Inc.
PO Box 708
Adams Basin, NY 14410-0708
Visit us at www.thewildrosepress.com

Publishing History
First Champagne Rose Edition, 2012
Digital ISBN 978-1-61217-268-2
Print ISBN 978-1-61217-348-1

Published in the United States of America

On the way up her stairs, Jack stayed a few steps behind her. Probably looking up her skirt. Good. She'd worn the new thong.

She turned to Jack at the door, and their bodies clashed full-on for the first time. Desire wrapped around them and squeezed. But the thong was damned uncomfortable. She'd never liked them.

"Sorry," Jack said.

She just smiled. He loved sweets and she'd made his favorite. The perfect way to win a man: sexy underwear and fresh baked goods.

"I know you just had dessert, but I made you a batch of chocolate chip cookies." Seriously out of practice in seduction, she needed another sip or two of wine before whatever was going to happen between them.

"I'll be just a sec." She headed into the bathroom, where she slid off her thong and threw it into the hamper. She checked her reflection in the mirror, smoothing gloss over her lips while predictable Jack scouted the kitchen for cookies. "Would it be inappropriate to ask for a glass of milk?"

"Sure." She left the bathroom and moved around her kitchen, pouring milk and wine, whisking the plastic wrap from the plate of cookies she'd set on top of the fridge earlier.

Jack came up behind her as she worked at the counter. He pressed against her, grabbing a cookie. His appreciation of the glimpse of thong on the steps made itself known through the thin material of her skirt. He bit into the cookie and kissed her on the cheek. He didn't move away.

"Crumbs." She wiped her face with her hand and turned around. Their eyes met for a long moment, and then, for the first time since she'd known him, Jack Karris put down an unfinished cookie. And he kissed her.

Praise for *THE PARIS NOTEBOOK*

"*THE PARIS NOTEBOOK* was totally unputdownable. I LOVE IT! It was so fun to drop everything and read it—I have done almost nothing else since I got it, inhaling it like a yummy plate of nachos because I was enjoying it so much. The likeable characters are so likeable, the villains horrid, and all loose ends are tied up so well and thread the plot perfectly."

~Becky Wolsk, author of contemporary fiction
~*~

"Want to know the reason why I'm up late??? I couldn't stop reading *THE PARIS NOTEBOOK*! I loved it! I'm an avid book reader and this is wonderful! I laughed, I cried. I almost woke the kids up laughing out loud!"

~Em Woods, author of contemporary fiction
~*~

"Each time I begin a new book, I realize that I may have to read through a few pages in order to be 'grabbed' by the story and its characters. And yet, in the case of *THE PARIS NOTEBOOK*, I was grabbed within the first few paragraphs. The instant emotions of Deena's thoughts and feelings are amazing. And Jack is the reason that I love Romance novels. Make a note to read *THE PARIS NOTEBOOK*. You'll be glad you did."

~Sharon Horton, multi-award nominated romance author

Dedication

To Al

Chapter One

Deena Smith leaned against the office door she shared with Jack Karris, watching him work. Instead of his usual button-down shirt, he wore a black t-shirt. As he entered a grade into his laptop, his cut biceps flexed, tightening the material.

The stack of papers in her arms started to slide. She rushed to dump them on her desk, but a few flopped to the floor. The donut she'd snagged from the faculty lounge rolled out of its napkin onto her mouse pad. She grabbed for it, knocking her coffee cup full of colored pens over. She righted the cup and stuck the pens back into it. When she turned to retrieve the wayward essays, Jack handed them to her. He stood so close she saw the glint of the tiny diamond in his ear.

"Hey you."

Deena took a step away from temptation.

"Music?" she asked, moving to the corner where they kept an ancient P.C. for streaming internet radio.

"Sure."

She brought up their favorite station, keeping the volume low in deference to the rest of the English department.

When she turned back toward the desks, Jack stretched backward, showing an inch of rock hard abs. Even over the music she heard a loud crack when the kink in his back straightened out.

Refusing to be flustered by her flirty office mate, she tucked herself, and her composure, into her chair, grabbed a purple pen, pulled an essay from the pile and started grading. A new song came on the radio, catching her attention. She parked her pen behind her ear and focused on the music, listening harder. The guitar stuff sounded like Ian. When the words started coming through, she recognized Ian's voice.

His voice brought it all back. She'd finally gotten over the jerk and here he was again, filling the room. Her gut tightened and her throat swelled. She looked up and blinked, holding back the tears, listening to the song. Familiar, but not from the album. If this song was new, why did she know it?

Gradually she realized. The words were hers.

"Son of a bitch." Deena glared at the old P.C. She pulled the pen from behind her ear and threw it toward the machine.

"Is it the speakers?" Jack closed his laptop. He didn't like grading. He'd said as much many times and would use any excuse to put away his work for the day.

Deena took a deep breath. She didn't know where to start.

"Shit for sound." Jack glanced toward the computer and shook his head. "We could go halves on a set of Bose."

"I don't believe that bastard."

"So we're talking about Ian Hensley?" Jack's eyebrows cinched together as he flicked his gaze from her to the P.C. and back again.

"He stole my lyrics." But now that the song was over, a part of her doubted her own ears.

"You gonna eat that donut?" Jack wore a hopeful look on his face. A beat later, he asked, "You write songs?"

"Lyrics only." Nobody at the university knew about her past. It wasn't like she'd be penalized for it. No big deal. "I wrote all the words for Yellow Star's first album."

"You're kidding."

"No."

Jack came from behind his desk, grabbed the plastic chair they kept for student meetings, and placed it directly across from her.

"I want to know how Ian Hensley met a girl like you." Jack leaned his arms on her desk.

Despite her anger at Ian, Deena's heart fluttered at Jack's compliment. *A girl like her.* He didn't know her. Not really. "In college." The next part was harder to admit. "When Ian told me he was in a band, I said I wrote songs. I lied."

Jack shrugged. "I once told a girl I'd been accepted to Harvard just so she'd go to prom with me."

Jack never judged her, no matter what stupid mistake she made. And Deena's first year of teaching had included plenty of mistakes.

"But back to Yellow Star." He moved her papers to the side of the desk and leaned in closer. "How did you go from fake songwriter to Grammy-winning lyricist?"

Jack had never been this intense around her. It was flattering. They usually stayed behind their own desks and Jack coming so close stirred something inside Deena. Something she'd kept a lid on all year. She lowered her eyes to the essay in front of her, hoping he couldn't sense how vulnerable she felt right now.

"I went back to my dorm room, tore apart some old poems, added rhymes and refrains, and called them song lyrics. I showed them to Ian the next day after class."

"So, you're a poet?" He sat back in the chair. "How did I not know any of this?"

She looked up, meeting his eyes again. "Because I'm not a poet or a songwriter. I'm a teacher."

"But why did you stop writing poetry?"

3

"It was a phase. Don't all English majors write poetry?"

He shook his head, his eyes steady on hers. "No. No, they don't. They might try. With tragic results. Like the girl they wrote the poem for laughs, thinking it's a joke." He picked up her Shakespeare action figure and pulled the quill pen out of the bard's hand, pointing it at her. "You, Deena, have talent. A gift."

"Thanks." Jack's praise warmed her. She didn't think of her writing that way, and Ian never had either.

"Realistically, taking that lyric back might be tricky. A new cut from Yellow Star? Probably on iTunes by now."

Emotions tumbled against each other through Deena's body. Gratitude to Jack for listening. Anger at Ian. Sadness wove through the other feelings, making it hard to sort them out. But the fact remained—Ian had already recorded her words, already laid claim to them.

"Ian Hensley is a plagiarizer," she said.

"What a dick," Jack agreed.

Deena appreciated Jack's support. It helped ease the hurt and betrayal coursing through every cell of her body. Her writing was a sacred thing. It belonged to her alone unless, *until*, she permitted its use. Jack understood that.

"Have a donut." She handed him her treat and watched as he bit into it with utter absorption.

While Jack inhaled the donut, she downloaded the new Ian Hensley release into her phone, popped in her buds, and listened to the song with her eyes closed. Her words. She played the song again, just to be sure. But she hadn't been mistaken, despite the irritating but totally Ian-like title change from *Girl in Window* to *Blow Job*.

She checked her address book, even though it

was futile. All contact info connected to Ian, including his grandmother's address and the cell phone number of his sister in Toledo, had been deleted long ago.

Yanking her ear buds out, she pulled her laptop toward her and Googled Ian's name.

"My dad's an IP lawyer," Jack said. "He loves helping people like you. I can set up a meeting."

Deena heard Jack talking while she typed, but her mind didn't fully process the words, because a TMZ photo of Ian taken that morning at LAX popped onto her laptop screen. *Heading Home to Michigan,* the caption read.

"He's here." She moved the laptop so Jack could see the screen.

Jack checked out the page. Then he pulled his cell phone from his pocket. "You want that meeting?"

Deena closed her laptop and fought the urge to bang her forehead against the desk.

"Say the word, and I'll make the call."

"What exactly is an IP attorney?"

"Intellectual Property."

"So he can confront Ian with plagiarism and make him pay for cheating me?" Jack had a speck of jelly on the corner of his mouth, distracting Deena. She took the napkin the donut had been wrapped in, reached over, and wiped it off. "Jelly."

Jack smiled. She rested her face in her hands. Conflicting emotions swamped her. She'd done a good job at maintaining a professional distance from Jack since she'd started teaching here. But what difference did it make now? He was leaving soon for another job in another town, and she needed to feel the way his sweet words of praise were making her feel. Soft. Feminine. Smart. As opposed to Ian, who just pissed her off. A lot.

"You wrote the lyrics," Jack said. "Just bring your first draft, to, let's say, dinner tonight with

5

Dad."

"That's it!" Deena realized she could beat Ian now. "I gave Ian my Paris Notebook, but it's only a copy."

She'd gone shopping in Paris and bought a stupidly expensive notebook with thick creamy pages, bringing it back to the flat they'd rented and writing out a legible copy with painstaking curlicues on the tails of her Ps and Qs. Deena remembered the original scribble, the crossed out words, the writing in the margins, her fear that Ian would not be able to read it. Recalling the effort she put into that notebook made her eyes tear. She tamped down her feelings. Blinked away unshed tears. She'd been an idiot. She was over it. Better mad than sad.

"What's your Paris notebook?" Jack set his phone on her desk.

"I bought it there." Only a few years ago, but it seemed like another lifetime. "After a concert, I gave it to Ian. He told me he'd look at the lyrics later, but he never called, and he never gave the notebook back."

"So, wait. You were dating?"

"We lived together. But by then we'd split."

"Sucks," Jack said. "But Dad will know what to do."

"Ok, call him."

While Jack talked to his father's secretary, Deena powered up her laptop and clicked onto the Yellow Star website. The new album hadn't been released yet. Knowing Ian, he'd probably stolen the entire contents of her notebook.

"Dad's in a meeting, he'll call back."

Deena glanced at the clock over the door. "I've got class."

"I'll walk you over to Wilson Hall." Before they left the office, Jack put his professor jacket on over his t-shirt.

****

The minute Jack got home, he texted Deena, glad to report that his dad would meet them tonight at The Ash Creek Chop House. He stashed his messenger bag full of ungraded essays in the closet, shutting away school until his next class. Then he opened his laptop and pulled up his copy of Deena's course pack.

She'd titled it *MindSprings*, which he didn't love, but titles were easy to fix. She'd asked him to look at what she'd written for her student text over the winter break, and even without any hint of her songwriting past, he'd seen that her writing had commercial potential. He'd told her it was great and even considered sending it to a friend from college who worked in textbook publishing. But he hesitated because *MindSprings* had been missing something more than a title, something he hadn't been able to put his finger on.

The songwriting aspect was the missing magic ingredient.

He scrolled through the manuscript. Her platform as D. Smith was a game-changer. He'd send this to Don in New York, but first he had to figure out a way to integrate her lyrics.

Jack went to Yellow Star's website, but they didn't have the lyrics to the first album posted. It took him a couple of hours to find every lyric and cut and paste them into a document he could work from. While doing this mundane work, he hit upon a million dollar idea—find a line to quote before each chapter. He quickly found the first few, but matching song lyrics to freshman composition material was trickier than he'd imagined. He printed everything out and resolved to work on it later. Then he called New York.

While Don's assistant patched Jack through, he pondered if he might be doing the same thing to

Deena that she claimed Ian Hensley had done. He immediately dismissed the idea. Not the same thing at all.

It was just dumb luck that he'd landed a project that could be his ticket out of academia.

"How's it going, Jack?" Don asked in his terminally rushed tone.

"I've got this project you might be interested in." Jack explained about Deena's course pack and her past as lyricist for Yellow Star. "I'm editing it for her right now." Okay, so that was stretching the truth a bit.

"Does she have an agent?"

"I'm her agent," Jack said, even though he had no desire to actually become an agent. He wanted to be an editor, and this was an excellent stepping-stone.

Don said he'd take a look at the book after Jack completed the edits. He sounded very interested—of course he did. This project was money in the bank. Everybody would win. Still, he decided not to tell Deena his plans yet because he didn't want to get her hopes up. Publishing was extremely competitive right now, and even though he believed he had a dream project, there were still hoops to jump through. Once he'd cleared those hurdles, he'd surprise Deena with a book contract offer.

It was a win/win situation. She'd establish a multi-genre platform, and he'd have his first editorial work under his belt.

He went over the manuscript until his phone pinged with an incoming text. *Deena!* He checked her message.

"Wine first?"

"Okay," he texted back.

She'd never invited him into her apartment before. Jack had wanted to go out with Deena since summertime when she'd moved in next door. Once he realized they shared an office, he'd asked her out at least once a week. She always explained that no, she liked being friends. Now it made sense. She had been nursing a broken heart for her rock star ex-boyfriend. But Ian had earned her hatred, which meant there was a chance for Jack even before he laid a book contract at her feet.

Chapter Two

Am I insane? Deena stood, smack in the middle of Victoria's Secret, holding a thong bikini in her left hand and a demi-bra of the same firehouse red in her right. Even though she'd invited Jack over for a drink first, he and her underwear would not be meeting tonight, so why make herself crazy finding the perfect match?

She carried her items to the cashier. Inside her purse, as she reached for her wallet, her phone, with the download of her song, lurked. She shoved it aside and pulled out her wallet. She left the store, secure in the knowledge that this bout of shopping would banish thoughts of Ian's theft for at least a few hours. She hated waiting, hated sitting around the house wondering how a lawyer would win her words away from Ian. Stalking diversion at the mall burned off energy.

She browsed the bookstore until a portrait of an English lord on the cover of a historical romance caught her eye. She plucked the novel from the shelf, noting the model's defined cheekbones, dark blonde hair, and blue eyes. He looked like Jack without the diamond stud. She couldn't see the face of the raven-haired temptress the man clenched, but the idea of sex with Jack tonight popped into Deena's head.

She understood he wanted her. It wasn't such a compliment, considering the number of women he'd had in the short time she'd known him. But why should sheer numbers stop her? She'd lived with a rock star. She knew a few tricks of her own. And no worries that she'd lose her heart with Jack. He'd be gone in a month. Perfect. No relationship, no possibility of having her soul crushed again.

She left the bookstore and headed straight to Godiva. Chocolate never let her down. After paying for her gold box of candy, Deena stood outside the glass window of the store and tore off the cellophane wrapper. She imagined sex with Jack: safe and uncomplicated. A rebound guy. Quick and dirty tension relief. Finally unlocking her treasure, she shoved a truffle into her mouth on her way to the next store. She needed a really short skirt, the kind she never wore to school.

****

Jack poured kibble into his cat's supper dish and pocketed his phone. He stepped out into the starry night and looked up, not at the sky, but at Deena's place. Lamplight glowed in her window. He'd waited so long for an invitation inside, dating a different woman every week just to take his mind of her, until finally, she said yes.

He ran up the wooden staircase and lifted his knuckles to the patio-style glass door. Before he knocked, Deena appeared behind the glass as she moved aside a silky white curtain, clutching the filmy material in one hand, sliding open the glass door with the other. For a second he stood mesmerized by her slim wrist holding the white silk. She wore a military dog tag, a single charm on a silver bracelet. He'd never seen it on her before. Did she know someone in the military?

He recovered and stepped inside. Warmth and the smell of wine surrounded him. He noticed her reddened nose and puffy eyes. The unmistakable scent of Chardonnay wafted up from her body. Was she drunk? A wine bottle and glasses sat on a low table.

"I'm not drunk, you idiot."

"Damn." Jack hated it when he thought out

loud. "Sorry."

She shrugged.

This was not the romantic start to the evening he'd envisioned. He held out a bottle of his favorite Muscato to her, wondering if flowers would have been better. "What I meant was, well, when you opened the door, I got a strong whiff of alcohol. And your nose is red."

"Thanks." She set the wine on a table already cluttered with an open bottle of Chardonnay, two glasses, a cork, papers, books, pens, television remote, and a packet of Kitty Treats. His eyes wandered her living space. It was full of chaotic color and layered textures. Pink and orange, velvet and cotton, drew the eye to a fat bowl of yellow roses on a pedestal table. He sank into the sofa, feeling claustrophobic amid the candles, papers, and books covering every available surface. He'd entered a gypsy tent. Surely somewhere a crystal ball sparkled.

Deena sat next to him, thrusting a glass into his hand. "I attempted to pour this—" she picked up the bottle of chardonnay, "—and spilled it when your footsteps running up here startled me. And my nose is red because I was crying."

"Um, nice coffee table," Jack said, even though it was really a cedar chest painted white with some sort of gold streaks through it. He pushed the word "crying" away. Crying seemed like a bad sign on a first date. Not that meeting his dad for legal advice was an actual date, but it was closer than he'd ever come before.

"Thank you." Deena's face softened. "It's the only thing I have of my Granny's. She used to give me hugs when I was little."

Jack didn't understand the big deal about hugs. He'd give her one right now if he wasn't afraid she'd call him an idiot again. In his family, everyone gave hugs all the time. Maybe Deena would let him hug her soon. His eyes wandered over Deena's blue sweater again. And the wine staining it. He wanted to tell her to rub some club soda on the wine spots, but then she'd realize where he'd been looking.

"You know what?" she said, probably aware of exactly where his eyes had focused. "I want to change out of this sweater. Excuse me, just a minute."

"You might want to dab those spots with club soda." He watched her walk into the bedroom. Her short blue skirt was tight enough to show every one of her curves. Not one of her teaching outfits.

She came back out in a white tunic that came almost to the hem of the skirt. She didn't have the blue sweater with her. In his mind's eye, he saw it sitting in a heap in the corner, the stain setting in. Then he noticed the hint of red under her white shirt. She was wearing a red bra. He tried to clamp down the image that sprang to his mind. Didn't work. He needed to think of something else or he'd embarrass himself. So he focused on her stained sweater. His sister called him a neat freak, but he simply liked things in their proper place. *Clean* and in their proper place.

"So, where is it?" He stretched his arms out over the back of the velvet marshmallow she called a sofa, trying to sound casual. He was actually dying to get a look at those lyrics. Maybe he could use some of them on the project for Don.

"What?" Deena's eyes widened.

He now understood that look. She'd worn it daily when she'd first started teaching. At first, he figured she had the new job jitters. But then once, she'd worn a hair band that displayed her widow's peak and he said her face looked like a heart. A sweet heart. Her vulnerability was sweet.

The next day she had a new haircut. With

bangs. He still hadn't figured out why she needed to put up such a defense, but maybe it had something to do with Ian Hensley. Guy could play guitar, no doubt, but he was a jerk to steal Deena's lyrics.

"Where's the original notebook? My dad said to bring it." He resisted the urge to push her bangs back from her forehead. He wanted to soothe her, not rile her up. He wanted to surprise her with the gift of publication, not steal from her.

Deena searched under a stack of student essays that threatened to slither from their pile to the floor, and came up with a marble-pattern notebook, the kind the grocery store sold for a buck. She handed it, page open, to Jack.

He read words that told the story of a prostitute in Amsterdam, about a moment's connection between a woman walking down the street and one for sale in a window. About the exchange of information and compassion that happened in that moment. He never listened to the words of songs, except maybe the refrain by default, but the music he'd heard earlier today didn't fit the mood of these words at all.

Her course pack had impressed him, reading over the first album's lyrics had deepened his respect, but this notebook showed a marked maturity not present in the earlier lyrics. He wanted to blurt out his whole plan to her, but caught himself. He'd wait until Don gave his verdict. He didn't want to disappoint her. Ian had already done that in a big way.

"I checked the words. There are 134 of them in *Girl in Window*. Ian changed less than a dozen, but they completely erased my meaning. It isn't even my song anymore. Here, I wrote it out to show your dad where he did it."

Jack read, amazed by how in a few words, meaning could be changed, painted over into something very different.

And then he had another thought. What would his father think of a conversation that included the phrase *blow job*?

Chapter Three

Deena liked the warmth of Jack's hand on the small of her back as they walked into the restaurant. When he stepped up to confer with the hostess, she missed the light pressure, missed the tingle from his touch. She soothed herself by thinking about how later, if things went right, he'd put his hands all over her. She had a moment's doubt but then repressed it. What was wrong with finding a fun way to cope with the fact that Ian was back in town, hurting her again?

Pleasantly distracted by the thought of sex with Jack, Deena followed the hostess to their table. When they arrived, an older version of Jack looked up from his menu. He stood and hugged Jack right there in the restaurant, smiling at Deena. They sat, Jack next to her, his father across from them, as Jack made the introductions. "Thanks so much for seeing me, Mr. Karris." Deena shook the hand he offered. Something about the dark, polished wood of the table and the plushy upholstered chair relaxed her.

"Always happy to help a friend of Jack's, Deena." Jack had mentioned that about his dad. What a nice guy. "And please, call me Bill."

A waitress put a rock glass full of ice and clear liquid in front of Bill. Deena ordered a glass of Pinot Noir, which she intended to sip very slowly until dinner. She preferred hearing Bill's advice while sober enough to figure out a next step.

Bill pulled a legal pad from his briefcase and took a silver pen from his shirt pocket. Jack put his hand on her knee and squeezed it as if to reassure her. She put her hand over his for a moment, returning the pressure, wanting his touch. After a year of resisting him, she felt reckless. Ian's newest betrayal had released something wild inside her.

"You brought the notebook and a copy of the song?"

"Yes." Deena pulled the items from her red leather bag and handed them to Bill. While he looked through the file, Jack moved his hand a little bit above her knee. She turned to him and smiled, a little surprised at how easy it was finally to give in.

"I always wanted to know," Jack's voice went low as his dad read the notebook, "why Yellow Star?"

Deena rolled her eyes. She and Jack were of the same mind when it came to Yellow Star's name. She tried to keep conversation light even though she could hardly concentrate on conversation because Jack's hand was setting off little sparks down her spine.

"I know. He's so self-involved and clueless. He said he'd been bullied when he was a kid by his step-father, so he knew how persecution felt."

"What an ass. Who compares themselves holocaust victims?"

"I know. He wouldn't even visit the Anne Frank house when we were in Amsterdam. Said it was too depressing."

"Did you go?"

"Yeah. Alone." She'd been alone a lot in those days.

The waitress came for their dinner orders, and Bill requested an extra steak. "For my wife," he told the waitress with a tone Deena tried to place. It sounded like love...with something else.

Respect.

"You've got a couple of choices," Bill explained after the waitress left. "Sue Hensley, or the record company, or both. Or send Hensley a registered letter stating proof of plagiarism and willingness to settle out of court."

"Let's do the out-of-court thing." Deena let out a breath she hadn't known she was holding. The image of confronting Ian in a court of law scared her silly, but this would be okay.

"Good choice. Jack tells me this is a single, and the album is due to be released soon."

"Yes, and I've been wondering," Deena tried to speak her mind without sounding conceited or greedy. "I think he may have used my lyrics on the whole album."

"Why do you suspect this?"

"I wrote the words for the last album. Ian isn't much for words. To him, it's the music that's important. Words are almost superfluous."

"The lyrics for the first album got a lot of positive press."

Jack's praise was almost as good as his hand on her thigh. He'd been doing some research. She tingled from the admiration, or maybe the pressure of his hand, which moved up her thigh an inch.

"I gave Ian a notebook full of new lyrics right before they started recording again. Just knowing the kind of guy he is, I think he used them."

"I'll send the letter, but we might want to wait for the release of the album for any further action."

I don't want to wait. "Is there a way I can find out now if he used more of my lyrics?"

"You have the original lyrics." Jack looked from Deena to his father. "So it would just be a matter of comparing them. Can't you ask other band members to give you the lyrics to the new album?"

"Good idea," Bill agreed.

Deena didn't want to erase the happy glow from Jack's face by telling him that Toby and the others were all under Ian's thumb. She didn't say anything, but she smiled at Jack. He wanted to help, and the feel of his hand on her knee was deliciously distracting.

"I could request the lyrics from the record company, but they're under no obligation to give them to us. They're confronted with this type of charge all the time."

Deena peeled Jack's fingers away with regret. She couldn't focus when he had his hands on her. And with his dad sitting across the table, it seemed disrespectful.

Less than a minute after Jack's hands were back in his own space, her thoughts turned again to Ian. If only she could get him to confess. Or better, she could break into his hotel suite and find her notebook.

"I don't even know where he's staying," she said aloud. He probably still used the same fake name as he had when they registered at hotels together.

Bill pulled a cell phone from his jacket pocket, pressed a couple of keys, and spoke quietly to whoever picked up the other end.

Deena turned toward Jack like a flower seeking sun. In the last hour, a whole new world had opened between them. He placed his hand over hers, on top of the table this time, and squeezed. Her heart did a little involuntary flip. The lonely long time since she'd held hands with a man disappeared as she entwined her fingers with Jack's.

The waitress set their salads before them, necessitating the breaking of the handholding. How could she eat? She was already full, not of food, but of something. Longing, desire, anticipation. With a side order of aggravation at Ian.

Bill clicked his phone off and returned it to his pocket. He jotted a few notes on his legal pad, ignoring his salad. "I've got an address on Hensley,"

"What? Just now?" The lettuce in Deena's mouth

turned bitter. She sipped her water. She'd rather chug wine, but would maintain her dignity in front of Bill.

"Our firm's investigator. It's routine." Bill ripped the page from his pad and handed it to Deena. "I wouldn't advise contacting him, but knowing where he's at might give you peace of mind."

Deena stared at the address. Not a hotel, but a house on a quiet street in the Old Oaks section of town. She'd bet a million bucks her Paris notebook was in that house right now.

Bill and then Jack were talking to her, but it was like watching a movie with the sound turned down; she didn't hear a word. Her mind was on Ian again. Maybe he'd written over her original words. Any judge would nail him on that.

Both Jack and Bill looked at her, waiting for a response.

"I'm sorry. What?"

"Apparently Hensley's here with his band to do a local promotion of the single before the album releases."

"You're bound to run into him, Deena." Jack looked concerned. "He'll be here a while. This may be his home base for months. That's why he's renting a house, not staying at a hotel."

Deena didn't respond. All she could think about was how to bust her notebook out of Ian's house.

The waitress brought their steaks. "Would you like another glass of wine?" she asked Deena, who hadn't realized that despite her best intentions she'd chugged the Pinot like beer.

"Please." She sliced into her filet mignon.

Immediately after finishing his steak, Bill rose from the table.

"Mom's waiting for her dinner," Jack said.

Bill nodded and grabbed the carryout meal with one hand and his briefcase with the other. "Nice to meet you, Deena. Don't worry about this. That's my job now."

Deena smiled and her thanks, but as Bill left, she accepted the truth—getting the notebook back was up to her.

The waitress approached, bearing a tray of desserts. "The check's taken care of. Mr. Karris says order anything else you'd like as well. After-dinner drink? Dessert?"

Jack, of course, stared hungrily at the dessert tray. Deena hoped that later, he'd stare at her the same way.

"Everything looks so good." Jack finally chose a chocolate pecan tart for them to share. They both knew she'd eat one bite and he'd inhale the rest.

When the waitress left them alone, Jack leaned into Deena's side of the table and kissed her. It happened so quickly she was sure nobody around them noticed. But that little kiss shimmied all the way down to the seat of her chair.

"You taste better than any dessert." Coming from Jack, this was a huge compliment.

"What are you doing tomorrow?"

"I usually have lunch with my friend Patti." She avoided mentioning her actual plan, which involved Patti helping her break into Ian's house.

Chapter Four

In the minutes it took to drive from the restaurant to her apartment, Jack held Deena's hand over the gearshift. He didn't let it go, even when he downshifted.

"Your dad's so nice, Jack." Bill reminded Deena of Jack. A steady, married Jack. "Are you sure my case isn't too much trouble? Because handling Ian, well, let's just say I have experience."

"Not a problem," Jack gave her hand a squeeze. "He loves helping people . He's gotten me out of more leases…" He laughed low as he stopped for a red light.

"What? Why?"

"Oh, I, um, like to move around a lot."

Deena knew this, sort of. He'd talked of doing his undergrad work at Purdue, then transferring to another school in New York for his master's, and then to U of M for his Ph.D. He'd worked at two schools before he came to Ash Creek and he was returning to Ann Arbor in the fall.

"So, you must love starting over."

Jack gunned the engine as the light turned green. "Michigan offered me tenure track. But you're right, I get a buzz every time I do a geographic."

"No roots." Deena understood guys like that. To support their first album, Yellow Star toured a different city, even different European countries, for what had seemed like years. For a while, she'd been a vagabond with Ian, but always in her heart she wanted to settle down, have her own place. And now she did.

"I feel like celebrating. Come back to my house for a nightcap?" Lame, but Jack would understand what the invitation really meant. The vibe between them, thick with wanting, was almost visible.

On the way up her stairs, Jack stayed a few steps behind her. Probably looking up her skirt. Good. She'd worn the new thong.

She turned to Jack at the door, and their bodies clashed full-on for the first time. Desire wrapped around them and squeezed. But the thong was damned uncomfortable. She'd never liked them.

"Sorry," Jack said.

She just smiled. He loved sweets and she'd made his favorite. The perfect way to win a man: sexy underwear and fresh baked goods.

"I know you just had dessert, but I made you a batch of chocolate chip cookies." Seriously out of practice in seduction, she needed another sip or two of wine before whatever was going to happen between them.

"I'll be just a sec." She headed into the bathroom, where she slid off her thong and threw it into the hamper. She checked her reflection in the mirror, smoothing gloss over her lips while predictable Jack scouted the kitchen for cookies. "Would it be inappropriate to ask for a glass of milk?"

"Sure." She left the bathroom and moved around her kitchen, pouring milk and wine, whisking the plastic wrap from the plate of cookies she'd set on top of the fridge earlier.

Jack came up behind her as she worked at the counter. He pressed against her, grabbing a cookie. His appreciation of the glimpse of thong on the steps made itself known through the thin material of her skirt. He bit into the cookie and kissed her on the cheek. He didn't move away.

"Crumbs." She wiped her face with her hand and

turned around. Their eyes met for a long moment, and then, for the first time since she'd known him, Jack Karris put down an unfinished cookie. And he kissed her.

"Umm, so good."

She didn't answer, but kissed him back, opening her mouth to his.

He deepened the kiss, moved both of his arms down to hike her skirt up, grabbing her with both hands and moaning when he realized she was all skin.

She hooked one of her legs around his and slowly moved it along his calf. She put her hands under his shirt, running her fingers over the firm flesh on his back. Skin to skin. So good. *Too many clothes.* She pulled her top up and off.

Revealing the red lace of her bra broke the kiss but not the mood. For a second she glimpsed grateful surprise on Jack's face, then he buried himself in her cleavage, moving his hands up to cup her breasts. His thumbs rubbed her nipples, streaking lightning through her body. His tongue teased her skin, his fingers eased down the lace cups. She arched her back, wanting more.

"Come to bed," she said, relieved that she'd remembered to throw condoms in her night table drawer.

Jack shed his shoes on the way to the bedroom, and while she grabbed a condom from the drawer, he stripped. Before she could rip the package open, he unzipped her skirt. It fell to the floor.

"Oh God."

"What?"

"I have pictured you naked every day at your desk but this..." He did not finish the sentence, but instead kissed her mouth again. They eased onto the bed, Jack's strong body covering hers.

She kissed him, lifted her hips, let him fill the

empty space inside her. When he unhooked her bra and pulled it free, there was no more slowing down for Deena. It had been too long, and every cell in her body screamed with needing him inside her. Jack explored her body with his mouth and hands, and yes it felt good, it felt wonderful. But it wasn't all she wanted. Never more impatient than now, she reached down to stroke Jack, focusing on his pleasure. She spread herself open, arched her back, and guided him inside her.

Jack's slow build and smooth pace swamped her with desire. She couldn't stop herself. She pushed further, faster, until his furious rhythm became as urgent as her own. He came seconds after she did and collapsed next to her.

Later, she lay in the warmth of his arms, basking in contentment. She lazily imagined that sex with Jack was a storm that had been brewing all day, maybe all year, and now it had broken and settled, and they were together under this beautiful rainbow.

After a few minutes, Jack said, "Why now? Why today, after all this time?"

"Because you're leaving." Not the whole truth, but close enough. In her experience, men never whined about feeling used. They did the using and the leaving.

"Ann Arbor's not that far." He got up and pulled on his boxers. He folded his clothes neatly over her vanity chair, took the hanger from her closet door knob and hung up her skirt. He picked up her tunic and threw it with the sweater into her wicker laundry basket. Then he took the sweater out again. "Got any club soda?"

"I think, in the fridge."

He walked, sweater in hand, out of the room.

The shortest rainbow in human history. She pulled on her robe and followed him out of the bedroom.

He stood at the sink, finishing his cookie with one hand and blotting club soda on her sweater with the other. Her full glass of wine sat beside his half empty glass of milk. She approached, snaked an arm around his side, and took a tentative sip of wine. Jack kept at the sweater, ignoring her. She brought her wine over to the sofa and curled up with her cat. She stroked Shadow's silky black fur, wondering why the mood had shifted.

Jack always said she worried too much. So she wouldn't worry now. Except for his boxers, he was still naked. She noticed her own robe, a very worn and comfortable chenille number. She should have bought a new one, made of silk and lace, at the mall this afternoon.

She stretched her limbs in a long curling cat-like line. She wanted to purr. If Jack's behavior was less than lover-like, if he seemed the tiniest bit put off, her bones still carried a delicious warmth from his tenderly frantic loving.

Eventually, Jack left her sweater soaking in the sink and joined her on the sofa. He unknotted the belt of her robe. She must have imagined his moodiness, because he took her again, right there on the couch, as if she belonged to him.

Chapter Five

The next morning, Deena walked with Patti and Biff, Patti's little bullet of a dog, through the shopping district of downtown Ash Creek. They were alone on the street, and Deena knew why. It was damn cold.

"Look at Biff's legs, Patti. You're working him too hard." Biff's short skinny legs, black with white paws, had to pump overtime to keep up with the humans.

"My chin is frozen solid. Tell me again why we're walking around in sub-zero weather."

"It's hardly sub-zero, and the exercise is good for Biff."

"You're ten pounds of trouble," Deena told Biff, but he just kept trotting. "Since when has running around your loft not been enough exercise for Biff?"

"Since I can't fit into my jeans anymore."

When Ian dumped Deena, she'd holed up in Paris and wrote. When Ian dumped Patti, she hooked up with chocolate. Eventually Ian's exes bonded over French truffles. Now Deena willingly froze her ass off in the name of friendship. For the first block of their walk, Patti listened to yesterday's lyric story, called Ian an asshole, traitor, jerk.

Deena was about to suggest breaking in to Ian's house and stealing her notebook when Patti said, "I have a mountain on my belly and it won't get off!"

Patti joked about her weight, but Deena could see how much it bothered her. Why else would the queen of tight jeans be wearing baggy sweat pants? Deena looked down at her own jeans; their olive

27

color matched her army jacket perfectly. And they looked great tucked into her ten-eye Dr. Martens with steel capped toes.

"Ready for combat, I see."

"Yep."

"So, what did Jack's dad say?" Patti slowed her walk a little, for Biff's sake. Deena slowed down too, wishing she'd worn gloves. She shoved her hands in her pockets. So much for spring in Michigan.

"He thinks I might have a case, but it would be stronger if more of the songs on the album, which is not yet released, were also mine. And if I had the Paris notebook. He offered to write a letter for me."

"What did you tell him?" Patti asked, turning into the alley.

"I told him to go ahead." Deena took her hands out of her pockets and cupped her frozen chin. Her chin got warmer but her fingers refroze.

"So, did you finally succumb to Jack's charms?"

"I did. Three times." Deena warmed, remembering being in Jack's arms.

Patti sighed. "I can't have sex with anyone until I lose this weight."

"I don't know that walking around town imitating ice cubes is going to do it."

"You could be a little more supportive."

Deena watched her breath condense into puffs of icy smoke. She tried to figure out what supportive meant. Agree that Patti had put on weight? Deny? Finally, she said, "When you, ah, before you, ah, what did you do before to keep in shape?"

"Danced every night until dawn. Slept through breakfast. Coffee and cigarettes for lunch."

"That doesn't sound healthy. Maybe your body is just getting adjusted to eating actual food, and um, lunch."

"Maybe. When I quit smoking, I took up eating."

"Can't you do something else with your hands?"

"I used to." Patti stopped. "Let's turn around."

A few minutes later, they entered the warm cave of Patti's loft.

"I can't feel my face!" Deena plopped down on the sofa minutes later. Biff ran around in a circle before curling into an O on his doggy cushion.

"I'll make coffee. Or hot chocolate with whipped cream. And Bailey's."

"It's eleven in the morning."

"I'm sure it's noon somewhere in America."

"Coffee, please."

"I must be depressed." Patti searched the far side of the loft space for the French press. "I didn't make my bed today."

"Nobody can see it. You've got the bookshelves. And I never make my bed, but that doesn't mean I'm depressed."

"That's my point." Patti poured boiling water over the ground coffee in the glass carafe. "You never make your bed, but I always do. Did." She came over to the sofa and handed Deena her coffee. Watched her take a sip.

Bailey's Irish Cream instead of Coffeemate.

"I shouldn't, but this is good." The cup warmed Deena's hands, the liquid warmed her inside.

"I thought you'd need a drink."

"Why? What?" Deena imagined some dire scenario. Patti had cancer. Or she was moving to New Mexico. Or...

"Ian came into The Pub last night."

"Hmm." Deena's mind abandoned fatal images and went back to Ian. Patti had yet to hear Deena's B & E plan. "Maybe I can work with that."

"What? You should be freaking out."

"Yeah, I am, on the inside." Deena took a sip of her drink. "But if we act like friends, breaking into his house and stealing back my Paris notebook will be easier."

Patti's gasp gratified Deena. It was a bold plan. An excellent if hazy plan.

They finished their spiked coffees, and Patti peered into her cupboards, looking for treats. She brought a box of White Cheddar Cheese Nips over to the sofa and plopped down next to Deena.

"People don't see me anymore since I've gained weight."

Deena looked closely at Patti. Same long blonde hair, same big blue eyes. Maybe her cheeks were rounder, but it suited her.

"Stale." Patti ate a handful and tossed the box onto the coffee table with disgust. "Are you hungry yet?" she asked, after a minute.

"Dunno. I could eat, I guess." *Where's Jack right now? What is he doing?*. "What time is it?"

"11:30."

"Too early for Ian to be there, right?"

"Probably. He didn't come in until maybe midnight last night. Some sleaze attached to his arm, coke crusted on her nostrils."

"Ew. How twentieth century."

"Some people never grow up. I, on the other hand, just keep on growing."

Deena felt bad for Patti. "This is really bugging you." Patti's size seemed fine to Deena. "If you're so upset about it, why don't we go to the produce market and get some nice salad stuff, come back here and have that for lunch?" Even as Deena said it, she hoped Patti would refuse. It was too cold for salad. "Or, you could have a nice bowl of vegetable soup at The Pub," she amended.

"The only vegetables The Pub serves are deep fried and come with a side order of bleu cheese dressing. Besides, I don't want to slim down to be noticed. I want people to see me for who I am inside."

"I can relate to that." Deena wanted to make a

plan with Patti to get her notebook but if she changed the subject, would she be a bad friend? Maybe they were done talking about Patti's body issues now. Maybe if she mentioned the cover of the notebook, its swirling pink and peach tone and the French words imprinted in gold at the top, then they could brainstorm how to get into the house and search for it.

"Plus, I'm too hungry to shop. You know how they tell you to never go to a food store on an empty stomach."

Or maybe Deena could work that part out herself, after she finished cheering Patti up. "They also say you shouldn't have alcohol on an empty stomach, but that didn't stop us."

"Which is all the more reason why we ought to go and get something to eat. Soak up the liquor." Patti rose from the sofa, scattering Cheese Nip crumbs on the floor. She looked down at her outfit. "Guess I better change."

Deena waited, her mind clicking from Jack to Ian and back again. Jack's dad was supposed to have messengered the letter this morning. Had Ian even read it? She remembered lots of notes he had failed to read, lots of letters and phone messages he had left unanswered. She knew what Patti meant about feeling invisible. That's how Ian had made her feel. Even before he stole her song.

Patti reappeared wearing a plum colored velvet pants outfit. "I need to do some serious clothes shopping. This has an elastic waist. I couldn't even zip my fat jeans." She held up her hands in surrender. "Velvet in April! I feel like your sofa. The better for people to treat me like a piece of furniture."

"If you mean guys, get used to it. The good ones are few and far between."

"It's so superficial to look past someone because

31

of their weight."

"Yeah, it is." Even though Deena wanted nothing more than to plot out her assault on Ian like a battle plan, well, unless it was spending more time with Jack, she tried to think of something supportive to add. "I know! After lunch, we'll go to the mall. I'll help you shop for a fabulous new wardrobe." The mall route passed Old Oaks. No harm in driving by Ian's new place. Just to case the joint.

"It's a plan, but only if you keep me away from polyester and anything resembling a caftan."

"Deal." *Patti wouldn't mind a quick side trip to Old Oaks for a bit of surveillance.*

****

They used the back entrance to The Pub, a few feet from Patti's stairs. The only light in the long hallway came from the partly open kitchen door, so Deena's eyes took a moment to adjust to the dark. The first thing she saw when they did was Ian, sitting at the bar drinking a beer. Patti pulled Deena over to a corner table next to the stage. "I don't think he saw us," she whispered.

"I don't care if he did." Deena was shaking in her boots. One of the ideas she'd considered had been to make friends with Ian and get herself and Patti invited over to his place. But it was a half-baked plan. She saw that now. Ian would have gotten the letter. He'd be pissed. Maybe she could pass that off somehow. A misunderstanding. An over-eager lawyer. Get the invite, get the boys stoned, and conduct a search. It could work.

"Hey Patti! Deena!" Rick, the bartender, yelled. "Your boyfriend's back." He laughed. Guy thought he was a comedian.

Toby turned and waved. Deena saw the wave but did not return it. What was wrong with her? She needed to be friendly, that was the plan. But her body wasn't cooperating, probably because she was so pissed. Patti waved at Toby with enough enthusiasm for both of them.

Rick came over, still chuckling at his supposed humor. "Didn't you both used to date Ian?"

They didn't answer, just gave him their order. He strode back to the bar and popped open two bottles of Coke, which he slid toward Ian.

Ian walked toward them, Cokes in hand.

"I can't talk to him. I'm too nervous." God he had hurt her. She had loved him so much and he used her up and dumped her in Europe like trash.

"Tell him to speak to your lawyer," Patti advised.

Deena's stomach jumped.

"Patti." Ian nodded at her before turning to Deena. "Listen, Dee, babe, I got that letter from your lawyer." He set their drinks in front of them and pulled up a chair, straddled it backward. "It's a mix-up, honest. I don't even have that old Paris notebook of yours anymore." He shot her a twist of his lips, what passed in rock stardom as a smile, the same smile she once adored.

She wasn't adoring anymore.

"The guys, all of us, went back to Holland, and I remember now you wrote a song about that the first time we were there. Together." He looked at her and his eyes were honest, innocent enough to convince any jury. Shit, he was convincing her.

"But I wrote my own song." He maintained with perfect calm, perfect cool. "If you had the notebook, you could compare and see they're nothing alike."

Busted. He had no clue she'd kept her own copy of the lyrics.

"Although I admit our conversations have always inspired me." He smiled again, put his index finger on the hand holding her Coke.

Deena shivered at his touch, and her eyes went to his perfect mouth. Plump lips, even white teeth, soulful kisses. Too bad he was such a jerk.

Deena kept all intel on the original notebook to herself. She'd been an idiot over Ian in the past, but never again. Maybe this anger worked for the plan. His suspicions might rise if she made nice too easily.

"Talk to my lawyer." She tried to sound calm but her insides were erupting like Alka Seltzer.

"You don't want to do battle with me, Dee."

"This the guy who stole your lyrics?" Jack came up behind Patti. Deena ached to jump up and throw herself into Jack's arms, but unsure of his reaction, she just smiled and made room for him at the table.

"Your lawyer?" Ian asked, shooting Jack a look full of disdain.

"No."

Toby claimed the seat next to Patti. "Patti, Jack. Jack, this is Patti."

Jack and Patti exchanged hellos.

"Hey, Patti, you're lookin' good," Toby said. "Sorry about the mix-up, Deena."

"What mix-up?" Jack asked. He pulled a chair next to Deena and put a hand on her leg under the table. Her tight nerves relaxed. She wished Ian and this whole damn problem would disappear so she could spend every moment of the time until Jack left for Ann Arbor with him.

"Oh, Ian here claims he was inspired by a conversation with me when he wrote *Blow Job*. Also, he did research in Amsterdam. Twice."

"Not me," Toby told Patti. "That's not my scene."

Jack, inserted between Deena and Ian, put his arm around Deena and whispered, "Are you okay?" in her ear.

She nodded. His arm around her made the world right, especially since Patti seemed ready to defect to the other side with Toby.

Defeated for the moment, Ian stood. "Come on, Toby."

Toby, busy saying something to Patti that Deena couldn't quite catch, ignored him.

"Tob, I said let's go, dude."

"Coming." Toby lumbered upright, his eyes lingering on Patti. At the door, he turned around and winked.

"He certainly doesn't think you're invisible." Deena bit into the burger Rick delivered. Jack moved his arm away so she could eat and ordered his own sandwich.

"Yeah, I always got the vibe that he had a crush on me. But, well, you know how Ian just zeroes in and won't let you think about anyone else." Patti's huge tray of nachos took up most of the space at their small table. "Have some," she invited Deena and Jack.

Jack took a nacho, but instead of eating it, he held it midair, a puzzled expression on his face. Patti saved Deena an explanation. "I dated Ian for a while, after he and Deena broke up."

Deena glanced at the door, although Ian had disappeared. "I wonder if it really is just a coincidence about the song? He always did have the ability to read my mind, at least where music was concerned."

"I can't believe you bought that," Jack said, before crunching into the loaded nacho in his hand.

"I'm not sure I do." She didn't believe Ian for one minute, but telling Jack about the plan was not a good idea. He wanted her to let his father handle things. "I really hate having to wait for the album to find out just how many of my songs he stole."

"You'll know soon enough."

Deena was torn between having Jack on her side and keeping her real plan a secret.

She could probably balance both, Jack in the boyfriend area and Ian in the problem-to-be-solved spot.

With Jack's help, Patti finished her nachos and started in on Deena's fries.

"Help yourself."

Deena had lost her appetite.

Chapter Six

Ian paced the living room of his rented house. He needed to get out of here; he needed a drink. Or ten. He grabbed his jacket and pulled it on. He reached into the pocket for his car keys and came up with the letter from Dee's lawyer.

Damn, he didn't like being back in Ash Creek. If it weren't for the fucking interviews their lame ass manager had set up with the local media, he'd be out of here yesterday. Wasn't that the point of fame? That it got you the hell out of your hometown?

He closed his fist over the legal warning. After the album's release in a few weeks, Deena would no doubt realize he'd borrowed some of her material. If she could catch it on *Blow Job* she'd be sure to notice it on the others. It pissed him off. Words were free. They didn't belong to anyone in particular. It wasn't as if Dee's phrases were anything special.

"Hell, I don't know what the big deal is," he told Toby, who sat on the sofa scrolling through his phone. "She always said writing lyrics was cake. She just thinks them up, one right after another. Why should she care if an old friend uses them?"

"Royalties." Toby sent a text and threw his phone on the coffee table. "Think Patti will go out with me?"

"No. And why do you want her? She got fat."

"She reminds me of Marilyn Monroe. Nice curves."

"Marilyn Monroe was fat" Ian started to form the germ of an idea. "But, if you really like her, I guess you could ask her out. She works nights at

The Pub."

"Maybe I'll go by there tonight." He stared at the coffee table littered with phone, beer bottles, Taco Bell bags, iPods and a portable recorder. "We should clean up, man."

"Let the chicks do it."

"What chicks?" Toby looked around as if babes would suddenly appear out of the kitchen. He could play the hell out of the bass guitar but was a little slow on the uptake with most other things.

"Whoever comes by first."

"Yeah, well, if they don't mind, I guess." Toby stood up. "Hey, let me see that notebook you got the lyrics from, man."

Ian went back into his room, put the letter in the drawer of his nightstand on top of Dee's precious Paris notebook. He opened and closed his dresser drawers without looking inside them. Opened his closet, stood there a minute, closed it.

"I can't find it, dude." He stepped out of the bedroom. "It must be in a box downstairs." Their manager had rented the place a week ago and had their things shipped. The basement contained several boxes of personal crap.

Toby stood there like a belligerent mountain. "If you used any of her ideas or words, you should give Deena co-songwriting credit."

Ian was not about to back down. "Do you not believe me when I say her fucking notebook was of very little actual use to me? That I changed the few things I did use enough so she'll never know?"

Toby sat down. Ian walked into the practice room. He'd won that round. He mentally reviewed his plan. If Toby could get next to Patti, and he could get next to Dee, maybe she'd agree to let him use her ideas before the album dropped. He'd get her to sign something. Yeah, wine her and dine her. Leave that loser lawyer dude in the dust. He understood Dee better than anyone. He could read the language behind what that army outfit of hers meant. He'd fight her and win.

****

Deena sat at the desk in the living room finishing her make-up with a slick of gloss. Teacher woman, ready to face the world of freshman English.

When she reached the office, Deena dumped her mail on her desk, picked up a stack of graded essays, and headed out for her morning class. She hardly noticed the sunshine and the mild day as she fretted about how to find out if Ian had stolen any more of her songs from the Paris notebook. Could she just call the record company? Would they even talk to her?

She took the stairs up two floors to her classroom, and threw her book bag onto the desk before she noticed that one of the professors who had been on the hiring committee was sitting in the back row of seats. Only a few students had straggled in, most holding paper cups of coffee.

"Dr. Marchant." Deena took off her coat before approaching the professor, who had a leather binder and pen on the desk, as if he were ready to join the class. "Can I help you?"

"Your first year observation was scheduled for today. Don't you read your e-mail?"

"Of course." Deena reconsidered. "Unless, did you send it yesterday?"

"My secretary takes care of that." Marchant didn't answer her question, she noted. Yesterday had been her day off, and this morning she had not yet had time to open her mail. Faculty deserved more than one day's notice.

"Fine." Deena moved to her place in front of the class.

She flipped on the P.C. and projector at her media controls, plugged in her Power Point, and passed out graded essays before explaining the appeal to ethics in an argument. Her hands shook as she moved through her slides, but as she spoke, her voice grew confident.

After class, Sarah Stevens and Dr. Marchant approached her at the same time.

"Sarah." Deena glanced at Marchant. She was sure he'd want her to deal with her students before any consultation. Students were the priority, after all. "How can I help you?"

"It's about my next essay." Sarah hesitated, glancing at Professor Marchant.

"I'm sorry, young lady, but you'll have to see Professor Smith during office hours." Marchant stepped in front of Sarah, holding out a sheaf of papers.

Deena took the pages but called to Sarah, who was already half out the door. "Sarah, if you wait a minute, I'll walk you to your next class."

Sarah didn't wait.

"At your leisure, please peruse."

"So, how did it go, do you think?" Deena was confident she'd done a good job despite the fact that Marchant had an unfriendly glare pinned on her for the entire class.

"You started class four minutes early."

Not really. She'd been passing back essays. But whatever.

"You ignored numerous student violations of the food and drink code."

She couldn't say anything to that. Guilty as charged. Sometimes even she brought coffee to her early class.

"Your text was not in evidence."

"Uh, yes, yes, here it is." She pushed an annotated copy of *MindSprings* toward him.

"I wrote it over the winter break. It's more user-friendly than anything I've previewed. The bookstore prints copies and sells them to students."

"I'm familiar with the route of the course pack." He glanced at her text and then away, as if embarrassed. "You used four mini-lessons for this class session, when one more in-depth presentation would have sufficed."

"Research indicates that today's students like a fast pace in the classroom. Keeps their minds from wandering."

"Nevertheless, you failed to follow the lecture/discussion format indicated for observation. Perhaps if you attended faculty meetings, you'd be more up to speed on the demands of the department."

"Oh, well, sorry. They were pretty vocal during brainstorming."

"Brainstorming is not discussion. No critical thinking skill required."

"They used critical thinking on the handout. And creativity is a necessary writing tool," Deena spoke to his retreating back.

"We are not here to be creative, Miss Smith." With that parting shot, he walked out the door.

Deflated, Deena glanced down at the evaluation sheets. From what she could tell, on a scale of one to ten, she'd scored about a three and a half. She shoved everything in her book bag. She had a couple of hours until her next class in Wilson Hall. Time enough to take a trip through Old Oaks. She'd been itching to check out Ian's house.

Lack of progress with the Paris notebook plan annoyed her, but the end of the semester and all the work it entailed, was perhaps not the best time to plot the downfall of a rock idol. Or learn how to break and enter.

Jack met her on the campus square, coming from Wilson Hall. "Wilson's closed."

"Why?"

"Somebody used pepper spray upstairs. They're airing it out."

"Campus security should find out which class was having a test, and then ask the prof what student is failing the class."

Jack laughed. "Or maybe someone just wanted to enjoy the day."

Deena had been so preoccupied, she hadn't noticed until this moment that the breeze today was twenty degrees warmer than yesterday. It felt like springtime in Paris.

"Anyway, classes are cancelled." A huge smile covered his handsome face. "Going back to the office?"

Revealing her intention to stake out Ian's place didn't feel right, so instead she said, "I was thinking of going somewhere off campus, for a large glass of wine."

"Why, what happened?" Jack put his arm around her. They started toward the east parking lot.

"Creativity died. Academic freedom, too."

"You had your first year observation."

"Yep."

"Who? No, let me guess. Marchant." Jack squeezed her shoulders. "Let's get out of here. Go have lunch or something. I'll drive. We can come back for your car later."

She wanted him much more than she'd wanted anything or anyone in a very long time. Ian could wait. She settled into the passenger seat. "Jack, do you like teaching?"

"Not much. It's a job. For now."

"Then why do you do it?"

"I need a paycheck while I look for right work."

"What's your dream job?"

"I'd like to edit a magazine, something that covers politics and popular culture."

"Wow." That was pretty specific. Deena understood now why Jack moved around so much. He hadn't found his comfort zone. "Your place or mine?"

Jack glanced at her, a grin on his face. "We haven't christened my bed yet."

"And mine's not made." The truth, but perhaps not the best image to evoke for a compulsive neat freak like Jack. She smiled, already tingling in anticipation of messing up his pristine bedding.

As they pulled into Jack's driveway, Deena noticed Professor Bluet, who lived downstairs in the house Deena bought, outside washing windows. Deena waved, hoping to avoid a conversation. She liked Professor Bluet, but Jack's bed beckoned.

Professor Bluet stopped washing the front window, headed toward Deena and Jack. "Hello, professors. Have they discovered the culprit who closed down Wilson Hall?"

"Not as far as we know."

"In all my years at Ash Creek, I've never heard of such a thing. Oh, we've closed for snow or the odd power failure, but this is ridiculous."

"Yeah, except on the plus side, we get a free day." Jack slid his arm around Deena, tucking her tight against him.

"Which I'm using to clean these windows one last time."

"Oh, that's right," Jack said. "I saw something in the faculty bulletin about you retiring."

Deena hated to be rude, but she wanted to scream. Jack seemed in no hurry to get inside and get naked. Maybe he'd like to invite Myra Bluet in for tea so they could chat about her plans after retirement.

"Ms. Smith made the first decent offer on my house since I put it on the market."

"Deena bought your house?"

"Not only bought it, but allowed me to live on the main floor until I retire. I was planning to move in with my son, but Deena said she'd be fine living upstairs for a few months." Dr. Bluet smiled at them and returned to her window washing.

"You own that house?" Jack looked at Deena's place, dropping his arm from her shoulder. He walked ahead of her and unlocked his door, not standing aside to let her enter first. She followed him inside, pulling the door closed behind her. Jack walked though the kitchen into the living room. This house was a smaller than hers, one story, built a decade or four after Myra's more solid Queen Anne. Deena followed Jack into the living room.

"All the time we worked together, sharing an office, and you never said you *owned* the house next door. I thought you rented from Dr. Bluet." He came up and smoothed the hair on her forehead, moving it back so her widow's peak showed. "Why didn't you ever tell me?"

"I didn't think it was important. We closed on the house with the stipulation that Myra would rent the main floor from me until semester's end." Deena shrugged. She didn't get how any of this mattered to Jack.

"But you might have mentioned..."

"Jack, come on. We didn't talk about stuff like that. We talked about school, our students. Other faculty."

"I asked you out at least fifty times."

"And I explained that I didn't want to date someone I worked with."

"But we're dating now."

"Well, not really." She flopped on to the black leather couch. "More like a business dinner. Then we had sex afterward."

"So the sex part was my finder's fee for getting you a lawyer?"

44

"See…" Deena took her shoes off and put her feet on the coffee table. "This is why I don't like to date."

"What? Why?"

Jack lifted up her feet and put a pillow under them. Whether it was for her comfort or so that she did not smudge the immaculate coffee table, she wasn't sure. He sat down next to her.

"This. Miscommunication. Nasty little digs."

Jack got up and went into the kitchen. She heard him opening the fridge, a cupboard. He came back with a glass of wine, which he handed to her.

"You're not having any?"

"That's the end of the bottle."

"Oh, you're sweet. Sometimes." Deena took a long sip and handed the glass to Jack. "We'll share."

"Was that our first fight?"

"Minor tiff."

She'd rather have make up sex with Jack right now, but she guessed from his expression that he needed her to share some personal info. Okay, so maybe they were dating after all.

"Yellow's Star's first album made a lot of money. And I was a credited songwriter. Even after living in Paris for a year, I still had enough money to buy myself a house and a car. Of course, they aren't paid for. Thus, the real job, as my dad calls it."

Jack set the glass of wine down, leaned in, and kissed her. She fell into him, already addicted to how his kisses made her feel. After a minute, he pulled slightly away, picked up the glass of wine and gave her a sip from it.

Then he kissed her again, and their lips and tongues and the wine meshed together until she was drunk with it.

Jack's kisses made it difficult to keep her clothes on, but before they could do anything about it, the front bell rang.

With a groan of remorse, Jack let her go.

Before he even got to the door, a woman walked in with the baby in her arms and a toddler clinging to the diaper bag over her shoulder.

Chapter Seven

"I saw your car was home, and we decided to invite you to lunch." The woman looked from Jack to Deena with a smug smile, as if she had uncovered a delicious secret.

"Uncle Zak!"

Jack kissed the woman on the cheek and picked up the little boy. He turned to Deena. "This is my sister Leslie, and her son Tyler. The baby's Ashley." Tyler waved hello, disbursing cookie crumbs all over the white rug.

"Hi, Deena, my mom told me all about you."

Oh God. Now his whole family knew about her. Once, she had believed she could keep things simple. Three separate and distinct tracks. Jack, sex track. First year of teaching, employment track. Ian and the notebook, revenge track. In her mind, they'd all run parallel and on their own times. But instead they'd collided in ways she hadn't planned, couldn't have predicted.

"Nice kitty." Tyler squirmed out of his arms, reaching for Derrida, who made a swift exit with Tyler hot on his trail.

"Say hi to Deena, Tyler." Leslie's voice stopped the toddler in his tracks.

"Hi, Xena."

"Hi, Ty."

Tyler giggled.

"We were just going to have some lunch. Why don't you guys stay?"

"Well, if it's okay with Deena..."

What could she say? She had a feeling that

"Please leave so I can quickly fuck your brother before I break into my ex-boyfriend's house" would probably be rude. Equally rude would be bailing on the afternoon now. So she said "Oh, of course," and held the baby while Leslie set the table and Jack made them all sandwiches.

"I've got ham, Swiss cheese, peanut butter, jelly, and tuna fish. What's everyone want?" While Jack organized the sandwich orders, Deena sat on the sofa with the baby on her lap. She'd never held a baby before. The little girl was cute, even with her lower lip wobbling. Tyler stood next to them, looking from Deena to the baby and back again.

"She's getting weddy to cwy," Tyler observed.

"I think you're right." Deena liked Tyler better than Ashley. At least he wasn't afraid of her.

"Stwanger. Thass why."

"I figured as much." She smiled at the baby, whose eyes were now starting to fill with water. Just like that, Ashley's bottom lip stopped wiggling like Jell-O and her face bloomed with a smile even while a teardrop ran down her pudgy cheek.

"S'okay now." Tyler took hold of the arm that was not holding Ashley. "Bwing her by Mommy." He pulled Deena toward the kitchen.

Deena turned Ashley around in her lap so that she'd see her mom the minute they entered the kitchen. She stood up, hugging the baby to her hip with the arm Tyler wasn't tugging on.

"You do that like an old pro," Leslie noted. "Got kids?"

"No, no. I'm not married."

"Yeah, but you could be divorced. Lots of people are."

At the sound of her mother's voice, Ashley started waving her hands and pumping her feet. "No, not divorced, either." Deena happily handed the baby back to her rightful caretaker. "She's adorable."

"Thank you."

"Wha'bout me?" Tyler demanded.

"You're adorable too," Deena told him.

Tyler beamed.

"So, Deena, Mom tells me you write lyrics."

"Oh, not really. I used to..."

"I know, the plagiarism debacle." Leslie held Ashley on her lap with one hand and ate with the other. Tyler sat on pillows. Deena wished she had a sweater. She felt a little exposed.

"Dad's taking care of it for Deena. She just has to let the wheels of justice turn," Jack supplied.

"They turn so slow," Deena said. Bill hadn't heard from Ian or his manager yet. He'd asked Deena if she wanted him to take further action, but she'd said no. She didn't want to antagonize Ian, in case the idea of befriending him and getting into his place that way worked out.

"So, Ann Arbor in a couple weeks?" Leslie looked pointedly from Jack to Deena.

"It's not that long of a drive." Jack said.

"Only two hours," Leslie said

"An hour and a half." Jack scooped another sandwich from the plate.

"If you break the speed limit by about 30 miles an hour." Leslie turned toward Tyler, who had been tugging on her arm.

"Mommy, I ready for my tweet."

"How about a cookie?" Jack asked Tyler.

"You got chockit chip?"

"I think I do."

"Unless you ate them all." Leslie winked at Deena.

"Deena just made them the other day for me." Jack brought over the Tupperware container that held the end of her batch of Toll House.

"Wow, home-made. Impressive."

Deena bit into a cookie, trying to convince

49

herself that this collision of tracks in her life was something she could handle. Jack would be gone soon. School would be over. Then she could focus on Ian and the notebook.

Tyler squished his nose. "Mommy that baby poops too much."

"Come help me change her, and then you can have your cookie."

"So, do you like kids?" Jack asked, as his sister and kids left the room.

"Yeah." Deena stacked the empty sandwich plates on top of each other. "I'm not exactly comfortable around them yet, but I do. I always wanted a baby sister."

"And your parents didn't comply?"

"My mom died when I was young." She folded her hands in her lap. "My dad never remarried."

Jack got up and took the stack of plates to the sink. He came back, gathering glassware. "Your dad's a plumber, right?" He took the glasses to the sink, slotted everything in the dishwasher.

"Yeah." Deena wanted the conversation to stop without exactly knowing why. But she struggled with the urge, and forced herself to continue. "And a volunteer fireman."

Jack came back to the table with a sponge and a dry dishtowel. "How could he handle both jobs? Did he work all the time?" Jack asked, buffing the smoked glass table with the towel.

"For about the first year after my mother died, my dad sat around eating potato chips and watching daytime television." She stopped and fingered a button on her sweater. Sharing childhood memories always made her uncomfortable. Maybe that would be enough.

"That had to be a sad time for both of you. I don't know how I would handle losing my mom."

"Well..." She looked at him briefly, then away.

This fun little affair was turning into something else.

"So does your dad like being a plumber?" Jack asked.

"I guess. He's always busy. Work. Gym. Doing the fire thing on weekends. I didn't see much of him growing up."

Jack took Deena's hand just as Leslie brought a sweet smelling Ashley in and put her on Deena's lap. "I've got to go help Ty." She left the room again.

"Look at Ashley's little hands, such tiny fingernails," Jack said.

"Do you ever think about having kids, Jack?" Deena asked. Talking about her hopes of having a family someday had always cooled Ian right off. Didn't all guys hate when women brought up the subject?

"Some day, sure."

Deena stopped stroking Ashley's fingers and put her face to the baby's soft cheek. "I haven't had much contact with babies. But I think I'd like one. I really would." When she said it, she realized she was trying to push Jack's buttons, or trying to push him away. But also, she was telling the truth. Her desires were in conflict with each other.

"Most women want kids." Jack was starting to sound a little bit uncomfortable.

Deena sighed. She'd scored her point, but victory wasn't all that sweet.

****

The next day, Deena made it through class somehow, even though she'd stayed awake most of the night, looking for the college's protocol on delivering the correct response to Sarah Stevens's essay. The campus had a set of actions professors should take in the event that something like this would come up.

Sarah's essay had been so personal it shook

Deena to her core. Her student had heeded the larger assignment requirement by addressing an ethical dilemma, but the actual pages were more like a private confession and a call for help. They seemed ripped from her inner self, a far cry from the composed and proper essays she'd been writing all term.

Last night, Deena had finally unearthed the handbook she'd been given when hired and had memorized what she needed to do. This could go one of two ways. If Sarah would agree to see a counselor, Deena would not have to report that Sarah's essay had included an ink-blotched paragraph admitting she'd considered suicide.

Sarah wrote that she had gone to a party, taken Ecstasy and ended up partnering, without protection, two guys in one night. Horrified by her behavior, Sarah had stopped partying. She considered suicide. Then found out she was pregnant.

Deena returned essays, and dismissed class, keeping Sarah's essay with her until the rest of the class disbursed. Sarah sat in her seat, looking at Deena, ready to cry, and Deena had to convince Sarah to get counseling at the Health Center.

She sat down next to Sarah, who blurted, "What should I do, Ms. Smith? What would you do?"

"Have you spoken to your parents about this?"

Sarah nodded. Deena could see her misery intensify.

"My mom wants me to have an abortion, but I don't want to." She sniffed, holding back the tears. "Nothing against other women who make that choice, but I can't." Her voice was choked with tears, and now a few spilled from her eyes. "I just had a feeling you wouldn't judge me," Sarah cried between words. "What would you do?"

Deena leaned over and put her arm around

Sarah's shoulder, mustering a tone of confidence. "I'm so sorry for what you've gone through. But I can't tell you what to do. And neither can your mother. You're of legal age, right?"

Sarah nodded. "I'm nineteen."

Deena took a deep breath. *Here goes.* "Maybe seeing a professional would help."

Sarah shook her head. "I don't need a shrink."

"It's not like that. There are trained professionals right here on campus who deal with this kind of thing all the time. Someone will help you sort out your feelings. I'm sorry, hon, but I'm just not qualified."

"I can't go to counseling. Even if I wanted to, I don't have the cash. I got fired from my waitress job because I barf all the time." Sarah's sobbing intensified. A few students arriving early for the next class wheeled right back around and out of the room when they heard her. Sarah tried to gulp back the storm of sobs, and mostly got herself under control.

"The first three sessions are free to students. Maybe you'll only need a few sessions, just to get perspective."

"I know what I want. I need a friend, not a counselor."

Deena remembered that Sarah's group of girlfriends had shunned her after the party. They had spread rumors of what she'd done all around school and were all against her. It was no wonder the poor girl was so isolated. "I'll be your friend, but I strongly advise you seek guidance, too." Deena reached into her purse and pulled out a Kleenex, then handed it to Sarah, whose tears were starting to subside. Deena noticed when the prof using this class next came in. He ignored Deena and her distraught student, pulling out his books and materials and laying things on neat piles at the desk. A few students came in and took their seats.

"Let's talk more outside." Deena stood.

Sarah slowly followed Deena's lead.

Deena steered them toward the Health Center. "Honey, there's another reason you should see somebody today. If you don't, I'm required by campus rules to take your essay to the dean of my department."

"You're shitting me."

"No. It's to guard against lawsuits."

"But you wouldn't do that to me."

Deena still had Sarah's essay in her hand. Now, outside the building, Sarah grabbed it from Deena. Deena didn't tell Sarah that she'd already made a copy. That had been in the faculty handbook, too.

"It's not my choice. I'd lose my job if someone found out I hadn't taken measures to ensure your safety."

Sarah drew a ragged breath. "Okay."

The weight of the day fell from Deena's shoulders. And they were already in sight of the Health Center.

When it came time to part, Sarah looked frightened. "Can't you come in with me?"

"No. You have to do this on your own. Willingly."

"But I can't tell them what happened. What if it's a man? I'd be so embarrassed!"

"You can request a woman." Deena's thoughts sped through a solution that would get Sarah in there today. "Why don't you just ask her to read your essay?" Deena gestured toward the now ragged set of pages. They'd been cried on and twisted and worried over, but they told the story.

"They would do that?"

"Absolutely. Ask for an emergency appointment." Deena had no idea if the person who would see Sarah would read the essay, but she hoped so.

"I'm so ashamed."

"Don't be. Everybody does things they regret. Especially young people. You're human. You made a mistake. That's all."

Sarah slowly turned to face the doors of the Health Center. "Thanks, Ms. Smith."

"You're welcome. And I meant that about being your friend. If you ever need anything, please call me."

"I will. Thanks." Then Sarah marched up the walk to the Health Center, opened the door, and vanished inside.

Deena stood there a minute, trying to put herself in Sarah's shoes. At nineteen, she'd have been just as frightened and confused.

****

Jack walked fast across campus, his mind on the morning's email from Don. His friend had asked for a proposal for Deena's book so that he could start circulating it in-house and create buzz within the company. Given Deena knew nothing about the idea, he doubted she'd be willing to submit a proposal. Asking her would ruin his surprise too. In the name of ethics, however, he supposed he should ask. He could guide her in what to write so they could nail this sucker down.

"Make sure you exploit the Yellow Star angle. That's the hook." Don had written.

Jack walked through the proposal in his head as he walked toward the library where he could work on it in peace. He almost passed Deena without seeing her.

"Hey, Jack."

"Oh, hey, Deena." Jack reached for her hand just as he noticed they were in front of the Health Center. He dropped his hand without connecting to hers, his heart skidding like a sled on ice. "You coming or going?" Condoms had been known to leak.

"No, I ah, just walked a student over."

Relief flooded through Jack. "Going home before your afternoon sessions?"

"No. I don't know. Listen, can we talk?"

Jack had promised the proposal to Don first thing tomorrow. He didn't want to be late with it. The idea of using his editing of Deena's book as leverage out of teaching wouldn't let him go. This could be his best chance. And he should probably speak to Deena about his ideas before going ahead with the plan. But she seemed troubled about her student, and he didn't want to burden her further. Looked like he'd have to write that proposal after all. Don wanted it pronto. Deena didn't need the added stress.

"Want to walk over to the library with me?"

"Sure." Deena's brow wrinkled. He had the urge to smooth it with his hand, but she started walking toward the library before he could touch her.

"A student mentioned suicide in a paper."

He felt like he'd been punched in the gut. It took every ounce of his willpower not to shut down and walk away. He put his arm around her. "That's rough." His mind flashed on an image of Theresa, his first serious girlfriend. They'd met in high school and had both been college freshman when they broke up. The result of that breakup, Theresa's attempted suicide, had hung around like a dark shadow for years. He shook the feelings off. He was past all that. Freshman writing students often confided private, sometimes terrible, things. In his short career, he'd had students write about being gay, about being beaten up or molested, about cutting themselves. He'd even read of cases where students confessed to murder in school essays.

"She went in voluntarily?"

"Yes, but it took some persuading."

Deena leaned into him. The horrible feelings his

memory of Theresa brought back, even his excitement over finally changing his life by editing Deena's book—everything washed away when Deena was with him. Being with her was all that mattered.

"Where are we going?"

Jack passed the library, heading toward the nature trails. "Let's take a walk."

"Didn't you need to go to the library?"

"It'll keep." Not for long. But he could always write the proposal tonight or get up early in the morning. Maybe he could get Deena to show him the new lyrics again. He'd have to tell her why he wanted to see them, but that was okay. Except right now he wanted to focus on her. "Tell me about your student." Jack didn't want to hear about an attempted suicide. But Deena needed someone to listen and that outweighed keeping bad memories at bay. It outweighed the whole editing her book discussion that must come soon.

Chapter Eight

Jack and Deena started down the curving path that led to the college's vast nature area. Sunshine glinted through the trees. A profusion of chartreuse buds pulsed on the tips of branches, ready to burst into leaf. The wind played with Deena's hair. She was pretty and kind and completely unaware of both of these things. They talked about her student, and Jack assured Deena she had done the right thing. He took her hand, entwined their fingers, and swung their arms in tandem as they walked. Usually Jack was uncomfortable being silent with a woman. He always tried to keep the conversation going, even if it was a struggle to find a topic. But with Deena, he was comfortable when they fell into silence.

They walked down trails past the football field and the wildflower meadow, over a footbridge and across a brook that flowed through this end of the campus.

"I hear they want to make this section of the wetlands into a golf course."

"I hope not. Jack."

Something in her voice put him on high alert.

"I need to talk to you about something."

The way she took her hand out of his, the tone of her voice. Bad signs, both.

"We've been having a great time together."

"Yes." Was he being dumped? His mouth turned to cotton, and his heart beat like he'd run ten miles. He patted his shirt front, searching for a stick of gum.

"I think it would be easier on both of us if we

just ended things when you went to Ann Arbor."

"Oh." He didn't expect her words to hurt, but they did, and he wasn't sure why. Leaving girls behind was generally part of the plan when he did a geographic. "It seems a natural breaking point." His agreement sounded hollow to his ears.

"Yes." He searched her face for signs that her sadness matched his own. He didn't find any.

"I don't do well with long distance relationships," she continued matter-of-factly. "I don't do well with relationships in general. But long distance, no."

"What happened with you and Ian?" Jack figured he might as well know. He didn't really want to know, because he wanted Deena now, wanted to have sex with her here, outside. Or at least fool around. But this was obviously an issue for her, and so they'd better get it out on the table. Then maybe later they'd get naked. And he'd tell her about the book proposal.

They weren't breaking up yet. They still had a lot of love to make before moving day. And with this book proposal, anything could happen. He might be moving to New York instead of Ann Arbor. So probably she was right. They should break things off cleanly when he left. But he didn't have to think about that now. He'd deal with it later.

"We were in Europe when I realized I couldn't stand touring anymore," Deena answered the question he hadn't really wanted to ask. "I stayed in Paris, settled into the place Ian had rented there as a home base."

A group of rowdy kids filled the path, walking backward, not noticing they took all the space on the brick pavers. Jack pulled Deena aside, onto the grass, until they passed. She waited to finish her story until the kids were well out of sight. Finally, their booming exuberant voices faded.

"And he did come back to Paris when he could. On one trip, he asked me to get a shirt out of his suitcase, and I found some pictures of him, naked, with various women, also unclothed. Doing stuff."

He might be a great musician but as a person Ian was a total asshole. Who in their right mind would treat Deena that way? The wind moved her hair from her face, and his breath caught in his throat at the sight of her hairline and the widow's peak she usually tried so hard to hide. Right now, caught up in memory, she didn't notice.

"He said they were souvenirs, that the women didn't mean anything. He told me that I had to accept that women were a natural part of the road, or we were over. So, we were over. I stayed in Paris for a few months while he finished the tour. We'd already paid for the place, and he didn't care."

"What did you do there all alone?" The image of her in a foreign country, far from home, without friends or family, pierced him. "Do you speak French?"

"Not really. You pick up enough to get by in restaurants and stores. And they have a great bookstore that sells English versions of the French authors. So I read Baudelaire and moped. I read Colette and felt better. I wrote the notebook, the one Ian stole my lyrics from. When they finished up the tour with a concert in Paris, I gave him the notebook, well, the copy of the notebook. You know the rest."

They walked over to a huge old tree. He pulled her down to sit on his lap. He tilted his head back, leaning on the rough pillow of bark.

"You must have figured out by now that I'm nothing like Ian Hensley."

"I have." She smiled and smoothed his hair behind his ear. "But I want to make this time between us just for now. It's easier on me that way."

Maybe she didn't know it herself, but Jack understood that Deena was afraid of getting hurt again. She was afraid he'd be unfaithful in Ann Arbor. And by breaking up, she avoided it. *Maybe she doesn't feel she has the right to ask for a real relationship.* He should feel lucky, because she completely let him off the hook, but for some reason he only felt sad.

His arms drew her closer and they kissed. Her sweater scratched under his hands. He moved under the wool to feel her smooth skin. He skimmed her breasts through her light cotton bra. Her nipples tightened, and she collapsed into his embrace, moaning low, spilling the sound into his mouth as they kissed.

He would miss this. Miss every part of her. But she was right. He didn't have a great record at long-distance relationships either.

"Sorry."

A Frisbee landed on Jack's left foot. A student laughed, came across to the tree, and picked it up. He slid his hands out from under Deena's sweater as she hid her face in his shoulder.

Once the Frisbee people were safely past, Deena jumped up, still blushing. Jack laughed.

"I know you've got work to do."

Right. He did. His heart twisted in his chest. She was the first girlfriend he'd had who really cared about his work. And the first one who ever wanted to end things before he did.

****

"You'll never believe what happened at The Pub last night," Patti said.

"What?" Deena came into the loft with a copy of the classic *Legally Blonde*. She'd really wanted to see Jack tonight, but she'd been ignoring her friend.

"Toby asked me out!"

"You going?"

61

"Of course! What should I wear? And I need another outfit for the benefit concert."

"Concert?"

"Yeah, Yellow Star agreed to do a thing at The Pub."

I could sneak in their house and steal the notebook while they play the concert. But that only made her feel guilty. She needed to watch Patti's back. She didn't want her best friend screwed over again by yet another musician. Toby seemed a decent enough guy, but he'd jump off a bridge if Ian told him to. Still, maybe this could work in her favor.

"We'll look over your wardrobe choices after the movie," Deena watched her friend gather movie supplies. Popcorn, extra butter. Cokes. Mars Bars chopped up on top of a bowl of chocolate almond ice cream.

"No ice cream for me." Patti eyed Deena like she was a traitor to chick flicks. "Okay, just one scoop. But no candy on top."

Two hours later, the credits rolled, the bottom of the popcorn bowl contained a scatter of unpopped kernels jelled into a half inch of butter. Deena gathered empty ice cream dishes and finished Coke cans off the coffee table.

"We could be Elle and Vivian." Patti referred to the best friends in the movie.

"At least they ended up in better places than Thelma and Louise."

"You're Elle. You do the same things she did."

"What?" Since Deena had never attended law school, gotten a manicure, or brought a little dog to class, she didn't see what Patti was talking about.

"Elle didn't want to be a lawyer, she only went to law school because Warner was there. And you weren't a songwriter. You just told Ian that so he'd date you."

"But Elle ended up being a pretty good lawyer.

And I wrote the lyrics to a platinum record."

"So then why are you teaching instead of writing songs?"

"Because I'm not a songwriter. And I'm not a fictional movie character." Deena stacked dirty dishes in the sink and squirted liquid into a flowing stream of warm water. Patti didn't have a dishwasher, but she was a neat freak, like Jack.

Patti put the empty Coke cans under the sink and grabbed a clean dish towel. Deena always washed and Patti always dried. "If you don't think you're a songwriter, then why are you fighting Ian about who wrote the lyrics on his new record?"

"It doesn't matter if I'm not a professional songwriter. I wrote those lyrics, by whatever fluke, and I want to be paid for them." She plunged her hands into the sink and scrubbed, before handing the popcorn bowl to Patti for a rinse 'n' dry. "Where's your hand lotion?" Usually, some pretty bottle sat right next to the lemon-scented Joy.

"In the bedroom. And let's pick out my date outfit now, please."

Deena searched Patti's massive antique armoire, flipping past old Laura Ashley dresses and anything with glitter on it. She pulled out a soft pair of black denim leggings.

"What about these?"

"Elastic waist! They'll probably still fit." Patti pulled off her sweatpants. "Look at how fat I am." She grabbed the skin around her belly.

Deena reminded Patti that Toby was a big guy, too.

"In case you hadn't noticed, he loves to eat. I bet he adores your figure." She tugged at an oversized white shirt, refusing to police Patti's ice cream consumption. "This is stuck." She pulled harder on the sleeve of the white shirt.

Something big and dark rushed forward from

the back of the wardrobe and landed with a familiar twang at her feet. The cuff of Patti's white shirt was still hooked onto a beautiful Martin acoustic guitar.

"Wow." Deena picked up the guitar, handling it with the respect it deserved. She blew dust off the fretboard. "What a beauty. Is it yours?"

Patti's face paled. She didn't answer, just grabbed the guitar, loosened the white shirt, and shoved the Martin back into the closet corner, covering it with clothes. She put on the shirt.

"Nice." Deena complimented the outfit, wondering about the deal with the guitar. Patti hadn't answered her question, had shoved it away like the guitar. Not like her to avoid answering like that.

"I have a belt that would be perfect with this." Patti looked into her dresser mirror from every angle. "I think we're done in here. I need to get to bed." Patti turned her back to Deena, sorting through her collection of nightwear in a dresser drawer.

Deena, wired after two Cokes plus chocolate, asked about the guitar again. "Patti, where did you get that gorgeous Martin?"

"It was a present, okay?" Patti slammed the drawer she'd been looking through and stomped out of the bedroom.

Deena followed. She hadn't even known Patti played.

"It's lovely. Who gave it to you? Not Ian?"

A ridiculous stab of envy pierced Deena.

Ian had never allowed her to even touch his guitars.

"No, my parents. Birthday present. The big 13." Patti popped the DVD out of her player and put it back in the case, then handed it to Deena.

Patti stood there, and Deena got the distinct feeling she wanted her to leave.

Why? She seemed as wide awake as Deena. She must not want to talk about the guitar.

But why not?

They told each other everything.

Chapter Nine

"Do you play guitar, Patti?" Deena thoughtfully eyed her best friend.

"Used to." Patti didn't sound like herself. She was too quiet. Too subdued."When?"

"You know. Before. Long time ago." She wasn't making eye contact either.

"When you were 13?"

"Before that." Patti scoffed, plopping down on the sofa, abandoning the ruse of sleepiness. "My first guitar was plastic, an Easter present when I was four. Then, in elementary school, I played. Everyone did something. You either sang or played an instrument. I picked the guitar. I played chords before I could multiply."

Deena sat. "Why did I not know this?"

"Because it's all in the past, before we met." Patti's bare toes played with the fringe on her afghan.

"Does Toby know? Does Ian?"

"Yeah." Patti's face contorted, like she was trying not to sneeze. Or cry.

"Jesus, what's wrong? Why did you stop playing?"

"No, it's okay." Patti's face relaxed, and the tears fell. She pushed them away with the tips of her fingers. "It's stupid, really."

"Tell me."

"It's nothing."

Deena tried to make this new part of Patti fit into the pattern she'd come to know and love. Patti seemed ten times more miserable than when she

66

talked about being fat.

"Those leggings look really good on you," Deena said, again. It was lame, but this awful, sad silence was worse.

"Yeah." Patti smiled. "They hold me in like a girdle."

"But they don't pinch, do they?"

"Nope. They feel good."

"Good."

"Yeah."

"And the white shirt isn't too ordinary?"

"No."

"Did you stop playing guitar when you were with Ian?" Deena leaned forward in her chair.

"Yep." Patti curled her legs up on the sofa.

"Why?"

"I wasn't any good."

Deena found this hard to believe. No one played guitar their whole life and then found out at twenty-five that they sucked. And Patti's parents wouldn't have bought her such an expensive guitar unless she was skilled enough to appreciate it.

"You still got a copy of *Thelma and Louise?*"

Patti nodded.

"Feel like watching it again?"

Instead of answering, Patti found the disk and stuck it in the DVD player.

****

By the time Deena made it home, it was well after midnight. As she got out of her car, she saw someone, a shadow in the night, sitting at the top of her stairway. Jack.

"I missed you," he said, when she reached him. He hugged her tight.

"I'll give you a key," she said, without thinking.

"I guess that means you missed me too."

They went inside. Deena had assumed Jack was on a booty call, and she was wondering how she should feel about that, when he surprised her.

"I think we could make it work." He accepted the glass of wine she offered.

"Make what work?" She was pretty sure what he meant, but it was better to be positive.

She sat on the sofa with her own glass of wine. He sank down next to her. Without thinking, she curled herself up against his side, and he put his arm around her.

"See how good we fit?"

She nodded. It was true. They were made for each other. At least physically.

"We should try to work it out. This. Us. After I move."

Deena stared at their glasses of wine, both untouched on the cedar chest.

"It might work." She wasn't promising anything. "We've got a couple of weeks. Let's see how it goes."

Jack picked up both of the wine glasses and held one out to her. "To us." He clinked her glass with his.

"To us," she agreed. "May we live well and prosper."

"Did you just quote Spock?" Jack laughed, and she did too. He always made her laugh. "Wasn't there a baby doctor also named Spock? Wrote a book?" Deena asked.

"Yeah. My sister says he's awful."

"Well, she's doing something right. Her kids are adorable."

Jack smiled, and she watched to see when his smile would fade and his look became guarded. It didn't happen.

"So, kids, huh?" Jack sipped his wine and looked completely open to the direction the conversation was taking.

"What about them?"

"You want some."

"Yep. It's not going to be simple."

"Why not? How many?"

"Let's see. The reason why not is my age. Women are most fertile in their twenties and I'm past thirty by a couple of years. So I'll take however many I can manage before my biological clock runs out." Now she had absolutely blown it. Tick tock. Men hated that. "What about you? Do you want kids someday?" She hoped that was enough to make him forget she had a timeline.

"I really haven't thought about it much. Until you brought it up the other day. Two seems a good number. One of each. Like my sister."

"I'd take any gender as long as they're healthy."

Jack nodded and sipped his wine. "Are you on the pill?"

"No."

"I read somewhere that women on the pill have a harder time conceiving."

"I didn't know that." Apparently Jack was not as allergic to talking about babies as Ian had been.

"That scumbag Ian would be a horrible dad."

So Ian was on Jack's mind too. Ian, who had taken her best years, torn them into tiny pieces, and blew them all away.

"Yeah, you're right. He's not the married-with-kids-type." She looked at Jack. Was he? A few weeks ago she would have said no. Now she wasn't sure. He was showing her a completely different side of himself tonight.

She drained her glass of wine. Her heart rate had been slowly accelerating during this conversation. Could Jack be discussing babies with her for a reason? And did that reason include a future together, one in which they were married, with children?

Guys did not bring that kind of stuff up unless they were seriously interested. Right? To cover her confusion she got up to refill their almost empty glasses. Jack followed her into the kitchen. She started to open the fridge, but he put his hand over hers, gently pulling her away and into his arms. Then he kissed her.

****

The next morning, after Jack left, Deena cleaned the apartment in search of a missing folder of exams. She wound the vacuum cord and rolled the machine back into the closet. She retrieved furniture polish from the depths of her kitchen cupboard. Her cleaning spree had nothing to do with the fact that Jack now had a key to her house. It was a direct result of finals week and the missing folder.

Just as she pulled an old dish rag from a drawer, right between her feet, Dr. Bluet banged on the floor. The professor's ceiling.

"Give me a break," Deena muttered. "It was only a vacuum cleaner."

As she cleared clutter and shined spaces, she found the missing exams, but also heard more banging from below. After a few minutes of listening to steady pounding, Deena headed down and around to the front door and knocked. No answer. She skirted shrubbery to peer into the big picture window at the front of the house. Through an opening in the heavy draperies, Deena saw someone on the dining room floor.

"Professor Bluet? Are you all right?" Deena yelled.

"Come in, door's open," the professor shouted back.

Her voice was strong at least, Deena noted with relief.

She entered the other half of her house. From the viewing before the sale, she remembered that the foyer led to the living room and the living room opened to a dining area. Still, she hesitated.

"Professor?"

"In here," Dr. Bluet commanded. "About time," she added.

Deena moved toward the voice. Professor Bluet lay on the dining room floor, a broom next to her.

Dr. Bluet looked up as Deena entered. "I can't put weight on my right leg."

Deena rushed to Dr. Bluet's side and bent to make eye contact. The professor's face showed obvious pain. "I'm calling 911."

"Yes, fine, but call my son, too. Tell him to meet me at the hospital? He's #1 on speed dial."

Deena dialed 911. They asked a couple of questions, but when Dr. Bluet seemed too confused or in pain to respond, they decided to send an ambulance. Then she called the next number.

"Mr. Bluet?"

"Yes, this is Dave Bluet. How can I help you?"

"This is Deena Smith. I live above your mother. I'm with her. She's had an accident, and she wants you to meet her at the hospital." Deena already heard the ambulance's siren.

"Is she okay? Can I speak to her?"

Professor Bluet's hand reached for the phone. After a minute or two of terse discussion, she handed the phone back to Deena, gritting her teeth. "I'll need my purse."

"Where is it?" Deena asked, letting the EMS guys in with their stretcher.

"On my dresser. My keys are in there too. Would you lock up for me?"

Deena ran to get the purse as the emergency technicians asked Dr. Bluet a series of questions. When Deena came back with the purse, they'd carried the professor, flat on a stretcher, outside.

Deena checked the purse for keys. In the middle of locking the front door, she heard the siren resume. She still held the professor's handbag.

Okay, no problem. She'd drive to the hospital

and hand it over to David. She walked back inside, called the university physics department, cancelled Dr. Bluet's evening class, then raced up the stairs to her apartment, got her own purse and keys, and headed out for Memorial Medical Center, where she inquired after Professor Bluet.

"Are you Deena Smith?"

"Yes."

"She said you'd have her Blue Cross card."

"Is her son here yet?"

"No."

Deena pulled a wallet out of Dr. Bluet's purse. This was such an invasion of privacy. She quickly scanned Dr. Bluet's stacked cards. Since she had an identical one, she quickly found and handed it over. Before she could even close the wallet, a man in his mid-thirties rushed up to the information desk.

"My mother's been admitted. Myra Bluet."

"Oh yes, Mr. Bluet. The doctor is looking at her now. He will be out shortly."

"David?"

"Yes? Deena?"

She nodded.

Dave Bluet wrapped his arms around her tightly. "Thank God you were home."

"I have her purse." She handed the bag over with relief. "They have the insurance card and your mom's driver's license."

Chapter Ten

Jack used his special black pen to make the final edits on his proposal for Deena's book. He'd changed *MindSprings* to *Writing Like a Rock Star* and added Deena's bio, something the course pack didn't have. He found perfect lyric lines to use as headers for a few sample chapters he'd included in the proposal, and had noted that a website was in the works. It wasn't, unless you counted the idea of it in his head, but he planned to talk to Deena about all of this tonight.

He checked his phone for the time. Dinner with Deena in ten minutes. Good thing she lived next door. He hated being late and wanted a perfect, relaxed night.

They met at his car. Just seeing her made him feel happy again.

"Hi." She hugged him and fluttered a light kiss on his lips before ducking into the car. "I'm starving."

"Me too. Let's check out American Paris. I hear the food's great. And they have awesome desserts."

"Myra's son owns that restaurant."

"Myra?"

"Professor Bluet. You know, I told you she fell and broke her hip. I met her son, David, at the hospital. He owns American Paris with another guy, the chef. They dreamed of opening a restaurant together since their high school fast food jobs."

"Oh." Jack noticed a red light ahead and pressed his foot a bit more firmly than necessary on the brake. Guy could be gay. Not that there was

73

anything wrong with that. "Did you have enough of the Bluets today? Do you want to go somewhere else?"

"No, no, it's fine. He won't be there tonight, anyway. He's staying with Myra. She can't get out of bed."

"Oh that's too bad." Jack revved the engine.

"I know. I'm helping them out. It's the least I can do. I mean, I bought their family home out from under them. Oh! That reminds me. David and I opened the door."

"What door?" The light turned green, and Jack stepped a little too hard on the gas. The car shot forward, and he had to brake in order not to hit the bumper in front of him.

"You know, that dead-bolted door in my apartment. It goes down to the main floor." He braked again for a woman who had slowed to a crawl in order to fix her hair in the rear-view mirror.

Walking into the restaurant, Jack shook off the tense driving experience. David Bluet didn't worry him much until he saw the place. No chintz or soft pastels or flowers in evidence. Instead the restaurant featured dark wood, white linen, lit candles in clear crystal holders. Classy but not feminine.

The hostess led them to a booth. Jack's plan was to ply Deena with great food and then broach the subject of changing up *MindSprings* and submitting it. He'd already sent Don the proposal and had done a ton of editing, so he should get her to approve the idea before the night was over. Was it wrong not to tell her? He finally decided no, he had been trying to spare her the pain of rejection.

He loved looking at her, loved the sexy, charged glance she threw his way while a server took their drink orders. When they were alone, she reached for his hand and took it in her own, thanking him for bringing her here.

"I love this place."

And I love you, he thought. But he didn't blurt this time. Instead he buried the words and suppressed the emotion.

"You seem preoccupied." She reached across the table and took his hand. The waitress brought his martini, and he broke away from Deena to take it from the server's hand.

"I'm not." He quaffed vodka to make it true. He needed a few drinks before he could tell Deena what he'd done. "Thinking about the new job. Disappointed to leave you, that's all."

"Which is why we need to have fun while you're here."

"I agree."

"So, you never told me. What will you be teaching at Michigan?"

"Same old freshman comp. That's depressing. For sure." He drank again, draining his glass. The golden handcuffs of tenure squeezed tighter. But maybe Don, after he saw Jack's final edits, would call his contacts and pull a miracle editing job out of a hat.

He focused on Deena. She wore the bracelet again, the one from their first date. He reached over, touching the shiny dog tag.

"Your hands are cold." She flinched from his hand.

"Ice from my drink."

The server set down their steaming dinners, and Jack tucked into his Beef in Wine Sauce, thinking that after the meal, maybe as they were perusing the dessert menu, he could lead into the book project idea with something romantic, not the L word, but maybe, "You're very special to me, Deena."

He looked across at her, a fork full of garlic mashed potato raised to her mouth. Her eyes went all soft, like melting chocolate, and the tender affection in them made him realize he'd said it out loud.

"You're special to me, too, Jack." She spoke before putting the fork full of potatoes into her mouth.

After they'd finished and ordered dessert, David's name came up again.

"I need to stop by Myra's after we leave."

It was weird how Deena avoided claiming ownership of the house. She'd been so upset that Ian stole her lyrics, but she was not at all bothered that someone else was living in the biggest part of her house.

"She needs a cup of tea with her last dose of medicine for the evening, but David has to get home to his kids."

"Oh. He's married?" The idea appealed at least as much as the Crème Brule the server set before him. He tapped through the brittle crust and dug right in.

"No, he's a widow."

Jack took another bite of the custard. "Older guy?"

"No, he's right around our age. Myra says he's a wonderful dad." Her eyes went all soft like melted chocolate again. Jack scraped the sides of the tiny soufflé dish. Deena wanted children. This guy had some. It seemed an unfair advantage. He needed a second dessert.

All the way home, he obsessed about David Bluet. This guy could be serious competition. There had to be a way to lock down Deena's love now.

Why was it so difficult with her? Why was she so different from other women he'd dated, women who professed their undying devotion after one date?

He pulled into his driveway.

"Come in for a while?" He hoped she'd say yes.

"I can't. Myra. Remember?"

How could he forget? Myra, David's mother.

They got out of the car, and he came over to her side to kiss her. She was digging in her purse for the house keys.

"I can wait upstairs for you."

"It's been a long day." She used the back of her hand to hide her yawn. "Another time?"

"Sure. See you tomorrow then?" He hated how his question came out sounding like begging.

She finally found her keys and looked up long enough for him to kiss her. Maybe a kiss would change her mind about continuing the evening. But she broke off way too soon. Oh, man. This was not good. His kisses usually had far better results.

As he locked his door and turned out the kitchen light, he remembered that he hadn't spoken to Deena yet about the book project. Damn. His mind had been full of Deena and this David person who would be here in town with his no doubt adorable kids and full access to Deena. He, on the other hand, would be in Ann Arbor. Or Manhattan. Very far away.

Chapter Eleven

Ian ran through the ballad with Jenny a final time. When she left the practice room, he sat there alone for a few minutes. This would get Dee back. He knew it. He just had to convince her to give him the words to *Girl in Window*. If she didn't give them to him, she'd wonder how he got them, and he'd be fucked. Dee could be so stubborn. Stubborn and yet endearing. The army outfit was just the latest in her cute attempts to make her outside match whatever she was feeling inside at the moment. His little Dee, ready to do battle. She'd never win, of course, but she'd put up a hell of a fight. He almost looked forward to it.

He still had his guitar in his hand. Without giving it much thought, he started singing about an army girl, putting it to the melody that had been running around in his head the last few days, ever since he decided to get Dee back. He stopped singing for a second, turned on his tape recorder. Then he strummed his guitar, making up the words as he went along. Why not? That's the way Dee had always done it. Didn't she have a song that said so in the Paris notebook?

Cal came into the practice room. "This place is a mess." He looked around at the empty beer cans and coffee cups.

"I was fucking working dude!" Writing a song for Dee would win her for sure. Chicks loved that shit.

"Oh, yeah. Sorry. New song?"

"Yeah. I want to preview it at the gig." They listened to the playback.

"Could be a song. Got a name?"

"*Army Girl.*"

"Hmm. I like it." Cal rewound the tape, listened again.

"Jenny ready?"

"Oh, yeah."

"I still don't know if this is smart."

"It's perfect." Why was Cal was their manager when he did all the real thinking himself? Then Ian remembered why he needed Cal—to deal with the record company dudes. Ian hated those guys.

Cal walked out of the room, leaving Ian alone again with his master plan and all the tools he needed to carry it out. Between Jenny's performance and *Army Girl*, Dee would come running back. He'd get the local radio people in, ignore any bootleg recording, insuring a video clip or two. With underground buzz, the label might hold up the release of the album until they added *Army Girl* as a bonus track. That would give him more time to work on Dee about those other songs.

Everything depended on her. She had to give him those words.

****

Deena heard the knock from her bedroom. She came out to her living room, hoping to see Jack. Patti stood with Toby at her side. Even though Deena wanted to make nice, or at least pretend to, her anger at Toby rose up at the sight of him.

"Hey Deena." Toby handed her a bottle of wine.

"This a bribe, Toby? Why'd you bring him here, Patti?" But Deena let them in.

"I didn't know about the songs. Honest."

"So it's songs, plural?" Deena took the wine. "I knew it!" She held the bottle of wine like a billy club as the words flew out of her mouth.

"Shit. I...well...I don't...I can't really say. I was wondering if you had the words anywhere, and I could look them over and maybe tell you."

"What does Ian say?" Deena modulated her tone and softened her stance.

"He says he didn't steal your lyrics, Deena. He says it was a coincidence. He admits he read your notebook though, and maybe borrowed a few ideas. He's always admired your ideas. That's all this is about, really. If I see the lyrics, I can tell you for sure."

Deena suspected Toby was here on a fishing expedition for Ian. Poor Toby probably didn't even realize it. She pretended to consider his suggestion.

"What about at least the words to your version of *Blow Job*? That couldn't hurt anything."

This was a dilemma. She didn't want the band to know she had a copy of the notebook. How to act like she believed the band but not give them any information? Patti went into the kitchen area and came back with a corkscrew and glasses. She took the wine from Deena and led Toby over to the sofa. Deena sat across from them, wondering what she could do to act friendly but not reveal the truth about the second notebook. Jack would know what to do.

Where he was today? She'd missed him last night, and that had made her uncomfortable. She didn't like to rely on anyone too much. Especially a man. They tended to disappoint. Maybe she could call his dad? But Bill Karris would only tell her to sit tight until the album came out. Of course, he couldn't know that asking Deena to sit tight was like telling champagne not to fizz. She really wanted to know, right now, if Ian had used any more of her material from the Paris notebook.

Toby was a nice enough guy. Hell, he'd been like a brother to her when she was with Ian. But Ian remained the problem. Toby followed Ian's lead too easily.

"Tob, tell me the truth, then we'll talk about my lyrics to *Girl in Window.*"

"Yeah, sure." Toby took a deep drink of wine, and then screwed his mouth in disgust. "You got any beer?"

"Help yourself."

Toby went to the fridge like a homing pigeon, and Deena looked over at Patti. "You two are very cozy."

"We're crazy about each other is all. I want you to like him, Deena."

"I do. I'm just not sure I can trust him."

Toby sat back down, giving Deena a hurt look. "Ask me anything. I'll tell you. I already told Ian he should give you credit. Because he admits he read your notebook and that he got ideas from it."

"Have *you* seen the notebook, Toby?"

"No. I asked to see it, but we just moved in, and Ian can't find it."

Deena's mind whirred with possibilities. "Still unpacking, huh?"

"Yeah. He thinks it's in a box downstairs. When he finds it, I'll be as curious as you are to see the extent of this. We're just so busy right now, rehearsing for the show."

She decided on a false gesture of goodwill in order to get Ian to believe she bought his lies, and gave him a dose of his own dishonest medicine. "I figured out my words after I heard Ian's version. Not that many words were changed. I guess it would be okay to give you what I wrote. I mean, the damage has already been done."

She opened her laptop and printed out a copy of *Girl in Window.*

"You've got to come to the concert. Ian's got a huge surprise for you."

"And I'm hosting a pre-concert party in the loft," Patti said.

Deena finally agreed to attend, as long as she could bring Jack. Even then, she hated missing her best chance to break into Ian's house and search those boxes in the basement. She'd find another opportunity.

****

The lights dimmed, and the normal sounds of clinking glasses and loud conversation drowned in a fluid brick wall of guitar and drums. Jack sat at a table in front of the stage, his arm around Deena. He'd agreed to attend tonight's benefit concert to make sure Hensley didn't hit on Deena. Bad enough she'd have David Bluet and Hensley in the wings when he moved to Ann Arbor. He wanted it known that tonight she was his girl. Not that it worked. Hensley had flirted with Deena through the entire pre-show party in Patti's loft, ignoring Jack even though he stuck by Deena's side.

The waitress doled out another round on a table already littered with wet cocktail napkins and half full beer mugs. Jack checked out the select crowd of radio, press, and music people. The college kids had yet to arrive, although Yellow Star had given out random tickets on campus earlier that day. Hensley had actually gone to Deena's class and given each of her students a pass. Jack had seen him later in the halls, autographing notebooks and exam papers, surrounded by adoring co-eds. Jack's arm tightened around Deena's shoulders.

"I've been meaning to talk to you about an idea I have for your course pack." Jack pulled her closer as the song ended.

She turned, her shiny silver top catching the lights from the stage and putting stars in her eyes. "I told you, Jack, Ian said he was really sorry, he wanted to make it up to me."

"I bet." Deena hadn't heard a word he said. Maybe tonight wasn't the right time to tell her about the book deal. It was still in process. There would be time to bring it up another day. He lifted his beer mug and set it right back down when Theresa Richmond, the girl who'd left a permanent mark on soul, walked in.

Chapter Twelve

Somewhere in the middle of the set from Yellow Star's first album, a woman approached their table and said hi to Jack. His body went rigid and his smile looked fake.

"Deena, this is Theresa. An old friend." He gulped down half a beer in two seconds.

Theresa smiled at that description, and Deena figured she was an ex. Jack had a lot of them.

"Who needs a drink?" Jack asked. He got up and grabbed his empty beer mug, and he didn't wait for anyone to answer him as he walked toward the bar, Theresa following him.

Soon the set ended, but Deena couldn't fully bask in the glory of hearing her lyrics performed because Jack was still not back from the bar. The room was thick with people, and she couldn't see if he was still there or had gone off somewhere else with Theresa. Patti nudged her, and Deena saw that Ian was motioning for her to stand up. She wished Jack hadn't taken off. She'd love to have him by her side right now.

"This is Dee Smith, the awesome chick who wrote those words you all seem to know." Applause rolled over her. It felt so good. It almost made up for the fact that he'd stolen her new lyrics.

Where was Jack?

As the crowd settled down, a woman came onto the stage holding an acoustic guitar. She sat down in one of two chairs that Cal had brought up from the floor. Yellow Star, all except Ian—who sat in the chair next to the woman with the guitar—left the stage. Ian took his twelve string from Cal, and looked right at Deena.

"This is another one Dee wrote. Jenny Galaxy's gonna sing it for you."

Toby appeared from backstage and sat next to Patti. He grabbed Deena's hand for a minute and squeezed. And, to Deena's astonishment, Jenny sang *Girl in Window* just the way Deena had always heard it in her head, with Ian backing this slow, moody version on acoustic guitar.

After the song, the stage lights went dark and the crowd roared for more.

"We'll be back," Ian promised.

"Time to go meet the press." Toby stood. He looked at Deena. "I told you he wanted to make it up to you."

"Thanks, Toby." Deena's heart wanted to burst with joy.

"Why don't you do the interviews with us?"

"No, no I...you know I'm no good at that." She wished Jack were here to lean against.

"Ian does most of the talking. We just sit there having our beers and chiming in every now and then. But if you're sure?"

She nodded and he left.

"Did you know about this?" she asked Patti.

"I swear I didn't. But isn't it cool?"

"It sort of is."

"Where's Jack?"

"No clue."

"Think he's jealous?"

She didn't. It was something else. Something with that friend of his, Theresa. "Not Jack. Not his style. He probably ate too much candy at your party and went out for some air."

"The make-it-yourself sundae bar was a hit."

"Too bad Jack ate all the M&M's." Deena noticed a group of her students trying to make their way over to her. "Patti, I'm just going to say hi. Those are my students."

"Yeah sure, I'll order us another glass of wine."

On the way to meet her students, a female press person, perhaps the only one who wasn't backstage getting quotes from Ian, waylaid Deena. "Ms. Smith, Cheri Croft from Detroit Woman Dot Com. Is *Girl in Window* on the new Yellow Star album?"

"No, yes, sort of."

"How does it feel to work with a genius like Ian Hensley?"

"Difficult." The crowd tightened around them, making it impossible to move.

"I understand you two were once an item."

"Ancient history."

Cheri said something else, but Deena missed it because she noticed Jack talking to Theresa. Where had they known each other from? College? Or was it high school?

Jack had his back to Deena, but she had a clear view of Theresa's dark hair. No smile on Theresa's face, Deena noticed with relief. Why relief? Had she been just a tad jealous? Maybe a little. Theresa tossed her long hair and aimed her eyes into Jack's.

Jack put his hand on Theresa's arm right before the crowd moved, blocking Deena's view.

"Listen, I've got to try to grab a quote from Ian, but I'd like to talk to you sometime. Maybe do an article. Get some pictures. You have quite a fan club."

Deena's students surrounded her. She took the card Cheri Croft held out to her. "Not fans, Cheri, students."

"Interesting angle." Cheri turned toward the backstage area.

"Hi you guys." Deena scanned the faces of her students. "Having fun?"

"I can't believe you're THE D. Smith," a sweet

guy from her Wednesday class said.

"Now I know why Ian Hensley came to our class today," another girl added.

The band returned, breaking into the opening chords of *Blow Job* without preamble. After ripping through a rendition that had the kids dancing like a single entity on the tiny floor while shouting the chorus, Ian started to talk. The crowd parted enough for Deena to head back to the table and Jack's still empty chair.

"Did Jack ever come back?" Deena asked Patti.

"Nope. Shhh. He's talking to you."

Ian's hair shone in the spotlights. He'd had it cut and styled in the old way, the way she loved. It fell over his eyes as he found her face. Then he smiled.

Her guard went up. Sure, the music and the way he sang the words made the two songs sound totally different, but Deena had been listening. The words were the same.

If he hadn't treated her like shit in Paris, and if not for Jack, she might be falling for his act all over again. But she smiled back at him, keeping the plan to get invited over firmly in mind.

"This song, I don't know how many of you caught it, but it's sort of like my answer to Dee's song, the one Jenny just sang. Dee continues to inspire me, whether she writes the words I sing or not. And Dee..." Ian looked from the stage at her. "This is one I wrote just for you. I call it *Army Girl*."

Deena tried to hear all the words, but she couldn't quite concentrate. Despite the fact that Ian had finally written a song for her, and that this insured there'd be no problem getting invited over to his place, she kept wondering where Jack and Theresa had gone.

****

Deena and Patti, in Deena's Miata, crept slowly

up the long line snaking around Mr. Pita's drive-in window on the gorgeous May morning after the concert.

"Did it bother you, seeing Ian and Jenny Galaxy play that song last night?" Deena asked Patti. She still hadn't gotten to the bottom of why Patti had given up the guitar, but it seemed connected to Ian.

"Nope." Patti changed the subject. "Can you even believe Ian wrote that song for you?"

"What were those words anyway? I was having a hard time concentrating." Deena handed the drive-in clerk at window number one money and pulled up to window number two for their food.

"Distracted by Jack?"

"Yeah. Something strange went on last night. He was gone for an hour at least with Theresa, and then when we went home, he barely kissed me goodbye." She took the bag of food and the two drinks, passing everything except her Coke to Patti.

She merged into traffic, which was light this weekend morning. She stuck her straw in the plastic lid's slit and took a deep sip before setting it in her cup holder. "It's not like Jack to turn down a blatant offer of sex."

"You said *wanna have sex*, just like that?"

"No, but I wore my silver cami and leather mini skirt. That outfit screams *easy lay*."

Patti snorted.

"Maybe he's jealous of Ian. *Army Girl* was all about how great you are." Patti took a healthy bite of her Mr. Pita. A plop of steak smothered in sauce fell onto Patti's sweatshirt as Deena turned sharply onto University Drive.

"Sorry. I can't believe I'm coming here on my day off."

"Tell me again. Why are we doing this?" Patti asked, wiping at her shirt with a napkin.

"You asked me to sponsor you. You said you

wanted to get in shape." Deena pulled up in front of the campus fitness center. "I'm being supportive. It's a friend thing." She turned the car off. They sat, both staring with loathing at the gym. Muscled athletes in cut off sweat pants fist bumped as they swarmed in and out of the club.

"All those guys are going to see me out of shape. Without makeup. Can't we come back another day? When they're in class?"

Deena looked over at Patti, who was perfect. A little more of her than there used to be, but it suited her. "It's okay if you don't want to do this, because I don't either," she admitted.

"But I do. Just not today. Look at me." Patti pointed to the spot on her sweatshirt. "I'm a slob. I've got sauce all over my top, my hair's a mess, and I don't think I got all my mascara off last night."

"You're not a slob, you're hung over. Maybe this wasn't such a great idea after all." *How can I bring up the guitar thing again?* "Anyway, it's too nice to be cooped up inside lifting heavy equipment."

"Bet my stomach would be the heaviest thing in there."

"Don't say that." Deena thrust the car into reverse. "Listen, I was thinking, maybe you took up eating when you put down your guitar." It was easier to say when driving, because she didn't have to look at Patti's pained expression.

Patti was quiet for a few minutes, listening to the radio. "No, I don't think so," she finally said. "I gave up the guitar when I was with Ian, and I didn't eat hardly anything back then. The food thing started after he dumped me."

"I still think it's all related." Deena didn't want to push Patti any further. It didn't take a genius to figure out that Ian had something to do with Patti quitting guitar.

"Ian really had me going when he had Jenny

sing *Girl in Window*." Deena decided to approach the subject from another angle.

"What do you mean?"

"Well, you know when you and Toby came to my place and I gave you a copy of *Girl in Window*? That was like, day before yesterday, right?"

Patti nodded, chewing her pita.

"So I told Jenny I thought it was great that she'd perfected the lyrics so quickly."

"Yeah." Patti audibly sucked the last bit of her Coke through a straw. "It was awesome, Deena."

"Well, yeah, but Jenny said she'd been practicing for over a week."

"So?"

"How could Jenny have practiced *Girl in Window* before I gave Toby the words? Ian's got my Paris notebook. It's not lost or packed away in a box somewhere." Deena drove fast, her anger making her less than cautious around corners.

"I don't think Toby knows. Ian must be lying to him."

Deena agreed. "Ian lies about a lot of things. Maybe he lied to you about your ability with the guitar." Patti didn't say anything.

"He doesn't like anyone else taking away from his spotlight. That's why he loves Toby. Good old background man. Somewhere in Ian's lame ego, he obviously saw me as a threat, and that's why he doesn't want to give me lyric credit. Maybe he figured you'd become a threat to him, too."

"Where are we going, anyway?"

"It's such a nice day." Deena gave up with the guitar thing. Patti obviously didn't want to discuss it. "What do you want to do?"

"I don't care."

"Visit Ian and Toby?"

"You hate Ian."

Deena glanced at Patti, who had peeled off her

sweatshirt to reveal the Yellow Star T-shirt underneath. Patti lifted an eyebrow as she fluffed her hair.

"So, what's up?"

"Okay, I've got a plan. But don't tell Toby."

"I won't." Patti swung the rear view mirror over to apply two coats of mascara.

"It's not a great plan. It just occurred to me that if we catch them still in bed, and they haven't had time to clean up the practice room, that maybe the notebook's in there. Or at least the copy Jenny used of my song. The copy I didn't give Toby."

"That's a pretty good plan, Nancy Drew."

"Thank you, Bess."

"Of course I get to be Bess. She's the chunky one."

Chapter Thirteen

"I never really wanted to date Ian," Patti said. "I wanted to be him. It sounds weird when I say it, but I think I was attracted to him because he had a band, and I wanted to be in one."

"And let me guess." Deena grew more pissed off at Ian with every mile she drove toward his house. "Ian didn't want to hear you play. Ian dismissed your talent. Ian wouldn't even jam with you. Am I right so far?"

"Pretty much. I never got around to asking him to play with me or anything. But whenever I picked up my guitar, he'd leave the room. He never said anything...he just wasn't interested in that part of me. Period."

"Because he's a self-absorbed jerk."

"Well, yeah, but at the time, I took it to mean my playing sucked. It seemed like it actually pained him to listen to me play. Like he was embarrassed for me, or something."

"Yeah, I know how that feels." Deena told Patti the short version of her run-in with Professor Marchant. "That's exactly how Marchant treated the text I put together for my students. Like an embarrassment."

Deena realized that she'd felt just like Patti with the guitar. As if only idiots printed their own course pack in their first year of teaching.

"We're a couple of losers," Patti said, as they pulled up to the curb in front of Ian and Toby's rental house.

"Not for long." Deena turned off the car and

marched with determination up the front walk.

They knocked, but no one answered. Patti ran around to Toby's room and knocked on his window. He opened the shade, looking all rumpled from bed, but delighted to see her nevertheless. He lifted her right inside. Patti giggled, The Plan obviously far from her mind. They kissed for what seemed like five minutes before coming up for air and noticing Deena standing outside. Patti whispered something to Toby, and he offered to come out front and let Deena in. Before she could reply, her phone beeped. Jack had sent her a text.

"Is Ian awake yet?" Deena asked Toby.

"You're kidding, right?"

Ian had probably partied until dawn.

"Well, if you don't mind..." She'd go in and check out the place while Ian slept. But a quick glance at the text from Jack asking if she wanted to meet him changed her mind. "No, I'll wait 'til later."

She waved goodbye and turned toward the street and her car. As jerked around as she'd been over not being able to search the house for her notebook yet, she couldn't be totally bummed. She was seeing Jack, and the leaves were all out on the trees, washing the morning in bright new green.

She buckled her seatbelt and drove to meet Jack. After his weird behavior last night, she was relieved that he'd texted. She called him back.

"Where are you?" he asked.

"I just left Ian's." She didn't think of how this would sound until the phone line went into a dead-zone silence.

"Jack?"

"I'm here."

"It's not what you think." *Could he actually be jealous?* "I just dropped Patti off. I didn't even see Ian."

"I'm at the DQ. Want to meet me?"

"Okay. Sure. I'd love it." Maybe he'd tell her where he and Theresa had disappeared to last night.

Ten minutes later, she sat down across from Jack and his half-eaten banana split.

"You want anything?"

"It's a little early in the day for me. I just wanted to see you."

He gave her a look she tried to read. Cool. Assessing. He'd never looked at her exactly this way before.

"I can't believe you fell for that jerk's line."

"I didn't." She assumed he referred to Ian and the whole charade of *Army Girl* last night. But Jack jealous? It seemed improbable, although she could think of no other reason he'd be acting this way. Jealousy, she could fix. She took his spoon and dug herself out a chunk of pineapple covered in chocolate. Before she put it in her mouth, she told Jack about her plan to pretend friendliness with Ian to get her notebook back.

"Why don't you just let my dad take care of it?" If not completely defrosted, his voice at least sounded warmer.

"Let's not talk about Ian."

"Fine."

Over ice cream, Deena chatted about Patti and Toby, seeking to repair whatever had gone wrong last night. She didn't quite have the nerve to bring up Theresa, and Jack hadn't mentioned her either.

Deena decided to forget Theresa and Ian and get back on track with Jack. They had a limited amount of time left together and needed to spend it doing happy things. Like making love.

"What are your plans for today?" she asked.

"I need to talk to you about something important."

"Okay."

****

Jack was happy that Deena had not brought up Theresa or his disappearing act last night. Seeing Theresa again had upset him, but as they talked outside the bar, he realized she was happy. She had a family. She'd moved on. He needed to move on, too. One way or another. "I was talking to a friend of mine." Jack finished the last spoonful of his ice cream before finishing his thought. "About you."

Deena's smile lit up her face. Jack thought this was a good sign. He believed she deserved this shot at publication. She deserved more respect than the university or Ian had ever accorded her.

"What about me?"

"Your book. *MindSprings*." Jack wanted to say all of it and get it out right. "I think it has potential. An old college buddy edits for a major textbook publisher. So I told him about your book."

"Whoa. It's not a real book. It's a course pack."

"But it could be a real book, with just a few changes."

"Really? You think so?"

One of the things he found so endearing about Deena was the way she always downplayed her strengths. She was so humble. She didn't seem to get that she was quite talented.

"I know so." And Don agreed with him. Based on the proposal, Don was excited to see Jack's edits. Now he just had to convince Deena to feel the same way.

"You need to incorporate your D. Smith persona. Use Yellow Star's popularity to increase your own visibility—"

"Wait, wait, wait! I don't want to do that. I like keeping my teaching separate from my short career as a lyricist."

"But why? And if the new album uses your lyrics, and you're credited, everyone will know anyway. Hell, after last night, everybody knows already."

Deena sat across from him, shaking her head no.

"Okay, you're right that people know, but I don't teach kids to be songwriters. I teach them to write college essays and use standard research methods."

"Yeah, but, don't you see, *MindSprings*, or whatever we end up calling it, has potential to be so much more than a primer for freshman comp."

Deena seemed baffled. "Whatever WE end up calling it?"

Jack had to tell her now. "I've got some editorial suggestions, starting with the title."

"So now you're my editor?"

"Only if you agree. And I'm acting, unofficially, as your agent, too. Don't you see? This will be so great for both of us."

Deena put her elbows on the table and cupped her chin in her hands. "I don't think so, Jack. I mean, I appreciate you talking to your friend and all, but right now, I've got too much going on to mess with the course pack."

"But you wouldn't have to do a thing. I'll edit it for you."

Her phone rang, and she looked at the screen. "Ian." She picked it up and said hello. She listened for a few minutes, nodded yes a couple of times, and held her index finger up at Jack. Disgusted, he stood to leave.

"Just think about it." And he walked out, leaving Deena to her chat with Ian. At least he'd told her about the project. After she thought about it, she'd come around, he was sure.

What he was not so sure of was their future. If she published her book, if he got a job editing in New York, would she move with him? Did he even want to ask her? Seeing Theresa last night had made him remember the negative side of being in love. And Deena's interest in Ian, no matter how innocent, didn't help.

****

Deena's phone chimed. "I've got to get this," she said to Jack. "It's Ian." Crap. Wrong thing to say. Before she could even say hello to Ian, Jack gave her a disgusted look and walked out the door.

Goose bumps rose on Deena's arms. How could Jack just leave her sitting there? Especially after last night's weirdness. It couldn't be jealousy. Jack was not the jealous type. So then, what was up with him?

"I'm sorry. Say that again," Deena said to Ian, who had been babbling about being sorry he missed her this morning. She'd lost the thread of where they went from there.

"Never mind. Just knowing you're my girl is enough."

Deena left the over air-conditioned Dairy Queen, still on the phone with Ian. She wanted to say "I'm not your girl." But that wouldn't make it any easier to get invited inside his house.

"Who's that frat boy you've been hanging with? What does he mean to you?"

This hot and cold routine of Jack's gave Deena a headache. Or maybe she'd had one too many glasses of wine last night.

"His name is Jack. We're dating." For now. Maybe.

"Dump him. You're mine now."

Deena was most definitely not Ian's and never would be again. But he had to think he stood a chance or her window of opportunity to find her notebook would close.

"He's leaving town in like, a week. We already decided to end things then." It was the truth, and Ian didn't need to know Deena wished Jack wasn't moving. Ian didn't need to know that maybe she and Jack were breaking up now. Today.

"So get back over here. What frat boy doesn't know won't kill him."

Ugh. There would be no way to search the house with Ian by her side, and she had no reason to go over there except to find her notebook.

"I have papers to grade. It's almost end-of-term, and I'm swamped." True enough again. Although when she'd met Jack this morning, checking papers had been the last thing on her mind. She lost track of whatever Ian was saying again. To cover, she told him *Army Girl* had really moved her. True again. She wasn't exactly lying to Ian. She was just telling him the parts he wanted to hear.

Chapter Fourteen

Deena heard pounding on the door. The police knocked, telling her through her glass doors that there had been a mistake, and the baby was not hers after all. "But I gave birth to her," she said. They didn't seem to hear her, and she tried to talk louder, but the words stuck in her throat. One of the policemen grabbed her baby, and Deena tried to get up out of bed, to follow him and bring her baby back, but she couldn't move.

Deena came awake realizing that she had not, in fact, given birth and nobody was stealing her baby. She'd fallen asleep while reading in the middle of the afternoon.

Another knock. Maybe it was Jack. Should she brush her teeth before answering the door?

Deena removed her cat, Shadow, from her legs under protest and made her bleary-eyed way to the living room. The drape across her glass door gaped open, so she clearly saw Sarah Stevens standing there with three paper grocery bags at her feet and a pink iPod in her hand.

"I'm sorry I woke you, Ms. Smith." Sarah hesitated at Deena's door.

Deena opened the door wide and waved her student inside the apartment. "It's okay." She tried to smooth down her unruly hair, wiped sleep from her eyes. "Come in. She grabbed one of Sarah's bags—*Clothes? Why?*—and brought it inside, waving Sarah inside, too. "Are you all right?"

"Oh, yeah, I'm cool. I just need to talk to you about some things. My therapist is out of town for the week, and you said, like, if I ever needed you...So, my brother dropped me off."

"How'd you find out where I live, anyway? Oh, never mind. I need coffee. What about you?"

"No thanks." Sarah patted her tummy. "But if you have herb tea..."

"Sure, I think so. Sit here." Deena gestured toward the sofa and went to sort out a tray of tea and coffee. In the middle of getting things together, she heard Sarah start to cry.

"Oh, sweetie." Deena ran over and sat with Sarah again, taking her hand and patting it. She felt like an ineffectual idiot. Sarah continued to cry. Deena jumped up to find tissue. When she sat back down, Sarah threw herself onto Deena's shoulder. The teakettle whistled, and the coffeepot gurgled to a halt. Once her shoulder was sufficiently soaked, Deena pulled a little away from Sarah, patting her again for good measure. Nobody had warned her about how teaching spilled over into life.

She looked Sarah in the eyes. "It'll be okay." She didn't know how it would be okay or if indeed it really would be okay or what exactly she meant by "it" but she spoke the words anyway. They seemed to help Sarah, even though, to Deena, the statement seemed clearly false. She popped into the kitchen for the tray of drinks, then came right back to sit beside Sarah and poured cream into coffee.

"Do you take cream or sugar?"

"Yes. I'll do it." Sarah scooped four spoons of sugar into her tea.

"Now, honey, tell me what's wrong. I noticed those bags are full of clothing."

Sarah had apparently cried herself out, for now. She blew her nose. "I'm thinking where to start. My mom brought those paper bags into my bedroom last night and said to pack my stuff and get out. Because I won't get an abortion. So I guess I'm, like, homeless."

"You can stay here." The words were out before Deena had time to think.

"Can I? Oh, thank you!" Sarah's eyes welled dangerously again.

Deena was sure the department would get wind of this and make trouble about it. But, she didn't have the heart to take it back.

"I know girls right here at Creek who have their babies and keep their scholarships and get family housing..." Sarah's face crumpled and the hand clutching her mug of tea trembled.

"Are you hungry?" Deena asked, not knowing how to mother this young girl and falling back on food.

"I could eat," Sarah confessed. "I went to your website last night, and I found out you lived in the University subdivision." It took Deena a minute to figure out that Sarah was answering the question she'd asked earlier. "You said in your bio that you lived on Shakespeare Street, and how perfect it was because you love his sonnets. And I saw your Miata in the driveway. Remember you told us in class you drove a red Miata?" She smiled, satisfied with her deductions. "I knocked downstairs first and some guy told me you lived up here."

They moved into the kitchen.

"The guy downstairs is David." Deena popped bagels into the toaster, set out the cream cheese. She remembered that she had promised David she would look in on Myra today so he could take his children to the zoo.

"He's kind of cute for an old guy."

Deena just smiled. David was around her age. The bagels emerged from the toaster, golden and crisp at the edges. Deena slathered on cream cheese and brought the plate to the table. Sarah ate both bagels and drank two more cups of sugared tea.

"I'm pretty tired," Sarah said, after polishing off her tea. "I've been up all night. Where can I sleep?"

Deena, for lack of a better idea, led Sarah into her own bedroom where the girl immediately settled in among the crushed bedclothes and drifted off. Deena backed out of the room, closing the door behind her, wondering what she'd gotten herself into.

****

Deena and David got into the easy habit of using the inner staircase as they team-tagged Myra's care. David had a full plate running his restaurant and caring for his three little ones. He often brought the kids to visit Grandma, and most of the time, he brought dinner from American Paris, too.

Deena left Sarah sleeping upstairs, going down to check on Myra, who most of the time refused to use the aluminum walker David had rented for her. But she would take Deena's arm to hobble to the bathroom, and she would allow Deena to run her dishwasher and washing machine and make her cups of tea. Myra was awake when Deena peeked in on her, but she didn't look happy.

"I almost got the broom out again." Myra pointedly looked from her bedside clock to Deena. "I hate being dependent like this." They heard the front door open and three squealing voices yelled, "Grandma! We brought dinner."

Myra looked at Deena. "They're early! Please shut the bedroom door. I need to shower and get dressed before I go out there."

Deena closed the bedroom door and helped Myra into the bathroom adjoining her bedroom. Before Deena closed the door, she slid the walker in. Myra didn't comment, but neither did she swear in French as she had done the first few times she'd had to use it.

Deena straightened the blankets on Myra's bed.

When she heard the shower start, she laid out a freshly laundered pair of slacks and a cotton pullover on the bed.

Before the kids banged on the door, Deena opened it and told them Grandma would be out soon. Then she came out into the hall, shutting the door behind her. One of the things Myra missed most was her privacy.

The subtle aroma of fresh vanilla wafted from David's vast carry-out order. He always brought delicious desserts. Deena went into the kitchen to help set up dinner.

"How's Mom?" David asked, hugging Deena. They'd quickly become fast friends and recently David had confided that he'd lost his wife to cancer shortly after his youngest child, three year old Julie, was born.

It was the saddest story Deena had ever heard. Before David's wife slipped into a coma several months into her pregnancy, she had made the doctors promise to keep her alive until Julie's birth. And they had.

Julie helped Deena set the table, carefully placing a paper napkin atop each plate, while the boys played hand-held video devices on Myra's sofa.

By the time Myra called for David, all that was left to do was plate the food. Deena took care of that while David escorted his mother, without the walker, into the dining room. Myra sat in regal grace at the head of the table, her sweet smile lighting her face as she talked to her grandchildren. She accepted a half glass of wine from Deena and dug into a plate with mashed potatoes, salad, and fried chicken.

"So how is this dinner French?" Deena asked.

"French Fried Chicken."

"French salad dressing." The boys both laughed at their jokes like they were the funniest things they'd ever heard.

The place smelled like heaven, in part due to the apple pie that warmed in the oven. "So are those apples in the pie from Paris?" Deena asked.

The boys laughed louder.

Either the laughter or the food smells must have lured Sarah downstairs. Deena saw her peek her head around from the kitchen.

"Deena?"

"Oh, Sarah, hi!"

"Join us," David said.

"Who you?" little Julie asked.

"Professor Bluet?" Sarah came into the room, too puzzled to remain shyly in the kitchen.

Myra looked blank.

"I had you for physics last year."

"Of course. Sarah Stevens."

Everyone introduced themselves, and David got up to bring another plate into the dining room. Julie demanded that Sarah sit next to her.

After a lively dinner, Myra retired to the sofa in the living room, the children drew pictures at her feet, and David and Sarah washed dishes. Deena cleared the table and after sweeping the floor, got an idea.

"Sarah," Deena asked, "didn't you say you just lost your job?"

Sarah looked from David to Deena, mortified. "It wasn't my fault. I'm just pregnant." Her face flushed, and a dish fell from her hand back into the dishwater.

"Honey, I know. I was just thinking." Deena looked at David. They'd talked about hiring a home health care aide for Myra, but Myra would have nothing to do with it. Too impersonal. She didn't want a stranger taking care of her.

David saw at once what Deena was thinking and quietly explained the situation to Sarah. "Would you be willing to help out?" He named a generous salary.

"I do need a job."

"And after Mom heals, you can come work for me. You were a waitress, right?"

"Yeah." Sarah seemed confused.

"I own American Paris."

"I'm not that kind of waitress," Sarah said, awe evident in her tone. "I worked at Hank's Polish Deli."

"Doesn't matter. You'll pick it up in no time." David smiled at her. "But first, what about Mom?"

"I, yeah, sure, I'll help her. I'm staying upstairs with Deena now anyway."

"We have empty guestrooms down here, and you're welcome to use any one of them. I know Deena just has the one bedroom upstairs."

Relief flooded through her. Now at least she didn't have to come up with a way two women would share one bed and one bathroom. Now she didn't even have to mention it. She and David were on the same wave-length when it came to caring for Myra.

"Honest to God?" Sarah looked ready to cry again. "I can't believe this. You all are so nice." Sarah sniffed, but held the tears back.

Deena figured Sarah wasn't used to being treated well by her mother. "You'd be helping us out. And I can give you a ride to school."

"This is so perfect. Thank you both so much. Now I better go and see if Professor Bluet needs anything."

Sarah left the room, and David and Deena beamed at each other.

"She's a very sweet girl," Deena said. "My student."

"I could tell Mom liked her, too."

Someone knocked on the kitchen door.

"Come on in." Deena called.

Jack walked in, looked at Deena standing there with David in his mother's kitchen, and seemed ready to bolt.

"David, this is Jack."

They shook hands. "Deena's told me a lot about you," David said.

"We ate at your restaurant last week. Food was awesome." Jack looked uncomfortable, but maybe it was only the sliver of pie left in the plate next to him on the stove.

"Thanks. Well, I'm going to round up the kids and head home."

"See you tomorrow," Deena said.

"I've been texting you and calling you for an hour," Jack whispered.

"I was down here. We were having dinner. One of my students is going to be staying here with Myra and taking care of her until she's better." Deena picked up the pie plate with one hand and pulled Jack into the dining room with the other. They ran up the inside stairs after she waved good-bye to David and his family. Best to let Myra and Sarah settle on a routine themselves.

When they came into Deena's, Jack looked at the open door with suspicion. He started to slide the deadbolt.

"We can't lock it. Sarah might need me. This is her first night. And her clothes are still up here. What were you texting, anyway?"

Jack took his hands off the deadbolt and shrugged. "Just wanted to see if you could hang out. I was thinking dinner, but clearly that's out now."

"Hey, why don't I go get the ice cream that we ate with this pie?" Desserts were Jack's favorite part of a meal anyway.

****

During finals week, Deena's students complained that they had no time to revise research papers because they were too busy cramming for exams. By the time Friday arrived, Deena could hardly wait for summer to start. She popped into the office to check her mailbox. Three late papers and a memo about posting grades online promptly greeted her.

She read the memo and made a joke about tardy teachers to Harriet, the secretary, when Dean Westingham stuck her head out of her office door. "Ms. Smith, I need to see you."

Deena's heart pounded. Something in the tone of Westingham's voice did not bode well.

"We've had a call from Mrs. Stevens. Sarah Stevens mother."

"Oh?" Deena had nothing to feel guilty about, she told herself. But the look on the Dean's face begged to differ.

"I understand Sarah Stevens lives with you?"

"No. Not exactly." Deena could at least answer this honestly. "Her mother threw her out of the house, and Sarah came to me for help. I found her a temporary job as a live-in nurse for Myra Bluet, the physics professor. Myra broke her hip last week."

The Dean made some notes, the frown that creased her forehead apparently a permanent wrinkle. Why was Westinghouse letting a parent get involved with an adult child's living situation? Deena was pretty sure that was against the law, or at least college policy.

"Sarah's mother claims you alienated her daughter with subversive course material. Further, she claims you talked Sarah out of an abortion."

Westingham's rigid posture held not an ounce of warmth or collegial solidarity.

"I don't—"

"I'll need copies of your syllabi and text." Westingham shuffled some papers. "Dr. Marchant's review indicates you authored a course pack for the class text."

"Yes, I—"

"Extremely unusual for a first year teacher. But, I'll look it over." She sighed with gusto and added, "Horrible timing for a complaint such as this." Then the Dean stood, indicating the meeting was over.

"I deny all the charges," Deena said, before Westingham rushed her out the door.

"Have your materials, such as they are, on Harriet's desk in five minutes." Westingham's final ominous words rang in Deena's ears all the way down the hall to her office. There, she quickly brought the required items to hand and speed-walked them back to Harriet. The unflappable secretary took the paperwork, tucked the syllabi into the soft bound copy of *Mindsprings* and said, "Betty's gone to lunch."

"Who's Betty?" Deena asked.

"Dr. Westingham." Jack rounded the corner into the office and checked his mail slot.

Deena followed Jack back to their own office and almost fell into her chair. She noticed Jack's tidy desk. Jack was always tidy, but it was the week before finals, and he didn't even have his laptop open, let alone a stack of research papers to grade.

"You're finished grading?"

"Graded and posted."

"Wow. So, what? You're done? Aren't you coming in next week to return papers? Aren't you allowing revisions?"

"Most students don't revise and don't care if they get their papers back. They just want their grade."

"But is that okay?"

"What's Betty going to do, fire me?"

"Good point." Deena, relieved that Jack seemed okay after their less than ideal weekend, blurted, "I think she wants to fire me."

"You worry too much." Jack moved her bangs off her face and kissed her widow's peak. That was a surprise. The last time she'd seen Jack, he'd walked out on her. The time before that, he'd disappeared for hours with who she guessed was an ex. She watched him throw a handful of textbooks into a box, add his minimal paper files and then his coffee cup. Deena dove back into her mile-high pile of term papers. She tried not to notice him packing up, continuing marking essays as he stood at the door with his box of stuff.

"I, ah, don't know how you want to handle this. I mean, you're pretty busy, but if you want to, you could help me move."

Deena looked up from her papers. She was stressed and annoyed. "I thought we were breaking up."

"We don't have to."

Deena sighed and stuck her chin into her palm, her elbow on the desk propping her head up.

He stood, probably waiting for her to say something. Someone knocked on the door. Deena looked at the clock on the wall.

Jack yelled, "Go Away!"

"Is Ms. Smith there?" the persistent student asked.

"Office hours are cancelled today. We're busy in here," Jack yelled.

****

After a couple of seconds, Jack heard the student shuffle away. Deena hadn't contradicted him about the office hours, so he set down his box of supplies and took out paper and a marker.

"Jack, what are you doing?"

"I'm posting a note on the door. We need to talk."

"No. I *am* having office hours. These kids need my help with revising. I promised them."

The look of stubborn determination on her face made the idea of trying to work out something long term with her seem crazy. But he was going to try, with both the business and the personal parts of their relationship. This had to work. He had to hope for more from his life than yet another move to yet another university doing the same old job and dating a new but somehow familiar set of women.

Deena was different. He really cared about her. And he knew she cared about him, too. Maybe more than she realized. So why did she put her feud with Ian ahead of him? She put her students ahead of him. She put the family who used to own her house ahead of him. He guessed that made him last on her priority list.

"Fine. Keep your office hours. But this isn't over. We aren't over."

He picked up his box with one hand, jerked open the door with the other. A couple of kids loitered in the hall. Obviously waiting for Deena.

Jack ran into some other faculty in the elevator, and after the conversation he'd just had with Deena, it didn't take much for them to talk him into going out for drinks to celebrate his last day at Creek. At least they cared. Unlike his supposed girlfriend.

Chapter Fifteen

At home that night, Deena closed her laptop.
The rumor she'd heard at school was true—someone
had posted Ian singing *Army Girl* on YouTube.
Seeing Ian on the computer screen didn't faze her
anymore. She wanted Jack, not Ian. Jack was
nothing like Ian. A long-distance relationship with
Jack wouldn't be a repeat of the Ian saga. Jack had
left the office angry with her, but if she told him she
wanted to stay together, they'd be okay again.
Derrida's howl penetrated Deena's thoughts. Jack's
cat was on her doorstep again, antagonizing Shadow.
"What are you doing out after dark, boy?" Deena
opened the door, and Derrida walked in as if he lived
there. Shadow hissed and hopped onto the sofa.
Deena checked Jack's driveway. His car wasn't
there. He'd left the office hours ago. Where could he
be?

Deena shushed Derrida's meows with a few
strokes on the head. Then she locked Shadow in the
bedroom and opened a can of tuna for Derrida. She
didn't want to call Jack's cell phone; he might think
she was checking up on him. So she texted, *Yr cat @
my place,* and pressed send. An irate howl from the
area of the bedroom signaled that Shadow smelled
the tuna and wanted her share.

Before Deena let Shadow out, she opened
another can of food and emptied it into a second
bowl. When Deena opened her bedroom door,
Shadow stalked over to the opening between the
kitchen and the living area, her black ears pinned to
her head. She spotted Derrida hunched over the food

and her back hairs went up. Her tail bushed out. She hissed. Derrida gave her a cursory glance, and then continued with his meal.

"Be nice." Deena picked up Shadow and held her cradled in her arms like a baby. She scratched her under her chin and stroked her fur. Then she sat Shadow down by her own food on the far side of the kitchen area.

Deena needed a shower, but was afraid to leave the cats alone together. When Derrida finished his meal, he hopped onto the kitchen sink, then up to the window. He stationed himself on the ledge where he had a perfect view of his front door. While waiting for his person to come home, he delicately washed his paws and face.

Deena made herself a cup of tea and settled onto the sofa with a worn book of poetry by Heather McHugh. She read a line four times before she realized that it was useless. She couldn't concentrate.

The whole episode with Dean Westingham this morning had wrung her out. And then she and Jack had argued. Plus she was no closer to getting her Paris notebook from Ian. Things just were not going her way.

Shadow growled at the kitty in the window.

Deena looked toward Derrida, saw that he'd come down to the sink. He sat there, blinking, asking permission to take the next step. Shadow didn't give it. Deena turned her open book face down, picked up Shadow, and went to take a shower.

After the shower, blow drying her hair, she heard Jack's voice. She threw on her robe and opened the bathroom door. Shadow escaped.

"Jack?"

He stood in her kitchen, scratching Derrida between the ears.

"Are you naked under that robe?" He moved

away from Derrida and grabbed Deena around the waist to kiss her. He smelled like limes and tasted like tequila.

"Where have you been?" She broke off the kiss, but he still had her clamped in his arms.

"Some people took me out for a good-bye drink. Okay, several good-bye drinks." His hand unbelted her robe in one quick motion. "You *are* naked."

"Not for long. Wait here while I put on some clothes."

He followed her into the bedroom and pulled the robe from her body.

The unmistakable meow of annoyance could only be an ignored Derrida. Seconds later, Shadow slithered in and added her voice.

"What will the kids think, honey?" Deena teased Jack.

He shooed the cats out of the room, closed the door, and came toward her, unbuttoning his shirt, unzipping his jeans.

An hour or so later, she opened her eyes, sensing Jack was looking at her.

"Oh, God, Deena, I love you."

"I love you, too."

And then he kissed her, soft and sincere. They were so in sync she followed him everywhere, even into totally illogical love.

****

The next morning, Deena woke to the sound of Jack humming in the shower. They hadn't talked yet about their fight at work, or about his move, or the L word. Her heart, beating overtime, skidded to a halt as he opened the bedroom door and walked in after the cats.

"Good morning. Hey, guess what? They've called a truce."

Jack fresh from the shower, shirtless, his jeans slung low and showing off his ripped torso, was better than any dream. He handed her a mug of coffee and sat on the edge of the bed next to her feet. The bored cats headed out in search of diversion. Deena sipped her coffee. Jack had remembered: she took it with cream, no sugar. Her heart did a little ping, then a bigger pang.

"Hi." Their eyes met.

"Hi." She smiled in spite of her banging heart.

"I'm sorry I'm leaving next week."

"Me too." They loved each other, but the words she wanted to say, that she had changed her mind, that she'd be willing to try a long-distance relationship, stuck in her throat.

"I need to tell you about Theresa."

It was about time he opened up about that. Deena gave him an encouraging nod.

"She was my high school girlfriend. I haven't loved anyone since we broke up, well, not until you." He stared at the floor, lightly squeezing her hand. "We were together for three and a half years. After we went off to different colleges, we tried to do the long distance thing, but it just didn't work. I didn't like it. So I broke up with her. That's when she tried to kill herself."

Deena set her coffee mug on the bedside table. "I'm sorry, Jack." His past explained a lot about his dating habits. At least before he'd started seeing her. They'd been together almost every night for a month.

He studied the rug on her wooden floor, not her eyes. "She was institutionalized for awhile. She never finished her freshman year at college."

"But she's okay now?" Deena patted his knee.

"Yeah. She's married. Has a baby." Jack looked at her. "I'd pushed all that stuff away a long time ago. It was difficult. I felt guilty for years. Guilty and depressed. But eventually, the bad feelings went away. Until I saw Theresa. Everything came

114

flooding back. I meant it when I said I love you. I do, but I think you're right. When I leave, we should end things."

Deena didn't say anything. She didn't feel like she had the right. After all, what could she really, when she'd been the one to demand they break up after Jack left town.

Chapter Sixteen

Jack stopped in the middle of rolling a wine glass in bubble wrap. Even though he finally agreed with Deena that their affair should end when he moved, he was still sad. He'd fallen hard for her. He consoled himself with the idea that he still had a few days with her, and that he had never been quite besotted enough to buy her flowers or candy.

He looked down at the bubble-wrapped glass. He had popped every bubble that remained unwrapped. "Hell with it." He continued to roll up the damn wine glass. Just to be certain, he finished with two strips of scotch tape. Then he went looking for the box of chocolate covered cherries his mother had brought him from the Morley candy factory.

Several cherries later, he still felt edgy. He called Thai One On and made a reservation. Then he called Deena.

She sounded awful.

"Are you sick?" he asked.

"No, I'm not sick. I'm tired, and I have cramps, but I'm not sick. I started my period."

"Oh." Jack understood now why she'd been so tense with him at work yesterday.

She hung up on him.

He must have said it out loud. He sighed. Redialed Deena's number.

"Deena, don't hang up! I made dinner reservations, and I need to know if you're coming. I made them for seven, but we can do eight if that's better for you."

"Oh Jack. I don't feel like dinner out. Getting all

dressed and putting on make up." She didn't say anything for a minute. He could hear her breathing.

"Why? What happened?" He didn't trust that damn Ian. Guy probably wrote her another song or something.

"Nothing, really. I've just been thinking."

"Always dangerous." At least Ian seemed to be out of the picture for now.

"Would you get carry out and bring it up?"

She sounded so down, so unlike the Deena he loved. If she had been just a little more cheerful, he would have talked her into getting dressed, getting her energy level up. But she seemed seriously bummed, so he called and changed the reservation to a carry out order. He stopped at a fancy wine shop and picked up a couple bottles of good wine, too. Then, because there were spring bouquets right next to the cash registers, he bought her some flowers to cheer her up. He threw a couple of bars of gourmet chocolate onto the check out counter as well. Everyone knew women craved chocolate at "that time" of the month.

****

Deena opened the door dressed in a pair of baggy gray sweatpants and a tight long-sleeved college tee. Her hair was pinned up off her neck, and her feet were tufts of pink fuzz.

"Hi honey, I'm here." He kissed her and handed her the flowers and candy.

Her face softened into an expression he couldn't read.

He put the food on the table and the white wine into the fridge while she stuck the flowers in a chipped *Fiestaware* pitcher. When she arranged them, the way the flowers spilled out made the chip disappear.

****

Deena appreciated Jack bringing over the food,

because she was starving and she had no energy to cook for herself. She sat like a sack of potatoes on the sofa and let him do all the work.

"So tell me about the new apartment." She took the glass of wine he'd brought her.

He gave her a funny look. She assumed she resembled crap warmed-over in the sweatpants, no make-up look. But really, at this point, why bother? He'd be gone in less than a week. Why should she even try? That is, if she had the energy to try. Which she did not right now.

"I've got to get the food out, or it'll be cold. Do you want to eat in here? You look too tired to sit at a table."

"Yes, thanks. It's been a hellish day." Deena stretched out on the sofa.

"You said that on the phone," he answered from the kitchen where he dished up two plates of curry. "What happened?"

"Nothing, really." She took a sip of her wine. It tasted like pears and honey. She took another sip. "I've been thinking. Obsessing, actually." She took the plate Jack handed her and tucked into shrimp and saffron rice.

"About what?" Jack sat down next to her and picked up his plate of food from where he'd set it on the stack of graded essays that cluttered the hope chest. She thought about moving the papers to her overflowing desk, but lacked the energy.

Say it now. Tell Jack you changed your mind, you want to stay together.

Deena set her plate down on a stack of essays. She grabbed a pillow and hugged it to her lap. It wouldn't be fair to either of them to try to maintain a relationship long-distance. Maybe if they had some kind of plan that would eventually bring them both back to the same place. But Deena's place was here. She had a house and a new career. And Jack, well, he'd said himself that he loved moving around. She couldn't stay here, waiting and hoping that one day he'd return. And he'd never asked her to go with him.

Deena reached for her plate, then let her hand fall.

"Honey, you're not eating."

Maybe it was Jack calling her honey. Maybe it was his concern over her appetite. But the tears slipped out despite her best effort. Jack slid his empty plate under hers, picked them both up, and carried them to the kitchen.

He brought her chocolate, and she ate a few bites while they cuddled on the sofa, sipping wine.

After awhile, she started to open up. "I never had to work at writing songs." She set her empty wine glass on the hope chest. "They just came to me. After weeks of hellish false starts, of course."

"Sounds like work to me. Maybe you worked harder than you give yourself credit for. When we love what we do, it feels more like play than work."

"I work at teaching, though. It's so much more complex than writing a song lyric. There are a thousand strands to weave together. Reading, planning, grading, lecturing, figuring out ways to engage students. When all that comes together for me, I feel so good."

"I wish I had your love of teaching." Jack pointed to her wine glass. "Would you like another?"

"Sure."

Jack refilled their glasses. "I want that freedom to do work I love every day." He swirled his wine, then inhaled the bouquet.

"You don't love teaching. But do you know what you do love?"

"I liked editing your book."

"Stop it. I can't deal with your pressuring me about that right now." What kind of edits was he talking about? She liked her book as is. She liked the title. She liked that it was about teaching freshman comp. She liked leaving the lyric writing out of it.

Jack seemed to be doing some sort of deep breathing, but at least he'd stopped talking about her book.

"Writing lyrics, that's unpredictable. I never know when I'll be inspired, and usually when I am, I am also miserable. I write my way out of misery."

Jack listened hard. She was finally getting through to him. "That's why I like teaching. It's reliable. Well, it was. I have a feeling the department is down on me. I don't want to lose this job."

"You won't." Jack came back to the sofa with the bottle of wine and refilled their glasses. "Some of them just like making you feel small. So they can feel big."

He sat down next to her. "But never doubt, they need you. They need dedicated people like you willing to work on a yearly contract for slave wages."

"I'll never get tenure."

"Go back to school for a Ph.D., and you'll have a shot. Or try a community college."

The idea of all the dry, scholarly research a Ph.D. would entail gave her a headache.

"What about your book? If you could get that published, that might go a long way toward job security."

"Publish or perish, huh?"

"That's the way it is."

"Except I'm not publishing in a peer-reviewed journal. Academics don't really go for the kind of assignments I design."

"That's just here. If a New York publisher picks up your book, offers you a contract, they'd have to pay attention to that."

Deena didn't reply. Why did Jack keep talking

about her text as if it was something people would notice? That wasn't going to happen. Not even if he tried out his edgy editing scheme. Which she had already said no to and did not want. Subject closed.

She leaned in to kiss him, to kiss her worries away and to kiss his crazy ideas away, and to create that little universe where it was all about him and her and what they meant to each other.

Chapter Seventeen

After Jack left the next day, Sarah ran up the interior stairway and bounded through the open door. She handed Deena a yellow flier with a huge star sketched into the middle of it. "It's an invitation to a party for Yellow Star Friday night! And I'm invited! What should we wear?"

Deena scanned the flier and swore.

"Don't you want to go?"

"I do, I really do," Deena said. Here it was finally, an invitation inside Ian's lair. Perfect. Except. "That's the day Jack's moving. I promised to help him."

"I thought you guys were ending things when he moved?"

"We are, well the dating part. We'll still be friends. We'll always be friends."

"That's cool. David thinks I shouldn't go in case there's a lot of smoke. Bad for the baby."

"Oh, you've seen him today."

Sarah blushed. "He texts about his mom."

"Well he's probably right about the smoke."

"I know. It sucks being a grown up."

"You'll get used to it." She really didn't have a choice.

****

"I'm sorry, Deena." Dean Westingham didn't seem sorry when she spoke the words the next morning. "But we're going to have to let you go."

Deena had been reading her student evaluations when Westingham spotted her in the office and demanded she come down for a chat. Deena couldn't connect the student comments she'd just read, many of which said things like *My best teacher ever* and *Ms. Smith actually makes writing fun,* with the words coming out of the dean's mouth.

"Letting me go? Do you mean I'm fired?" Deena hoped the dean would explain that no of course she was not fired, what she had meant by "letting go" was in fact...what?

"With a yearly contract, it's not a matter of firing." Dean Westingham, Betty to her secretary and probably everyone in the department except Deena, rose from her chair, a signal for Deena to gather herself together and get out. She stayed put.

"We are simply unable to renew your contract at this time."

"Why? Everyone else is coming back. All the other contracted faculty. And my evaluations are excellent."

"The wording of student comments, the plethora of praise, these type of evaluations signal trouble. Students like teachers who don't challenge them. They like the easy A."

"I had six four points out of eighty students! And they worked for those grades. They rewrote every paper more than once, using all of my suggestions..."

"Nevertheless, an unfavorable peer evaluation by Professor Marchant, a parental complaint..."

Deena sat very still. She held herself as straight as possible so as not to risk falling apart in front of beastly Betty, whose tone of voice grated more every minute. *She's probably late for her lunch date.* She should get up and go gracefully. But she couldn't move. To risk moving would be to risk everything.

"I also previewed your syllabus and text." Dean W. emphasized the word "text" as if she'd just sucked a lemon. "You have allotted far too much in-class writing time and your text..."

She paused, leaving her thought about Deena's

text unexpressed. Deena heard the message anyway, without the words. "Jack Karris came to me with the ludicrous notion that it might be publishable, or that your... " She trailed away, her lemon look returning to her face for an instant. "*Songwriting* might qualify as scholarly work."

Deena would not let Betty see her cry. So she left the building, carrying her box of personal books and papers, the bag with her laptop.

"Deena!"

Deena walked with her head down, avoiding the goose droppings that peppered the sidewalk. She stopped and looked up.

"Oh, hi, Myra. So you made it in for the last day after all."

"Yes. I'm fine. Good as new."

Even mired in her misery, Deena saw Myra's blatant lie. The professor clearly favored her injured hip, and she walked with a cane.

"Why the box?"

"I'm fired."

Myra cracked her cane on the sidewalk. "Idiots!"

All the way to the parking lot, Myra talked up the benefits of working at one of the local community colleges.

****

Myra and Jack leaving the same week was too much to handle, but Deena pulled herself together for Myra's send off, standing with everyone in the driveway while David loaded Myra's suitcases into his huge Jeep.

Myra asked the kids if they wanted to look over their dad's old toy collection and that gang headed out to the garage where Deena had stored those boxes for David. Deena left them to sort themselves out, and took a walk through her house, which was finally, and completely, her own place.

The parlor, as Myra called it, was empty. All the

rooms, except Sarah's and the dining room were empty shells waiting for paint, waiting for Deena's furniture.

Myra insisted the dining room stay with her. Furniture, china, and crystal—she gave it all to Deena. Even David didn't object, swearing he wanted nothing to do with the fussy Royal Albert china pattern or the ornately carved furniture. Deena loved it all, not so much for herself, but because it represented a piece of Myra that would stay here with her.

Deena heard the kids voices through the back kitchen door. She opened it and went outside where everyone had gathered.

"Daddy can we take it all?"

"Why not?" he replied. "But not now. We'll have to come back for it after we drive Gran to the airport. That okay, Deena?"

"Absolutely." She came further outside to say goodbye.

Sarah hugged Myra, burst into tears, and banged into the house through the kitchen door. David went in after her.

"She hates good-byes and so do I," Deena said.

"I think it might be a little more than that," Myra said. "She's in love with David."

"You're kidding? What about—"

"The age difference. I know. That's what's holding him back. But I've seen them together, and he won't be able to resist his feelings for very long." David and Sarah came out of the house holding hands. *That was quick.* Before they got close enough to hear Myra, she gave a large envelope to Deena. "My car. I've signed the title over to Sarah. Give it to her, would you, dear?"

"Sure." Deena assumed David would be picking up the car with his other boxes. She'd been looking forward to parking her Miata in the garage. "She'll be so happy." Deena took the envelope and smiled at David and Sarah, trying not to stare at their entwined fingers. Myra gingerly got herself into the front seat; David belted in the little ones. Julie begged Sarah to come with them, but Sarah leaned in and kissed her and said she'd see her later. Then they were off. Just that simple. Deena didn't want to think of the next good-bye. It would be harder because it was Jack. She followed Sarah into the house, knocked on Sarah's bedroom door.

"Come in."

Deena saw Sarah at the desk, writing something on what looked like a list. Jack liked lists too. It really wasn't Deena's thing. She mostly just let life happen.

"What's this?"

"A plan to get my life together." Sarah showed her the list. "This is everything I need before Sheryl gets here. Well, if she's a girl she'll be Sheryl."

Deena smiled.

"You're in luck then, because Myra just left you number one." Deena pointed to the first item on the list.

"What?"

Deena handed Sarah the paperwork for the car.

Sarah looked at it, her face beginning to glow as she read the words.

"How could she do that?"

"Maybe she'll buy a convertible."

Sarah jumped, heading out back toward the garage.

Deena followed her.

"Yeah. We'll have to talk about who gets the garage."

Sarah squealed as she opened the car door. "She put an infant car seat in here! A brand new one!"

"No kidding? You'll have to write her a thank you note."

And then Deena turned back to look at her house. She'd miss Myra, but finally taking full ownership made her want to dance. Or sing. Or both.

Then she remembered she wouldn't be receiving rent checks from Myra anymore. And she didn't have a job. She couldn't charge Sarah to live with her. The girl was working so hard to get a good life ready for her baby. Deena's savings account was in good enough shape. She'd be fine as long as she could find a job by fall semester.

****

Jack hung up the phone after coordinating moving day with his mother. He was sure she'd love Deena. Was it weird that Deena would finally meet his mom when she was about to become his ex? Probably. But his mother had been wanting to meet Deena since forever. She'd insisted on bringing a picnic supper to his new apartment after the movers left, and wanted to know if Deena was a vegetarian, or if she had a sweet tooth.

"No and yes." Jack chatted with his mom a few more minutes before saying goodbye, wondering why Deena didn't talk about her mother at all. Maybe she didn't remember her.

He looked around at the chaos of his half-packed house. Derrida loved the boxes, especially the empty ones, but they gave Jack a panicky feeling. Action would shake off his weird mood. He still needed to pack up his desk. He glanced at the work area where his edited copy of Deena's manuscript sat neatly stacked. It was stupid not to send it. She wouldn't thank him now, but later, she might. He opened his email and attached the document file to Don in New York. In the body of the email, he gave Don all of Deena's contact information, then hit send.

He'd started that project for Deena with such high hopes. For Deena, and for himself, too. But Don hadn't come through with even an interview, and

Deena had refused to consider the project. Fine. Let them deal with each other from now on. He picked up the manuscript he'd labored over in every free hour he'd had since the idea had come to him and let it fall with a bang into the bottom of an empty box.

Jack took his corkboard down from the wall and stuck it in the box as well. He wound his pencils together with a rubber band and put those in the box, then his pens. He had two unopened 500 sheet packets of paper for the printer in his bottom drawer. Those could go. He took out his pending files. The one marked *U of M* was crammed with new faculty information. Looking at it lowered Jack's spirits even more. He had to face it—he'd once again be teaching freshman comp. He sighed. Maybe it wouldn't be so bad.

He finished filling the box, and on his way to find the packing tape, stopped to grab four Oreos from the Tupperware container he kept his cookies in. As he poured milk, he tried to think positive thoughts.

He peeked out the window. Deena's car wasn't in the driveway. Before he could stop himself, he texted "Where R U ?" and hit send.

Chapter Eighteen

Fired. Myra gone. Jack on his way, too. Deena drove on auto-pilot to The Pub.

"Wine, Deena?" Patti asked when Deena sat down next to Toby.

"No, better make it a Russian Milkshake."

"What's wrong?"

Deena wanted to cry on Patti's shoulder. Wasn't that what bartenders and best friends were for? Instead, she had to share Patti with Toby.

Patti gave Toby a look, left the ice cream in the blender, and poured him another beer. She set it in front of him. "What's up, Deena?"

"Long story. Put lots of liquor in that ice cream, and maybe I'll tell it to you."

Patti poured vodka and chocolate liquor into the blender full of ice cream. Deena turned to Toby. "What's new?"

"Nothing." Toby took a long drink of his beer. "You coming to our party Friday?"

Deena hadn't thought about it more than a hundred times or so. But, she'd promised Jack she'd help him move. If she could just get that notebook before the party...

"I don't know."

Toby sighed into his beer. "You think she really cares about me?" Toby perhaps felt safe to speak his mind as the blender momentarily deafened Patti.

"She's crazy about you."

"She is?" Toby looked pathetically happy. "How do you know?"

"She told me. Day one when you and Ian were

129

here. She said she always liked you better, but you acted uninterested and Ian eventually wore her down."

"Really. Deena, you're a doll." Toby looked annoyingly happy. "I really wish he'd give you credit on the songs."

Deena didn't mention anything about the plural. She'd known all along that Ian had stolen more than one song lyric. Now she just had to prove it. Before Friday, if possible.

"Where's Ian today?"

"Out looking at new guitars." Toby still basked in the sure knowledge that Patti returned his love. His exuberence mildly irritated Deena until a cloud passed over his features. "I hope he locked the door this time," he muttered.

Patti set Deena's drink in front of her and poured the leftovers into a small glass for herself. The manager, Steve, wandered over and looked pointedly from Patti to the baby drink.

"Save it. I'm off in ten minutes anyway."

Steve started to walk away. "Hey, Steve, would you order us a Kitchen Sink?" Patti turned to Toby. "Hungry, babe?"

"Oh, yeah."

"Better make it a large. No anchovies."

Steve stuck up his middle finger, but he kept walking back toward the kitchen.

"It's pretty cool having a famous boyfriend and all. Want to have pizza with us, Deena?"

"No, better not."

"What were you guys talking about?"

"Nothing. Just Ian."

Deena figured this wasn't the time to tell Patti her troubles. However, as that window closed, another door opened. Downing her drink, she got the hell out of The Pub, accompanied by a slight case of brain freeze.

****

Ian's car wasn't in his driveway, so Deena went around to the back door. It opened easily when she turned the knob. Finally inside, she glanced quickly around the kitchen but dismissed it as an unlikely hiding place for her notebook. She saw the door to the basement, but decided not to go there either. Ian had the notebook out, not packed away. Jenny Galaxy had proven that.

She moved into the living room. Someone had recently cleaned. There were no newspapers or beer bottles in evidence. No notebook, or even a place to stash one. All the tables and a shelving unit were clear glass.

In the hallway off the living room, she spotted the bathroom, two open doors, and a closed one. The band room. She tried that door, only to find it was locked. She remembered that Toby's room had been on the side of the house. That meant the other one, the one in front, was Ian's. She went in and some residual of loneliness almost overwhelmed her. God, how she'd hating living with him near the end. Life on the road meant his presence was always yearned for, but not often actualized.

But she caught herself before going too far into those remembered feelings. She'd recalled just enough to harden her heart. She was *not* a thief. She would take back what was rightfully hers. She opened his dresser drawers one by one, reliving how she used to tuck his folded laundry into similar stacks with sickening devotion. Now the drawers were stuffed with all kinds of things, including but not limited to *Hustler* magazines, a pair of pliers, a pint of tequila, and photos of women proudly displaying their breasts. She rifled through it all. No notebook.

When a car door slammed outside, she shut the drawer.

Cal walked in just as Deena managed to whisk into the living room.

"Deena, hey."

"Hey, Cal."

She wasn't going to offer any explanation if he didn't ask for one. She'd just leave. Well, maybe she'd say something like "Tell Ian I came by." Something simple and short and then she'd get the hell out.

Cal unlocked the band room door and looked over at her, a question on his face.

"Just waiting for Ian," she said, right as Ian came in the back door. Her heart dropped, but she managed a smile. "Oh! Hi."

"Dee!" If she'd had any reservations about Ian thinking all was well between them, they disappeared when he grinned and held up a guitar case. "Wait 'til you see this." He ignored Cal, who had gone into the band room and closed the door.

"I ah, I really can't stay, Ian. I just came by to say thanks for the party invitation. Can I bring anything?"

"Oh cool, you're coming." He set the guitar down and closed the space between them.

She backed away, grabbing her purse where she'd thrown it on the sofa earlier. "Yeah. Yep. I'll be here. So, ah, do you need anything?"

He backed her against the wall and placed a hand on either side of her head. "Oh yeah." He moved his mouth toward hers.

She shoved him away, trying to laugh it off. "I mean for the party."

He seemed a little pissed about her pushing him away, but better he be angry than suspicious about why she was here. For once, his vanity worked in her favor. She smiled in what she hoped was an ingratiating way. The effort nearly broke her face.

"Just you, babe." He grinned back, but keeping

the distance she'd set. "What else is there?"

"Nothing I guess. Well, then, I'll see you tomorrow." She inched toward the back door and made her escape.

****

Jack leaned over Deena's soft old sofa and kissed her. Even though Myra had moved out this morning, they hadn't brought any furniture downstairs, because Deena wanted to paint first, so they were up in the apartment. Maybe for the last time. Tomorrow, he'd be gone. Somehow this time, his move to a new scene didn't energize him like it usually did. He hated leaving Deena.

"Jack." Deena broke the kiss.

"What? What's wrong?"

"Nothing. Well, not nothing." Deena sighed. "I got fired yesterday."

"I'm sorry, hon." This was bad news, but it could also be good. Because she'd be more invested in his ideas for her book. She'd listen if and when Don contacted her.

"There's something else I wanted to talk to you about."

Wow. Maybe she'd changed her mind about the book project. Maybe they'd stay in contact after he moved. He could still be her agent. He kissed her, and for awhile they both forgot there was anything else in their universe of two.

****

"I'm sorry, sir, we'll have a table for you in a few minutes if you'd like to wait at the bar." The hostess's perfectly pitched Midwest accent contradicted her heavily Asian features. She gave Jack a beeper for his pocket and turned back to her list.

They were late for their reservation, but that didn't bother Deena. They'd ripped each other's clothes off one last time and showered together afterward which meant another one last time after that.

They sat at the bar sipping their wine, Jack munching peanuts the bartender had set before them, Deena worrying about how to tell Jack she wasn't helping him move.

She decided to just blurt it out.

"Jack, listen, I, well, now that I'm unemployed, it's more urgent than ever that I get credit, get royalties, for my song lyrics."

"I know, honey. I can't believe Toby let that slip about the song lyrics. He probably doesn't even realize he said anything."

Deena took a sip of wine and twisted around on her barstool to face Jack.

"That's us." Jack took the buzzing beeper from his pocket.

As they followed the hostess to their table, Deena took deep breaths. It would be okay. Worst case scenario, Jack would order two desserts.

Five minutes later, after dealing with menus and drink orders, she started again. "So, I'm glad you agree that I should try to find my Paris notebook." Deena fidgeted with her silverware, moving each piece a tiny fraction away from her plate.

Jack cupped both her hands in his, soothing her nervous fingers.

"Listen, Jack, I know what I need to do about Ian now."

"What? Nothing crazy, I hope."

"No, but—"

"I don't want you to get hurt."

Every time she'd get to the point of confessing her new plans for tomorrow night, he'd interrupt. And she let him, because she was a coward. She didn't want this thing with Jack to end. Ever. And she for sure didn't want it to end with him angry.

"Ian's harmless. What's he going to do, press charges against me for stealing my own notebook?"

"I'm not so sure that guy is harmless. He's after you. He wants something. Either you or your song lyrics or both. That whole show at The Pub was intended to seduce you. It makes me really uncomfortable."

Deena didn't have the heart to point out that Jack was about to be her ex-lover and what she did from now on wouldn't concern him at all. She gave him an emphatic shake of her head. "All the more reason why I should get the notebook. Then I can stop pretending to give him the time of day and sue his dirty socks off."

The waitress set their dinners in front of them before Deena could break her news.

Jack took advantage of the interruption. "How's Sarah doing at her new job?" He smiled at his steaming plate of Stoked Pepper Steak.

"I think she likes it." Deena made a mental note to include Sarah in the party Friday night if she still wanted to go. More likely, she'd be working at American Paris or spending time with David. They'd hit it off despite the age difference.

Deena picked at her food, dreading the conversation she had to start with Jack before the night was over. "I told Sarah she could stay with me for awhile when Myra moves."

Deena told herself she only made small talk so she wouldn't ruin Jack's appetite, but she couldn't stand it, and blurted, "I can't help you move because Ian's having a party tomorrow night, and I have to be there to try to find my notebook. This is my best chance yet, and I have to take it. I'm sorry."

Jack didn't say anything for a minute. He played with the napkin inside the empty bread basket, avoiding her eyes. "Fine."

"Jack, I'm sorry. The timing sucks, I know. But

maybe it's better this way. This is kinda hard, you know?"

"I know."

Her savior, their server, approached with a dessert tray.

"Just coffee for me," Deena croaked over the lump in her throat.

Jack ordered a towering concoction of chocolate and coconut and asked for whipped cream and a cherry on top of his coffee.

They didn't talk at all while Jack ate dessert. They didn't say much on the drive home, either. Before she was fully out of the car, Jack was at her side. He grabbed her close and slammed the car door.

"I don't want to go." He spoke the words into her neck and then moved his mouth to her lips before she could say she wanted him to stay, too. The kiss was sweet and hungry. It went on and on, neither of them willing to be the first to pull back. Finally, she moved her face away. He still held her tightly with one arm while the other cupped the side of her face. "I'll miss you," he said.

She nodded and moved another inch away from his embrace. She couldn't say anything or she might start to cry. With a final effort, she pulled herself free and entered her house by the front door. Inside, she sat in her empty living room on the wooden floor, too stunned for tears. It was over. Really over.

Chapter Nineteen

"Not that one; it makes me look fat."

Deena sat on Patti's perfectly made bed, amidst approximately two hundred discarded tops. She held up a saffron colored gauzy tunic with adorable tiny beads sewn into the neckline and hem. "What about this? The neckline is low. With all those beautiful young things in their tight clothes you want a little bit of cleavage. Just try it."

Patti pulled the tunic over her head and smoothed the material around her hips. "You know, it doesn't look bad." She turned one way and another in the mirror.

"It's the spandex in the jeans. Like wearing Spanx."

"I'm not happy at this size."

"I think you look great. Have you played that guitar yet?" Deena had noticed the Martin had come out of the closet. Polished, too. Of course, everything in Patti's loft got polished every week, including the baseboards.

"No." Patti threaded an earring through her pierced lobe and changed the subject. "Maybe you're right." She checked herself out in the mirror, moving her head from side to side so that her hair spun around her face and her gold hoops flew back and forth like swings. "Maybe I do look great. Toby told me yesterday that he loves my thighs. What are you wearing?"

Deena looked down at her camouflage camisole. She'd paired it with some drab green hiking shorts. The dog tag bracelet she'd fashioned herself was on her wrist and her ten-eyed steel toe boots were laced up tight."This."

"You've got to be kidding." Patti looked dismayed. "You've got me all tarted up and you're GI Jane again? What's going on?"

"Everything." Deena put another coat of mascara on her lashes. "I need to be in combat mode." *And there are all kinds of armor.*

"Why don't we just ask Toby to get the notebook for us?"

"No way. He and Ian are so tight you could play drums on them."

"But he likes you. And he wants to do the right thing."

"Why? What did he say?"

"Nothing, except maybe Ian did use some of your words. But, since you won't let him see your lyrics, he has no idea how much. He's thinking it's very minimal. Ready to go?"

"No, yes. I'm nervous, that's all. Don't tell Toby about me trying to get the notebook tonight, by the way."

"I won't! I love him, but you're my girl." Patti glanced in her mirror. "You okay? I mean... Jack...the split..."

"Yeah. It hurts like hell but we both knew this was coming. We've known since day one. And now I finally have the time to focus on getting my notebook."

Deena wished she hadn't lost her job and Jack in the same week, but, in a way, it freed her up to battle with Ian. Maybe if she kept telling herself that, she'd believe it.

"What's that?" Deena pointed at the square of paper taped to Patti's mirror that read *All Will Be Well.*

"Affirmation. You should make one."

Deena followed Patti out into the living area to

look at book titles and get ideas. None of them made any sense, affirmation-wise. Patti favored historical romances with titles like *The Corinthian* and *The Rake's Revenge*. Not much affirmation material there.

Patti came over and handed her a glass of wine. "Well?"

"How about *Don't Mess With Me!* I tape this to my mirror and repeat it like a mantra, right?" Deena sipped her wine.

"That's what you do, but the thing is, an affirmation has to be positive. You can't have negatives in it like the word don't. You're an English teacher, can't you get the gist of that idea without a negative?"

Deena thought about it. She was a *former* English teacher. That hurt almost as much as losing Jack. She had to forget all that, find a phrase that would snap her out of it when she thought too much about Jack or work. "I guess *Mess With Me Not* is out. How about *Treat Me Right?*"

"A little Pat Benatar, but better."

"Pat Benatar rocks."

"Yes, she does. My apologies."

"Accepted. Let's get over there before the groupies tie up the bedrooms."

****

Ian fended off many tasty women waiting for Dee to arrive, but it had been worth the wait when she came in wearing her *Army Girl* outfit. She was into him, into the song and being his girl again. What she wore told everyone at the party she was his.

She looked so fresh, so damned cute next to all the sleaze and sequins that he telescoped to her heart from across the room. The music and laughter and loud false female screams faded. She was one in a million. He'd get her back. Make her see she was no songwriter, but better, she was his muse. And that was no small thing.

"Hey, is it true the twins are gonna make a sex tape later?" Jason, his drummer, asked.

"I heard they'd be here with film, dude." Ian headed straight for Dee.

****

Deena didn't search anywhere except the bathroom all evening, as Ian stuck to her like sweat in summer. When she went into the kitchen for a drink, he followed, pinning her against the fridge. His mouth came at hers so fast, the kiss was absolutely unavoidable. She faked liking it in the line of duty and pulled away when Cheri Croft snapped a photo.

She hoped Jack never saw that picture, but what were the odds? And she was pretty sure her face had been averted. While Ian gave Croft a quote for her article, Deena took the opportunity to rifle through the kitchen cupboards and drawers.

"Whatcha need, lover?" Ian asked.

"Cup." Deena said. "Corkscrew."

He handed her a crystal wine glass. "No plastic for my muse. And I ordered a case of Kendall Jackson just for you." He took the bottle of Two Buck Chuck from her hand. "I've got some KJ chilling in the fridge."

Damn. No notebook anywhere in the living room, kitchen, or bathroom. That left the band room, Toby's room, and the rest of Ian's bedroom, as she'd only had time to look through a few drawers. It wouldn't be in Toby's room.

She wandered, as if randomly, through the house. Ian stayed next to her, his arm around her neck. Like a noose. How had she ever found him attractive? He was so bone thin that his Adam's apple looked the size of an orange.

"Want to do a little coke?" When she shook her

head no, Ian persisted. "How about some weed?" He tried to lead her into the band room, where apparently the heavy drug action was taking place. Part of her wanted to go in so she could look for the notebook, but one glance inside at all the people snorting and toking and—was that girl really shooting up?—made Deena believe Ian wouldn't have left the notebook laying around in there. He'd put it away. In a drawer. In his room.

"No thanks, E." She used her old pet name for him, tried to put herself back on the old familiar footing without having to actually do anything sexual. He made it hard. So did the girls plastered all over the guys. Girls kissed girls and girls groped roadies. So not Deena's scene. Never really had been.

"Do you have any normal women here?" she snapped over the vintage blast of *Rage Against the Machine* from the speakers. Someone in the band room held a joint out to Ian, and he left Deena to claim it. She headed for the living room love seat where Toby and Patti sat, one of the few couples not indulging in a make out session.

"Where's Ian?" Patti asked, moving over so Deena could sit.

"In the band room."

"This place is trashed." Deena looked around.

"No kidding," Toby said. "I'm sleeping at Patti's tonight. You about ready to go, babe?"

Patti started to get up, but Deena grabbed her hand and squeezed it hard. "Treat me right," she said, as Ian joined them, a tightly rolled, still-burning joint in his hand.

Since the sofa was small, Ian couldn't fit. He sat down on a glass coffee table, crashing wine glasses and cups of beer all over the floor.

"Who's going to clean this shit up?" Toby said.

"We'll get Tina and Candie to do it. They'll do anything."

When both Deena and Patti raised their eyebrows, Ian shrugged.

"Why don't you get a real cleaner in here?" Patti asked. "I can get Maxine to come over once she's done at The Pub tomorrow morning."

"Not too early," Ian said. "Fuck, I got beer all over my jeans. Sit tight, doll, I'll be right back."

Patti smiled at Toby. "Can you get us another glass of wine, sweetie?"

"Sure, babe." Toby wove his way through the bodies lining the walls into the kitchen. As soon as he was out of earshot, Patti anxiously asked, "So did you find it?"

"Hell no. And how am I supposed to go through Ian's room with him crazy-glued to my side?"

"I noticed. Toby says he thinks you're his muse. Maybe the *Army Girl* outfit is working against you here."

"Who would've thought?" Deena took the glass of wine Toby offered.

Eventually, Patti and Toby left. Deena spent a fair amount of time fending off advances, curtly telling strangers that she was with Ian, despite the fact he'd checked into the band room about two hours ago and was still M.I.A. Which would have been perfect if some people weren't having group sex on his bed.

"No thanks," Deena replied to a wasted redhead offering a bared breast as if it were a rare treat. She had no idea what the etiquette of refusing a lesbian encounter entailed. Or if gender preferences even mattered during orgies. Man, this was so not her kind of party. But she had to stick it out. Anything for the notebook.

She went back to the living room, where almost everyone was wearing clothes, determined to wait this out. She'd sit here until the last partier was gone if that's what it took to get her notebook.

Chapter Twenty

Deena drove home from Ian's feeling tired and crabby with a horrible kink in her neck from falling asleep on his sofa. She'd woken up at dawn, checked the bedroom again, only to see Ian there with two blondes, all three of them passed out. She didn't quite have the nerve to open any closet doors or drawers with Ian right there in the room.

She parked in the garage and went in the kitchen door. A couple of boxes were on the floor, but she ignored them. Probably Sarah's stuff. Then she walked into the dining room and from there saw Jack sitting in the living room on his sofa, boxes stacked everywhere.

To add to the surreal quality of the scene, Derrida and Shadow lay next to each other in a patch of sunshine by the big front window.

"Where have you been?" Jack looked like her father when she got home after curfew.

"What? Why are you here?"

"It's a long story. Please first tell me where you've been all night."

Jack didn't seem exactly angry. His tone was more worried than mad. But what was he worried about? And why was he here with all his boxes?

"I fell asleep at Ian's. On the sofa. Alone. I didn't find the notebook."

Just then, Sarah came in from her bedroom.

"It's a girl. I am so stoked. Pink is my favorite color!" She looked from Jack to Deena and then turned around and went back into her room.

"That's great, honey," Deena called after her. "I

143

wish I hadn't gone to that stupid party last night."
Deena rubbed the persistent crick in her neck.

"Need some Tylenol?" Jack checked labels on his
boxes and opened one, bringing forth a bottle of pain
relief.

"God, Jack, what happened? Did the movers not
show up?" She asked over her shoulder as she went
into the kitchen to get a drink of water. She opened
a box marked glassware, pulled out a martini glass,
filled it with water, and downed the pills Jack gave
her.

She went back into the living room and sat next
to Jack on his leather sofa. It looked so out of place
with Myra's flowered wallpaper.

"So apparently, you didn't move yesterday," she
prompted.

"No. I tried calling and texting you. I didn't want
to just move my stuff in without asking, but you
didn't even answer my texts."

"The music was loud." The truth was she hadn't
looked at her phone once all night. She'd been too
focused on finding her notebook.

When she started to rub her neck again, Jack
took over. It felt so good.

"Don, you know, my friend in publishing in New
York, got me an interview with the editor of *The
Radical Tattler*."

"Who? What?"

"The magazine. From New York. You know."

She knew the magazine. It was part social
commentary, part political satire. She never read it,
but Jack had a subscription. She'd seen him reading
it in the office and bringing it into his house with the
mail. But she still couldn't connect Jack's stuff in her
house with a job interview.

"Did the moving truck cancel?" That had to be it.
They'd come today, or next week.

"No. I cancelled. I called the university and told

them I wasn't going to take the job after all."

Wow. She knew, of course, that Jack didn't like teaching much. But to give up such a golden opportunity for an interview? She took his hands off her shoulders so she could turn around and face him. She wanted to know what this meant.

"I gave up the apartment in Ann Arbor, too. I'm not moving. Well, not yet. Maybe I'll move to New York at some point."

Deena studied Jack's face full of happy anticipation. For one second she'd let herself believe Jack had rejected the post at U of M because he couldn't leave her. Ha. He just needed a free place to stay while he looked for a job even further away.

"You, ah, wouldn't want a roommate, would you?"

"Sure." All at once she was really tired. "What's one more?"

"I can help you around here. Painting. Cooking. Cleaning."

"Thanks, but there's still the issue of neither of us having jobs."

"True. I've got savings. I always do that, for summer."

"Where did you set up your office?"

"In Myra's den. Is that okay?"

"Yeah, I was going to use the sun porch to work. It's more cheerful in there." She yawned, not caring that her voice lacked enthusiasm. "Where did you put your bed?"

"In Myra's room. I hope that's okay."

Jack understood she wanted to paint before bringing her furniture downstairs. But he'd just offered to help. She didn't know what was wrong with her. She couldn't focus. "Any chance you gave me Tylenol P.M. by mistake?"

Jack went into the kitchen and returned with the bottle. "Yeah, sorry. It's P.M."

"I hardly slept last night." Deena could fall asleep right on the sofa. And she was really confused about Jack. Why would he quit such a great job? How had he snagged an interview in New York? Nothing made sense except hitting the closest bed, hard.

Jack walked with her into Myra's room. He pulled down the sheets and folded the duvet at the foot of the bed. Then he tucked her in and kissed her. She couldn't believe he was here. But for how long?

****

After Deena fell asleep, Jack went into Myra's kitchen, well, he guessed it was Deena's kitchen now, but she hadn't moved anything in here yet. He could at least get out the coffee stuff.

Sarah came in while he ground beans. She had the newspaper in her hand.

"Oh thanks." He reached for it.

"Where's Deena?"

"Sleeping. Myra's room. Guess we should stop calling it that."

"So, you're what? Moving in?"

"I just explained it all to Deena, Sarah, but yes, I'll be staying here for awhile. Hope that's okay with you." He couldn't help the note of sarcasm that crept into his voice. Deena didn't know he'd gotten the interview on the strength of his editing of her book, now retitled, *Writing Like a Rock Star*.

"For how long?"

Jack, busy rehearsing how he'd break the good news to Deena about her book, had forgotten Sarah. "I don't know. Does it matter?"

"It's just...Never mind." She left, and in another minute, he heard the shower. Then the cats came in, demanding food, so he opened a can of food and split it between two china saucers he found in the cabinet in the dining room. Then he refilled Derrida's water fountain.

Finally, he poured a cup of coffee, sugared and creamed it, and took his drink and newspaper into the dining room. It must have been a slow news day because Ian Hensley was featured on page one in a teaser for the media section. There was a tiny photo of Ian kissing a girl with the headline *Local Rock Star Gets His Army Girl*. Jack took a sip of coffee, feeling annoyed about Ian's positive press.

Jack's stomach growled. He'd seen bagels in the fridge. Surely Deena wouldn't mind if he just set his toaster on the counter for now. He'd help her clean up before they painted, he reconciled as he pulled his toaster from a box. He was feeling better than he had in weeks. At peace with his decision and happy to be here with Deena for however long it lasted. Maybe, if they did well living together now, he could talk her into moving to New York later.

Jack buttered his bagel and brought it into the dining room. He sipped his coffee and saw the teaser photo again at the top of the front page from the corner of his eye. *Local Rock Star Gets His Army Girl* floated through Jack's consciousness.

Ian had written a song about Deena called *Army Girl*. But surely, the girl kissing Ian Hensley in the tiny photo couldn't be Deena. Some other girls must have taken to wearing those quasi-combat outfits.

He pulled the photo closer. It was so small, he couldn't tell, but the girl did have on shorts. Her legs were obviously bare. And she had on Doc Martens, just like Deena's pair. The same shorts and shoes she'd had on when she'd walked in the door this morning.

Jack flipped through the paper to the entertainment section.

He studied the enlarged picture. He couldn't see the face of the woman kissing Hensley, but Jack had a sick feeling that it was Deena. There couldn't be two military ID tag bracelets exactly like the one that dangled from the familiar female wrist in the picture.

Worse, Deena seemed right at home in Ian Hensley's arms. Jack's stomach rolled, and he pushed the bagel away. They'd broken up. She hadn't done anything wrong. Not really. But still, looking at that picture hurt.

He read Cheri Croft's article, detailing Ian and Deena's history, Ian's success, and their breakup. "A mistake" the article quoted Ian as saying about the breakup. Ian then dished at length to Croft about his trip home. Croft herself claimed to be a witness to the "rekindling of the passion Ian and D. Smith once shared" at both the benefit concert at The Pub and later at "a private affair celebrating their coming together again."

What a load of bullshit. Deena despised Ian. Surely, she'd only kissed him because she wanted her damn notebook back. Then Jack remembered Deena had sex with him after he'd done her a favor regarding the notebook. She wouldn't go so far as to have sex with Hensley to get her notebook back, would she?

He didn't want to believe it, but the picture in the newspaper mocked him.

Chapter Twenty-One

Deena heard her name called from inside a very weird dream. She opened her eyes and stared at the picture Jack thrust under her nose. She rubbed her still aching neck. Jack dropped the newspaper and left the room.

She took one look at the picture in the paper, went into the living room where Jack sat on the sofa, and sat next to him. "I know this looks bad, Jack, but I did it for the notebook."

"Somehow that doesn't make me feel any better." Jack stood and began to pace the floor, kicking at boxes he passed.

"Kissing him was like kissing a lizard, cold and slimy. But why should you care? We broke up. Remember?"

"I still love you." Jack came and sat down next to her. "I thought if I stayed here, instead of moving to Ann Arbor, we could..."

"What?" When she'd walked into her house and seen Jack and all his stuff parked inside, she'd felt a quick piercing joy. He'd stayed. For her. Of course, that joy had dissipated when he told her she was just a way-station to New York. "You want to be together again? Until you move to New York?"

"I always wanted us together. I thought that if things worked out this week, you could move to New York with me." Jack kicked another box. "But now I don't know. I mean..." He sat down on the sofa next to her. "Just tell me you didn't sleep with him."

"When I left his house, he was in bed with two girls of barely legal age."

"Really? You didn't sleep with him?"

"No! God. What kind of woman do you think I am?"

"Well, you slept with me because my dad wrote a letter for you."

Did he really believe that?

"Jack, I slept with you because I wanted you."

"Also because you knew I was leaving and it would be easy to break things off."

"Or so I thought…" Deena sighed.

"Yeah, me too."

"I've been so sad about you leaving, and now here you are, and I'm not sure how long you're staying. Everything's a mess."

They sat quiet for a couple of minutes.

"Can we be together now?" Jack finally asked. "Or did I make a huge mistake thinking you'd take me in like this?"

Deena thought about it before answering. He was asking for too much, but if she said no, he would think she didn't care. The problem was, she cared too much. If he moved in, she wanted it to be for real. Forever. But she wasn't going to get that. Not now. Maybe never. Finally she said "We're cool on one condition. You never mention that photo again."

"Okay." He tugged on her arm, and she fell back against his chest on the sofa. They sat there together, his arms around her, her fingers entwined in his.

"Got any coffee cake?"

"No."

"Cookies?"

"Nope. But I think there's some whipped cream and strawberries."

"Hm." Jack kissed the side of her face and then her mouth. "You know what I'm thinking?"

Deena had a pretty good idea, since his hands cupped her breasts. She leaned into the press of his fingertips. "What about Sarah?"

"We still have the upstairs to ourselves, right?"

On the way up, they grabbed the strawberries and whipped cream out of the fridge.

****

Deena did not do mothers. Yet, here she was, meeting Jack's. He'd talked her into coming to his parents' place for dinner after they'd made love all afternoon. Worn down her defenses with sweet clouds of love. Jack saying he wanted her in New York with him proved how much he cared. They hadn't talked again about the job, but he wanted it. And her guilt about hoping he didn't get it stung. Hence, the capitulation on dinner with his parents.

As they stood in a foyer as big as Deena's front parlor, Melinda Karris hugged Jack. The ice in her large tumbler of amber liquid clicked. She held out a diamond-encrusted hand to Deena, but instead of shaking hands, Melinda pulled her into a close hug. Deena endured this overly-familiar gesture and thereafter studied Melinda, a well-kept middle aged women of a type she often saw slumming in the funky stores downtown, throwing hundred dollar bills around and cramming their BMWs with purchases.

"I'm so happy to finally meet you." Melinda smiled at Deena, then picked up her drink again. A diamond the size of a silver dollar winked on her finger. Then she excused herself as Jack's father came up. Bill Karris said hello to Deena while he hugged Jack, then ushered them into the family room.

Something about Jack's father and his rolled up, crisp white shirt sleeves made Deena feel safe, even nostalgic. She didn't think her father owned a white shirt. The nostalgia was most likely inspired by Ward Cleaver on *TV Land*.

Looking around the family room, Deena figured

they could play basketball if they got bored. The huge room had thick carpets, two sofas, an ornate wet bar, a cracker thin television hanging on the wall by the sofas, a fireplace on the other end of the sofas, and a baby grand piano in a corner. Despite the vastness of the room, all the little areas made it somehow cozy. Mrs. Karris, or her decorator, had chosen some interesting textiles that worked with all the dark wood and glowing lamps.

"Dinner in just a few minutes." Mrs. Karris poked her head into the room from around the corner. She held an empty tumbler in her hand and lifted her glass. "Cocktails, anyone?"

"I'll get the drinks, Melinda," Bill said.

"Just a beer for me, Dad."

"I'll have what Mrs. Karris is having." Deena needed something strong.

Bill's eyebrows raised.

"Please call me Melinda," Jack's mother said.

"Coming right up." Bill went to fill the drink orders.

"So, dear, I hear from Jack that you're a marvelous teacher."

Bill came back from the bar and handed Deena a drink. She sipped it cautiously, expecting scotch or maybe bourbon, but instead tasted ginger ale.

"My mom teaches too, Deena."

Melinda, with her discreet highlights and her carefully coordinated outfit, looked so cared for, so pampered. So not like a teacher.

"Yes." A soft look came into Melinda's eyes. "I finished college when Jack went away to Purdue."

"Melinda teaches kindergarten in Detroit," Bill said affectionately.

Deena had heard that inner city kids had discipline problems. Well, probably not *all* Detroit students. Certainly not kindergarteners. But still, teaching materials were scarce in the city and many of the buildings were in terrible disrepair. What kind of heart would lead Melinda daily into places that her life made it unnecessary to even think about?

"We're having pot roast for dinner. I hope you're a beef eater, Deena, I hadn't thought..."

Wanting to put the flustered woman at ease, Deena assured her she adored pot roast. Truth was, she'd never had it. Her favorite beef dinner came from McDonald's.

"I admire your writing so much." Melinda caught Deena off guard.

Had Jack actually given her a copy of Mindsprings? Then Melinda brought the sheet music from Yellow Star's first album over from the piano.

"I think it's just terrible that this Ian person is trying to swindle you out of your royalties."

Deena didn't know what to say, so she simply nodded.

"Bill will certainly see to it that that doesn't happen," Melinda added.

"I really want my name on the next album," Deena admitted. "But I can't think of a way to prove that he took more than the one song. It's stupid I know..." She trailed off, feeling dumb. Why had she opened up to this woman?

"I can see why you'd want to be credited, Deena. Any artist would."

Deena was no artist, and was about to say so when Jack took her hand and squeezed it. "Did you make pie, Mom?"

****

In the passenger seat of Jack's car, driving home from dinner with his parents, Deena tried to tamp down a feeling of pure and utter happiness. Her heart said, *This is the guy.* But her head said, *Not so fast.*

She ticked off the evidence, starting with the

fact that Jack's mom had confided he hadn't brought a woman home to dinner since college. That was a big one right there. Then, he'd talked about wanting children without any prompting from her. They discussed it like two people in love, planning their future. He'd told her he loved her. He was here, not in Ann Arbor. Okay that last one was a bit confusing, but he had asked her to move to New York with him if he got a job there. And his parents' house was huge. Why hadn't he stayed with them while waiting to hear from New York?

Part of Jack was still unsure about making a life with her. Maybe his extended dating lifestyle had rendered him unaware of his own desires. But she thought she could read his true intentions, even if he didn't quite get it yet.

Allowing herself to believe that Jack might be The One created an inner body tingling, a hyper-awareness from her fingers to her toes.

He pulled his car into her driveway.

"Here we are." His smile was lit by the light of the moon.

****

The next morning, Jack woke to a dangerous din from the kitchen. Deena must have been up for awhile. He threw on a pair of boxer shorts and ran out to see what all the racket was about.

"I love this juicer!"

She'd unpacked more boxes. The kitchen sink was littered with coffee grounds, orange rinds, egg shells, and potato peels. On the counter, Jack noted an open container of butter and a package that had once held shredded cheddar cheese. The stove boasted several pots and pans in various states of simmer and bubble. The juicer whirred. The coffee pot gurgled. The pan of potatoes fried.

Jack sat, stunned into silence.

Deena bustled over and placed a cup of coffee in

front of him. Then she turned all the various appliances off and came to sit opposite him with her own cup of coffee. "I was hungry."

Sarah came out of her room. "Something smells awesome."

"I...I..." Jack was not a morning person. He certainly wasn't a chatty morning person.

Deena and Sarah both looked at him, but he decided not to finish his sentence. What could he say? Please shut up?

"I'll get the paper. And I have something to tell you guys!" Sarah jogged out of the room, a buzz of energy.

Her sunny face and springy steps contributed to Jack feeling like an old crab. The three of them under one roof would take some getting used to. Always before, when he'd spent the night with Deena, he could escape next door to his own space. His silent, tranquil space.

"Isn't he adorable?" Deena indicated Derrida, who sat on the sideboard, washing his back. "He's like a yoga master the way he stretches his neck."

"Umm." Jack took steady, even breaths. Cats on furniture where food was served disturbed him. His head pounded. He drank his coffee, hoping caffeine would help.

"Hungry?"

"Yeah. Smells good."

As a rule, he liked two cups of coffee and some reading before breakfast, but he figured if Deena was eating she wouldn't be talking.

Sarah came in with the paper and slapped it on the table. Deena disappeared back into the kitchen, only to return with three plates. She slammed one down in front of him.

Wearing a smile as bright as the sun outside, Sarah dropped into a chair. "So, guys. I found an apartment."

Jack silently thanked heaven.

Deena and Sarah chattered away about Sarah's apartment, while Jack hid behind his newspaper, shoveling in the tasty hodgepodge of eggs, bacon, and potatoes that Deena called camper's breakfast.

Then, before he'd finished his cup of coffee, Sarah excused herself and Deena cleared the table. Suddenly, the house felt too quiet. The merest hint of anxiety began to creep into his consciousness.

Something was wrong.

Chapter Twenty-Two

"You okay, hon?" Jack came into the kitchen and up behind Deena at the sink. He put his arms around her waist and pulled her close.

She bent over the potato skillet, furiously scrubbing bits of browned egg away. "You said you wished I'd shut up. I forgot how you are in the morning, that's all."

Oh shit. There he went again, voicing his thoughts without realizing it. Smooth move.

"I'm sorry, love." Jack kissed her cheek and rested his head on her shoulder. "I'm a bear in the morning."

"You say what you're thinking. Right?"

"This is weird, living together, isn't it?" He found a stack of clean dishtowels in a drawer and dried the rinsed pan Deena handed him.

"You never lived with anyone?"

"Roommates in college."

"Of the opposite sex?"

"Nope." He stashed a pan under the sink. "You know me pretty well."

"I thought so."

"You know how I can be."

"Neurotic?" She looked as if she were softening. He pulled her away from the sink, drying her hands with a fresh kitchen towel.

"It'll just take me awhile to get used to sharing my space with someone. My mornings are usually quiet."

"Mine too! I hate it. That's why it's been so great having Sarah here. And Myra. Before I met them,

157

sometimes I would call Patti just to have someone to talk with over coffee."

"But, I don't hate it. It's restful to me." Jack held her hand and looked into her eyes while telling her this hard truth.

"Oh."

"Never mind. Let's go to Home Depot and pick out the paint for the house. A week should be plenty of time to paint this place."

"Have you ever removed wallpaper?" She had a secretive smile on her face as she asked him.

"No, but how hard can it be?"

****

At Home Depot, Jack tried to explain to Deena why she shouldn't paint her dining room burgundy, but she just ignored him.

"Yellow kitchen, blue bathroom, mocha bedroom, burgundy dining room continuing into the parlor on the focal wall...I think that's it." She held paint sample cards fanned out like a crazy rainbow.

They stood at the paint counter, Jack feeling like half of an old married couple. He couldn't decide if this was a good sign or a bad sign. If they *were* married, would he have more input on the paint colors?

"Married? You're thinking of marriage?" Deena dropped the paint cards into her purse.

"No!" Even as he said the words, they sounded harsh, but it annoyed Jack when he spoke his thoughts out loud. It was like revealing a poker hand. Maybe he could get hypnotized to make it stop. "Not really." He tried to gauge Deena's impassive face as they stood waiting for the paint guy to shake up her colors. "Just well, so you'd have to listen to me about paint," he whispered.

Deena didn't say anything, but she smiled at him. "I'll go to the grocery store later, while you strip the wallpaper."

"I mean, living together is a good first step."

"Until you get a job in New York."

"I don't know if it will work out. And you could always come to New York with me." He couldn't wait to tell Deena about the progress of her book through the ranks at the publishing house. Don reported that so far, things looked excellent. He hoped to have a contract ready to present within a few days. *Maybe it would be better to wait for the contract?* Probably. Deena had had many disappointments lately, what with Hensley stealing her lyrics and being fired. If he could present her with good news, her book contract as a done deal, that would be best.

****

Deena, in an effort to forget that Jack had mentioned marriage, spent the rest of the morning applying to community colleges online while Jack peeled wallpaper from the parlor walls.

Her dad called just as she finished. "When do I get to see this new house of yours?"

"You want to come over for dinner tonight?" The words popped out before she could think about it. Her dad didn't even know she'd been seeing someone, let alone living with him. She and Jack could talk to him together. Tonight.

"Sure. You want to me to bring take-out?"

Her signature dish was pasta with jar sauce. She'd do better tonight. "Nope, got it covered. Want to help paint my living room?" She couldn't imagine her dad and Jack in the same room for any length of time, but if they had a project, it might work.

"I'll be there," Dad said.

Deena went into the living room to tell Jack about her dad. She'd had dinner with his folks, now it was his turn to meet the parent.

"Honey, where are your cookbooks?" she asked, peeking into random boxes now covered in flakes of cabbage rose wallpaper.

159

Jack stopped stripping the wallpaper and located the exact box that held his cookbook collection. "Take your pick."

She chose *The Microwave Gourmet,* thinking that any cookbook with *microwave* in the title must have easy recipes. Jack loved shrimp, in fact he loved all seafood, so she decided on Shrimp Creole. Feeling like the epitome of organization, she made a list of ingredients and left Jack to the wallpaper.

She hunted in vain through the dairy case for shrimp butter, then threw a box of unsalted butter into her cart instead. She stopped at the fish counter to buy fresh unpeeled shrimp, since according to Jack it tasted so much better than the frozen, peeled kind.

She hauled the bags of groceries in by the back door and slid them from the little foyer area onto the kitchen floor. Shopping was way easier when she didn't have to climb steps with bulging bags. "Hi!" she called into the front room. "I'm home." No answer. She left her keys on the counter and walked into the living room. Jack had buds in his ears has his back to her, and sure enough, little bits and pieces of stubborn wallpaper still stuck to the walls. Jack dunked a sponge into a pail and wet one long, skinny strip, then used the scraper tool to remove all traces of the wallpaper. She put a hand on his shoulder and kissed his cheek. Only two or three dozen to go, she wanted to say, but didn't.

She went back into the kitchen to empty the bags of groceries onto the table. The cookbook was already turned to the proper page, held there by a chip clip. Deena read through the recipe again, noticing this time the embedded recipe for shrimp butter. Who ever heard of such a thing? She flipped to the shrimp butter page and freaked when she realized she would have to peel the shrimp and use the shells to make the butter. Her timetable had just been shot to hell by a bunch of shrimp.

One hour later, the shrimp peeled, the butter processed, the vegetables chopped, Deena threw the lot into the microwave and nuked it. She had to stand there with a spoon, uncovering and stirring and covering again. She read the recipe a third time and realized she had to make another ingredient, something called a roux. Deena read the roux instructions twice and still did not comprehend. Maybe because she was also listening to Jack swear at the wallpaper. Maybe she could skip this step?

No, she'd go slow, put the roux together step by step.

Turned out it wasn't that hard. A little flour, a little butter. But she was seriously behind on the dinner plan. Her dad would be here soon. She microwaved the roux for fifteen minutes while running upstairs to put on her makeup. She'd eventually bring her clothes and stuff downstairs, where she'd been sleeping with Jack, but for now it didn't seem worth it, with the painting and all.

She came back down to the kitchen just as the microwave binged, then beat the roux to death in the bowl before adding it to the recipe, which she damn well hoped was done. Looked like all she had to do was micro it for three minutes when they were ready to eat. Good thing she'd bought Minute Rice.

"You bought *Minute Rice*?" Jack came out of the bathroom all clean and relaxed. He'd given up on the wallpaper and taken a shower. His hair was wet. What would her dad think about her boyfriend's hair being wet? She'd have to explain about Jack staying here. She didn't look forward to it. Her dad was traditional.

"What? What's wrong with Minute Rice?" Deena asked, trying to get a spot of roux out of her top with a wet kitchen towel.

"It's flavorless and nutritionless. It's not a whole

food. It's overprocessed." Deena didn't get it. Rice was rice...until it came to Jack.

Jack took the kitchen towel from her hand and pulled the shirt up over her head. "I'll get the spot out. You go find another top." He kissed her.

At that precise moment, a heavy knock sounded, and a second later her dad popped his head in the kitchen from the tiny landing at the back door.

"Hi." His voice went flat as he gradually took in the fact that she was shirtless and freshly kissed. She scurried behind Jack.

"Hi, Dad." She had a couple of choices. Stay hidden behind Jack forever, act like wearing her bra and shorts was normal dinner party attire, or rush upstairs to her bedroom and let Jack handle it. After the Minute Rice crack, she chose the third option.

She waved. "Dad, this is Jack." Leaving Jack holding her shirt, she sprinted for the stairs. By the time she came back down with a new shirt on, her dad and Jack were bonding over beers and wallpaper removal stories.

"We won't be able to paint this room tonight," her dad said. "The walls need to completely dry first."

"Well, dinner's almost ready, so at least we can eat." Deena went into the kitchen for the final nuke of the meal. Her dad, unfortunately, went to view the rest of the house with Jack.

"You're living here?" she heard her dad say to Jack. "Since when?"

Deena placed the meal on the table and called the boys to their places.

Her dad didn't look happy.

"I'm sorry I haven't called. I have a couple of roommates, well, only one now. Just Jack. The other one, Sarah, moved out. She rented her first apartment. We're so proud of her, aren't we Jack?"

Jack nodded while guzzling his beer.

"Roommate? That's a nice way to say shacking up, Dee Dee. Didn't you learn anything after that last creep dumped you?"

"Is he talking about Ian?" Jack shot Deena an insulted look. "Please don't compare me to him, Mr. Smith."

"What are your intentions toward my daughter?"

Oh for Pete's sake—she should have known Dad would come up with something from the last century.

"I...um." Jack turned toward Deena. "I thought he knew!" He looked back to Deena's dad. "My parents know. They're cool with it."

"If Deena were my son instead of my daughter, maybe I'd be *cool with it* too."

"Dad, it's not what you think. Jack is between places right now, that's all. He's going to New York in a couple days for a job, and he needed a place to store his stuff, and my whole downstairs was empty, and he used to live next door..."

"This Shrimp Creole is delicious, Deena," Jack said. "Another beer anybody?"

Eventually, her dad calmed down. They painted the bathroom and Sarah's empty room. Jack worked on the bathroom alone, while she and her dad did the bedroom. Deena didn't have the heart to tell him she'd lost her job. That would send him over the edge.

Chapter Twenty-Three

Jack couldn't sleep. Deena's dad's words repeated themselves in an endless loop. *What are your intentions toward my daughter?*

He got up as quietly as possible so as not to wake Deena and went into the kitchen, looking for something sweet. Ah! Coffee cake. He sliced a huge piece and sat at the dining room table eating it, trying not to think. That worked for a minute but there wasn't enough coffee cake in the world to keep him from thinking about what came next with Deena.

Did she wonder the same thing as her father? Did she question his intentions? And what were his intentions? Why did people have to label things and cast them into conventional molds? How old-fashioned a notion: marriage. He could see living with Deena for a while, maybe a few years, and then deciding if his love for her was the forever kind. What was the rush?

He searched his memory for the expression on her face when they were buying paint and he thoughtlessly blurted out the "M" word. Joy had lit her face but had been quickly extinguished when he'd taken his words back.

So, he had been thinking about it. In some ways, he was right there with her. He didn't want to serial date forever. And he loved her. But things were so up in the air now. Both of their careers had derailed. Maybe when they got back on track, found jobs. If she would show her love by moving to New York. If it came to that.

There were too many *ifs* for them to be planning a forever future right now.

Still, he was happy to know she wanted it all—marriage, kids, career. And she wanted it all with him, not Hensley. He'd beaten out a rock star for her love.

****

"I read that most men who live with someone before marriage are less committed afterward if they do finally marry." Patti sorted through the salvage yard's pile of wrought iron.

"Who are you? My dad?"

"No, just saying."

"We're not really *living* together. He's only with me because the rent's cheap. And it's convenient."

"Not very romantic." Patti unearthed another piece of wrought iron and added it to their pile.

"What are you going to do with this stuff, anyway?"

"I'm going to make a cage for Jack." Deena worked on setting aside several thick stained glass windows in order to see the iron stacked behind them. "Actually, Jack and I talked about finances, and he has some money saved, and he wanted to help me with the house as a sort of housewarming present, so we decided we'd tear down that old set of outdoor steps that used to lead to my apartment."

"Yeah, okay, now I know why the house looked different when I pulled up this morning." Patti had swung by Deena's early with Toby's pick up truck.

"Some guy, Pete, from *Husbands for Hire*—he's helping Jack with the painting and steps and stuff—gave me the idea. You know how there's that sliding glass door up there? Right?"

Patti nodded. She was now adding slightly deteriorated pieces to the pile they'd acquired. Deena moved them to a separate pile. She didn't want to have to strip and repaint these things if she didn't have to. There was enough painting going on already.

"I bet that patio door looks funny now that there's no steps leading to it. I think I even got it on the video, but it didn't register."

"Yeah, it does look weird. So Pete suggested we make a balcony."

"Just like Romeo and Juliet."

Deena laughed. "And do you know how expensive new wrought iron is? Pete told me about this place." Deena checked the stacks of iron. "I think we're good."

"Excellent. I need to get the truck back to Toby."

"How is he? What's up with you guys?" Deena paid the cashier, and he helped them haul and load the wrought iron into Toby's pick up truck.

"He's okay." Patti drove the truck with easy familiarity back down to Ash Creek. "He's worried about Ian. There's something wrong with him."

"You can say that again. He's psychotic." Deena had decided to wait until Jack left on his trip before she attempted another phase of the Notebook Plan. This time, her strategy was fool-proof.

"No, besides his usual crazy. Something physical. Ian's seeing a doctor and everything."

Deena's cell phone rang. She checked the ID. "Hi Pete."

"Did you still want me to help Jack with the painting today, Ms. Smith?"

"Yes. And I got the wrought iron. I'm heading home with it right now. If you get there before me, and Jack doesn't answer the door, the back door off the kitchen is unlocked."

Pete laughed. "You call that a lock?"

Deena had noticed the lack of a deadbolt, but Ash Creek wasn't a hotbed of crime.

****

While Pete finished painting the dining room,

Jack drove to English Gardens, where he purchased four rose bushes for Deena. Painting her house was a good gift, but he wanted to give her something lasting and romantic. So that's why he also bought a trellis, because it reminded him of her. She should have a garden in the back yard, with a trellis and paths of shredded bark. She should have an old-fashioned swing under an awning. Maybe he'd buy that for her birthday. When was her birthday, anyway?

Deena opened the door while he wrestled the trellis out of the back seat of his car. He held it up as she stepped outside. "The rose bushes are in my trunk."

"I love this trellis!" Deena kissed him, and they walked around to the back of the house.

"The wrought iron looks great. That balcony will be awesome."

"I know." Deena smiled.

This project had energized her. It made her forget about being unemployed. She seemed less obsessed with Ian these days, too. Jack hugged Deena to him as they stood surveying the yard. "Something smells good."

"Shrimp Creole leftovers. Want a beer?"

"Thanks." Jack had just learned that shopping for rose bushes was thirsty work.

When Deena came back from the house with two beers, he hugged her to him and gave her a kiss, right there in the yard for all the neighbors to see.

Jack brought a couple of kitchen chairs and a battered T.V. table outside for them. Eating dinner outside in the warm air with sun shining on them beat the smell of fresh paint fumes any day.

After dinner, Jack sat his empty beer bottle on the little square of broken cement Myra called a patio and carried the rose bushes into the back yard, one at a time. He sat them next to the trellis, which was propped up against Deena's sorry excuse for a garage. Next project—sand and stain that peeling wood.

Jack stood for a minute, drinking his beer, surveying the yard. It would be fun to work with Deena fixing it up. They had such different tastes, but he had to admit, her colors looked good on the walls. Now she just needed some landscaping, then to extend the patio, put up a balcony, paint the garage or tear it down, and to gut the upstairs to make into a master suite. He could see it all in his mind's eye. He wanted to make a list.

Instead, he wandered into the kitchen where Deena washed dishes. They needed a dishwasher, too.

"Can I help?" Cans of paint, brushes, and rollers were stacked in a corner of the kitchen next to the table. "Should I move this stuff out to the garage?"

"Tomorrow." Deena handed him a serving bowl to dry. "Maybe I'll try another recipe from that book while you're in New York."

"I don't mind taking turns with the cooking, Deena. And I'm happy to clean house." Jack's face flushed. He didn't want Deena thinking her housekeeping skills weren't up to his standards, but she seemed oblivious.

"Cool. I hate housework."

He watched the careless way she brushed her hair off her face, revealing her widow's peak. She used to be so self-conscious about that. She used to be so stand-offish. And now here he was, living with her. It seemed like a miracle.

But it wasn't real.

Tomorrow he'd be in New York and anything could happen. New York was the big time deal, the break he'd been working toward his entire adult life. Going into teaching had been great training, but it wasn't the work he wanted to do. Now he had the perfect opportunity to attain the kind of job he could really love, the way Deena and his mom loved teaching. But somehow, the thought of leaving Deena, and this house which was their home now, gave him a pained pang. Or it could just be indigestion. Two nights in a row of spicy food maybe wasn't such a great idea.

****

Deena sat on the bed watching Jack pack his bags. She didn't want him to go, but also couldn't wait for him to leave. She had a new, unbeatable plan to get her notebook from Ian. This time she would find it or die trying.

"I'll be back."

"Maybe. Unless they love you and never let you go."

"I'll text."

"Me too."

"Not the same."

"I know."

"I'll call."

She nodded. He picked up his bag. This past week had been lovely. Living together. Learning new ways to please each other. She had to believe he'd be back. Who got a job and moved to another state all in a matter of weeks?

Jack. That's who. He'd done it before. Plenty of times.

Deena followed him out the door. He wouldn't let her drive him to the airport. It was easier that way, she guessed. He let his bag drop in the doorway and kissed her for a long time. She would miss his kisses. She clung to him like a dream she couldn't bear to wake from.

Then he took her arms in his hands and pulled her away from him. A minute later, he was gone.

Panicked suddenly, in the house all alone for the first time ever, she didn't know what to do. So she opened a bottle of wine and called Patti. Getting a second opinion on her brand-new Ian plan was better than pining over Jack.

****

The house Chianti flowed freely, the warm bread drizzled in olive oil was to die for, and Deena was ready for some girl talk. Maybe Patti would be able to figure out Jack's mixed signals.

As Patti tore apart a loaf of bread, Deena thought about how far they'd come from the old days when they'd both been heartsick over Ian. Well, they still had a ways to go in putting him behind them. She wasn't sure if she could pull off her most recent scheme for retrieving the notebook, but all Patti had to do was pick up her guitar and start playing again. How hard could that be?

"You need more wine." Deena gestured at the bottle.

Patti shook her head. "All the wine in the world won't convince me that it's a good idea for you to lure Ian to your house and sweet talk him into giving you that notebook back."

"But I'm a really good cook now."

"He doesn't eat anymore, and he's immune to sweet talk."

Patti was right. So, the plan needed more work. Fine. For tonight she'd try to forget about Jack and help Patti win her own battle against Ian. But she'd have to lead into it gently, because Patti was stubborn.

"When I first showed Ian the Paris notebook, he acted like it wasn't worth his time." She dipped her bread into the seasoned garlic oil and took a bite, to give Patti a chance to digest the nugget of intel.

"He's such an ass."

"It reminds me of the way he treated you when you tried to play guitar around him." Deena hoped her analogy had been subtle enough.

The waiter set down an enormous platter of salad and another of Fettuccini Alfredo. "Enjoy," he said, saving Patti from responding. But Deena hoped she'd been heard.

"Heart attack on a plate," the guy at the next table said.

Deena had noticed two men dining alone one table over when she sat down. The thing with Italian Stallion was, the tables for two were set close together. And the hostess always sat singles and same sex doubles in that section together. Made things interesting, if anybody was interested.

"Charming," Patti whispered.

Deena remembered the lovelorn days when she and Patti came here twice a week. No guy had even tried to make conversation. It was like males had this radar that allowed them to only want a woman if she was committed to someone else.

"Toby had quite an enlightening conversation with Ian the other day," Patti said between bites of pasta.

"About?" Deena drained her glass of wine and poured more from the gallon jug on the table. It was doing its job. All her sore spots mellowed. Jack away? Take a sip. Sarah on her own? Cheers to the young woman. But as far as Patti was concerned, Deena was still on a mission. Wine wouldn't deter her from getting Patti to pick up that guitar tonight.

Deena forked pasta into her mouth and listened to Patti's story.

"Ian thinks he's the driving force behind the band." Patti poured herself another glass of wine. "He told Toby, and I quote 'I'm the creative one, I write all the music.'"

"But Toby writes the music with him. They're collaborators. Always have been. From day one."

"Exactly."

Deena saw the parallel. "So, how'd Toby take

171

it?"

"Better than you'd expect. He's worried about Ian, says he's getting more and more messiah-complexish. He's not the same guy he used to be. And he's looking really run down. Way too thin."

This reminded Deena that Patti hadn't complained about her weight once the entire meal. Her self-esteem must be improving. Toby was good for her. Now if he would just tell Patti she was a great guitarist, everything would be perfect. Well, perfect for Patti. Which was almost as good as perfect for Deena.

"One thing he did admit—he thinks Ian is deliberately keeping the notebook from him. He's asked to see it several times. He even offered to go through all Ian's boxes in the basement." She took a dessert menu from the waiter. "Toby thinks the lyrics are probably a lot more yours than Ian's admitting to himself."

"That's what I've been saying all along."

Patti gave the waiter her dessert order.

"Hey." Deena looked closely at the waiter. "Aren't you Maxine's son?"

"Oh, yeah, hi." He smiled at her, a glimmer of recognition in his eyes.

"Ash Creek University. Freshman comp. Last fall." Deena grinned.

The kid's grin wasn't nearly as comfortable. "Oh, uh, sure. You want dessert, too?"

"No, but bring two forks."

Patti nudged Deena after the waiter disappeared. "I didn't know you taught Maxine's son. Maxine from the bar, right?"

"Yep." The plotting part of Deena's head started putting a new plan together.

Chapter Twenty-Four

Deena had finally hit on the right plan to get her notebook back. It all seemed so simple now. This time it would work. She leaned across the table and asked Patti, "So, is Maxine cleaning for Toby and Ian?"

"Yeah."

"How's that working out?"

"Fine."

"She's supposed to clean tomorrow morning, correct?"

"Yeah."

"And Ian's got that appointment with the specialist tomorrow morning."

"So?"

"I'm about the same height as Maxine. I could put my hair in a bandana like she does, wear her clothes, put on some glasses, leave off the make up—nobody will recognize me. I can bring a bucket and mop, go in and pretend I'm Maxine."

Maxine's son came with the dessert, and Patti and Deena stopped plotting long enough for him to present it to Patti with two forks.

When he left the table, Patti said, "Oh, man, that will never work."

"Yes it will," Deena insisted. This was it. This was the perfect plan. "The only people who might be there who really know me well are Toby and Cal. Toby can make sure he's out of the house with Cal. I'll just go in while Ian's at the doctor's office. It's perfect. Neighbors will see a little lady, same as usual, coming in to do the cleaning."

173

"It might work."

"It will work." Deena set down her espresso and took a bite of Patti's dessert. If she had any more food, she was going to explode. "We can't let Ian win. Me *or* you."

"I'm not. I simply no longer have the desire to play. Just like you no longer have the desire to write."

"I'm not done writing. I've just channeled it elsewhere. I write all the time for the classroom," Deena protested.

"I'll make you a deal." Patti, unfazed by Deena's logic, now wanted to bargain. "If you write some lyrics, I'll put them to music on my guitar."

"Why do you have to make it so complicated? Can't you just pick up the guitar and play something?"

"Well, I guess it wouldn't hurt." Patti pushed her Zabaglione away unfinished. "I'm too full. Did you want to go dancing or anything after this?"

"Not in these jeans!" Deena tugged at her ridiculously tight waistband. "I need to go home and get a Maxine costume together, and you need to fix it up with Toby. Also, I better call Maxine and explain the plan to her. I'll tell her to stand by. I'll call her when it's time for her to switch places with me."

Patti had a bandana, so Deena came up to the loft with her. She peeked into Patti's bedroom area. The guitar was sitting out, propped in a corner next to the armoire. She walked in and picked it up. She brought it over to Patti and set it down in front of her. "Why don't you play this thing for me?"

"Because I don't want to pretend I'm some rock star when I'm just another girl who plays guitar."

"So just be a girl who plays guitar." Deena held on to the guitar, keeping it poised before Patti's face.

Finally, Patti grabbed it by the neck and set it down on the sofa. "Gotta find a pick," she told Deena, going to her silverware drawer and rummaging around.

"Yeah, I always keep my picks with the forks and knives, too." Deena thought this was merely another elaborate ploy on Patti's part. To her surprise, Patti held up a blue pick. Her smile was wicked.

"I'm gonna suck, because it's been a long time, but you asked for it." Just then they heard the key in the lock, and a second later the door opened and Toby came in.

"Whoa, Deena, you're still here?"

"Yeah. Patti was just about to play her guitar."

"Patti? Guitar?" Toby looked as surprised as Jack had the day he found out Deena wrote song lyrics.

Patti stood frozen between the kitchen area and the living room. She'd put the hand with the pick in it behind her back, as if doing so would make it all go away.

"Toby, really? You didn't know Patti played guitar?" Surely there must have been times when Patti first started hanging out with the band that he'd at least seen her carrying her guitar case.

Toby came over to the sofa and picked up Patti's Martin. Patti walked to take it from him. Toby handed Patti the guitar and she moved back over to a kitchen chair and sat down, the guitar resting on her lap like it belonged there.

"I guess I do remember you with a guitar when I first met you." Toby took another seat at the table. Deena sat with them, waiting to see what Patti would do. So far, she hadn't said a word since Toby had come into the loft.

****

Instead of talking, Patti threw the pick on the table and used her fingers to play the opening bars to "Landslide." She kept her head bent over the guitar, looking at the strings. A couple of times, she made mistakes, smiled at the strings, shook her head, and kept on going. She didn't sing. She just played. To Deena's ears she sounded way better than a person who hadn't played a guitar in over a year.

After the song, Patti propped the guitar against the kitchen table. "Damn, my fingers are sore." She looked at her left hand, and then showed Deena the deep indentations on the pads of her fingertips where she'd held the strings down on the fretboard.

"No calluses," Toby said. "That's what you get for not practicing, babe."

"You're really good." Deena tried not to sound as amazed as she felt.

"Yeah, just need to practice, babe, work off that rust." Toby smiled as if he couldn't be more pleased to learn his girlfriend was a musician too.

"I don't know if I want to," Patti admitted.

"What?" Deena asked. "You play guitar your whole life, and suddenly you just decide you don't want to anymore?"

"It's not all that sudden." Patti pointed out.

"But—"

"Babe—"

Deena and Toby both protested at the same time.

"Listen, guys. I already told Deena this once, I'll start playing again when you two write me some songs."

Toby looked dumbfounded. His eyes went from searching Patti's face to Deena's.

Deena shrugged. "I've been trying to tell her I'm not a songwriter."

"And I've been trying to tell you I'm not a guitarist," Patti retorted.

"It's different."

"It's not," Patti answered. "Now let's tell Toby about your plan to get the notebook tomorrow morning."

****

The next morning, Deena called Toby from Ian's driveway before she went in. He and Cal were at a breakfast meeting, so Toby pretended he was talking to Maxine.

"Yeah, house is still full of people. Ian asked me to get them out before he came home from the doctor, but I didn't have the heart to wake them up."

"That's fine. Nobody I know, right?"

"Nope. You don't have to make them coffee, Max."

"Okay then. Thank you."

"I'll be home in time to pay you for the day's work."

Deena shut her phone and went into the house. She filled her pail with water in the kitchen and put a pot of coffee on. She looked through the cupboards to see what cleaning supplies Ian had. Or rather what cleaning supplies he lacked. Just about everything. Evidently, Maxine brought her own.

She had three rooms to check out—the band room, the office, and Ian's bedroom. Deena headed to the bedroom first, stepping over a crashed out couple on the living room floor along the way and carrying an old tote bag with rags and a feather duster sticking out of it. The tote had a far more useful purpose than just the disguise.

She stopped for a minute at Ian's open door. The smell of semen and stale marijuana assaulted her, but at least no girls slept on his bed. The night table was there, waiting, so she opened its drawer. She saw her notebook right away, under a sizable carton of condoms.

She reached for it as someone came up behind her. "Hey lady, what are you doing?"

Her fingers released the notebook, and she pulled her hand out of the drawer and shut it. She

177

turned and saw an unfamiliar man.

"Mr. Hensley requested that I start in here. This drawer was open. I was simply admiring his array of condoms before shutting it so I could strip the bed." And she began to efficiently do so as he stood watching her.

"Oh right, you're the maid."

"There's coffee in the kitchen."

"Cool. Carry on."

As soon as he left, Deena retrieved her notebook and stashed it in her tote. Then, she gathered up the soiled sheets. On her way to the laundry room, she pulled the rugs from the bathroom floor. The laundry room had a back door, so Deena went outside and began shaking rugs. She came into the kitchen, where a few people were up and drinking coffee. She heard the shower running.

"I forgot my Comet. Does Mr. Hensley have any?" When no one answered, she opened the cupboard that contained a box of dish detergent and an old Brillo pad. She made a show of opening a few more cupboards.

"I'll just pop over to the store and get some." Making a hasty exit, she retreated to her car, where she called Maxine.

"How did it go?" Maxine's voice sounded like she'd smoked a million cigarettes. Which, probably, she had.

Deena gave her a quick summary of events. "You'll want to bring Comet," she said before they hung up.

When she got home, Deena sat in her newly painted and de-boxed parlor. Guess she could start calling it a living room now. She and Jack had moved down her Granny's hope chest, and she'd brought some other things—candles and books and lamps—to mix with Jack's furniture. Somehow it all worked together.

She poured over the notebook with a sense of disbelief, and her anger rose every time she turned a page. Ian had merely crossed off a dozen or so of her words on most of the lyrics and inserted his own. She went through the book again, her simmering anger getting hotter by the minute. He hadn't even bothered to hide what he'd done.

The man had to be insane. Or just on the usual Ian ego trip. Something was wrong with him, because he seemed convinced that he was merely inspired by her poetry, not fueled by it. If he had used all the lyrics he'd marked up on the upcoming release, Yellow Star's latest efforts owed quite a bit to Deena Smith's Paris notebook.

Flipping through the pages, she noticed several blank sheets toward the end. Half the book was actually blank. She remembered that. She fanned through the blanks, staring at nothing, feeling numb.

Just as she prepared to set the notebook back on the hope chest, she saw Ian's handwriting on the last two pages. They were covered, front and back, with names and cities. First a woman's name, then a European city, and finally a phone number. It read like the final leg of Ian's last tour. The part after Paris. The first entries were actually Parisian. There were three. Then Rome, Milan, Venice, Warsaw, Berlin, Copenhagen, Amsterdam, and finally, London. At the bottom, Ian had scrawled *all four star fucks*. Some had the added notation *BBJ*. Deena's skin crawled.

Chapter Twenty-Five

Ian didn't like wasting time. He'd only come to this specialist to get Cal off his back. The guy took one look at Ian's throat, didn't even touch it, didn't even order X-rays, before he pronounced doom.

"What you have here—" the doctor pressed delicately around Ian's throat, "—is a thyroglossal cyst. May be benign, most of them are. We won't know until we take it out. Either way, it has to come out." He looked Ian over from top to bottom, checked his notes where the nurse had recorded his weight and height and blood pressure. "How long has the cyst been obstructing your eating patterns?"

Ian laughed. It was more of a bitter bark. The dude was a quack. "That's my Adam's Apple, man."

"I'm afraid not." The doctor shook his head.

"I'm not gonna let you cut me open on the strength of you poking me in the neck. Shouldn't you be taking X-rays or giving me a body scan or something?" Ian didn't like this feeling, like someone else was in charge. But since he was here, he might as well get the works, get the proof that this was nothing, and get Toby and Cal off his back.

"You're scheduled for various tests, but that's not going to change my diagnosis."

Bloody know-it-all, scribbling on his clipboard.

"I understand you're a singer."

"Yeah, dude." Ian's veins bulged in disgust. "Which is why I can't let you fucking cut me up."

The doctor seemed a little surprised, and this gave Ian a small measure of satisfaction.

"Has it always been hard to swallow? Painful?"

"I'm a singer, dude. I get sore throats. It's part of the package."

The doctor once again handled his throat. He pushed it in the middle, low. "This is your Adam's Apple. This—" he palpated the larger knob a bit to the left of center, "—is the mass that needs to be biopsied. By the time you come out of anesthesia, we'll know if there's a malignancy present." He stopped for a minute and looked Ian in the eye. "Your voice may be affected, of course."

Ian left the doctor's office seething. Damn fucking shit. They'd done the test, shown him the X-rays. There was no fucking doubt that he'd be going under the knife. No fucking doubt at all.

All these years, to protect his voice, he never smoked—well, not cigarettes. All these years, he took it easy on the hard stuff, no whiskey or tequila shots, to protect his voice. His voice was his fortune and lately everything seemed to want to fuck with it. First Dee, who wanted to claim a piece. Now a doctor, in need of a new swimming pool. Wait until he saw Toby. He'd started all this with his fucking concern. *Concern my ass.* Toby was out to bury him. Ian just didn't know why.

Ian phoned Cal and Toby, but neither picked up. Gradually his anger turned to frustration and then something he refused to call fear. He thought about phoning his parents. Mothers could always be counted on for sympathy. But his parents and their aging hippie routine really bugged him. Drove him up the fucking wall was more like it. Dee popped into his head. She'd always been a good little nurse. Maybe this was the thing he needed to finally get her back. How could she say no to a dude in his situation? He was fucked. She'd have some compassion for that. It was sort of perfect, if he didn't factor in the surgery part.

He drove his new XKR Jaguar over to Dee's,

refusing to give in to fear, keeping the idea of finally winning her back firmly in the front of his mind. He liked the car, liked the idea that he could buy any car he wanted. He'd worked hard to sit in this seat, behind this wheel. He just needed Dee back in his life so she wouldn't spoil things. He'd always been able to talk her around before. Now would be no different.

Back then, she'd wanted to be married. He'd scoffed at the idea. Now, it didn't seem so terrible. Lots of guys in bands were married. The wife stayed home, had the kids, kept the house in good shape, and waited for the tour to end. Perfect. He could see the two of them shopping for rings. The press would love it! *Hensley Marries His Army Girl.* Sales would shoot through the roof.

He drove through the streets of the city he and Dee had dreamed of getting out of, passed the university where they'd met. Finally, finally, her house. He had made that house possible for her by giving her songwriting credit. Now, he'd make an even bigger house possible by marrying her.

Dee's red Miata was in the driveway. He pulled in behind her.

Hell, he'd probably stay the night.

No one answered the door. He could hear music playing, thought maybe she couldn't hear his knock. He didn't want to risk yelling, didn't want to inflict any more stress on his throat. He tried the door, opened it, and walked right in. Beth Orton sang from the docking station. Deena and her chick singers. A black cat curled on the sofa opened one eye and gazed at him. Candles were lit everywhere. That was Dee, always the romantic.

"Hi honey, I'm home," he said, just as Dee came into the room holding a bowl of popcorn.

****

Deena saw Ian in her living room and flung the

bowl of popcorn into the air. Kernals flew in all directions, and the cats shot out of the room like two furry bullets.

"Jesus, Ian! Don't you knock? You scared the shit out of me."

Ian stared at her through all the candles.

"It was mine!" She folded her arms across her chest. "You lied to me, and you stole my words, you bastard."

"What?" Ian looked confused. He rubbed his throat.

"What are you doing here? Haven't you caused me enough trouble?"

Ian clutched at his throat. He seemed to be working something out. She could almost see the pieces of the puzzle fall into place. Her eyes went to the coffee table and his followed seconds before she scooped the notebook up and put it behind her back. "Get out before I call the police."

"You miserable bitch." Ian croaked in a voice so unlike his own chills rolled down her spine. "You'll pay for this." He kicked the screen door open, leaving her and her frantically beating heart alone.

****

After Ian left, Deena jumped in her car and drove the notebooks, both of them, over to Bill Karri's office. On the way, Jack called.

"Hello?" she answered as she turned a corner.

"I got the job." He sounded way too happy for a man about to move hundreds of miles away.

"How nice for you." Deena's phone beeped, and she checked the I.D.—Ian. "Jack. I gotta go. Ian's trying to call." Deena clicked over.

"You're dead, bitch," Ian said. Then he hung up on her.

When Deena pulled up at the lawyer's office, she had to sit in the car for a minute, because her legs couldn't carry her. Jack gone. Ian stalking. Man, she was so screwed.

After she finally regained control of her kneecaps, she walked into the law office. First she asked for Bill, then his partner, but both were in meetings. Deena felt compelled to babysit the notebooks until Bill's meeting was over, but she finally left them with his secretary, after stressing a hundred times how important they were.

Another awesome June day, and the last thing she wanted to do was return to her house. She'd kept all the windows open, but the place still smelled strongly of paint. Even the cats had noticed. They streaked out the door every time she opened it to take refuge in the June sunshine.

She looked at her watch. Almost lunch time. Circumventing her home, she headed for The Pub, where Patti was working. As Deena walked in, Patti waved from behind the bar. Deena dropped onto an open stool. "Ian just threatened my life. He knows I took the notebook."

Patti poured Deena a Chardonnay. "You call the police?"

"No. Should I? I mean, you know Ian. He's an ass, but he's not really gonna hurt me."

"Actually he's sick. Really sick. He's got a growth in his throat. It could affect his voice. It could be cancer. He's having surgery and everything."

For a minute, Deena felt bad about the way she had blown Ian off when he'd stopped by. "Oh my God." She realized then that he probably hadn't even known that she'd taken the notebook. "I blew it."

"What?"

Deena recapped the bizarre encounter.

"And to make it worse, Jack got the job in New York. He's positively ecstatic about leaving me behind. He didn't even try to fake it."

Patti poured more wine.

After Deena's fourth glass of Chardonnay, Patti

said, "You're in no condition to drive. Go upstairs and take a nap. I'll wake you when my shift is over."

"If I'm not driving, I'll have one more." She waited while Patti poured her a glass. "By the way, I think my affirmation needs tweaking."

And then her phone rang. She didn't recognize the number, so she let it go to voicemail, then listened. The secretary at Taylor Community College wanted to schedule an interview for Monday.

The prospect of a steady job lifted Deena's spirits. She pushed her full glass of wine away and decided to take Patti's advice before returning the college's call. She walked out of the bar and around back to the steps leading to Patti's loft.

****

Deena opened her eyes, disoriented. Something woke her, but where was she? Oh yeah. Patti's place. The sounds she heard were the door to the loft opening. People entering. She stayed hidden in Patti's bed, behind the shelves of books that divided the loft.

"I need a shower," Patti said.

Deena eyed her jeans laying just out of reach. *Shit, Toby's out there.* Good thing Patti had all those bookshelves between the bed and the rest of the loft. Especially since Toby wasn't out there alone.

"Chicks!" Ian said, after Patti went into the bathroom, and Deena heard the spray from the shower.

Why was Ian here?

"You said you'd be nice if I made you lunch," Toby said.

Shit. Now she for sure was staying put. Deena glanced at the bedside clock. Five in the afternoon. She had a headache from drinking wine so early in the day, and she needed to brush her teeth. She wanted a Coke really, really bad.

Toby asked Ian something she didn't catch.

Deena heard water running in the kitchen sink. Someone moved closer to the bookshelves. Biff barked, and Toby called the dog to his supper. So, Toby in the kitchen and Ian way too close for comfort.

Maybe he'd leave soon.

"So, how do I get that damn notebook back? The bitch stole my property."

Deena struggled to hear Toby's words over the sizzle of bacon frying. Inflection and tone were all she could catch. He sounded unhappy, even angry. But at who? Her or Ian?

"I'll do it, dude. I don't care about that bitch. She's trying to take what's mine. I might not be able to control this fucking thing in my throat, but I can damn well make sure all my stuff's in order before I go down."

The bacon smelled really good. She pictured Toby slicing tomatoes and setting them atop squishy slices of white bread. The smell of coffee wafted through the bookshelves, tormenting her almost as much as Ian's words.

Toby's voice got closer. "In a minute."

Deena heard Toby let himself into the bathroom and close the door. An electronic beep broadcasted Patti's ancient PC boot up process. What was Ian doing on Patti's computer?

Biff growled over the sound of Ian clicking at Patti's keyboard. When the printer started humming, Deena hoped he'd get what he wanted and leave.

A door opened, then another. "Changed my mind about the sandwich, dude," Ian told Toby. "Nice robe, for a fat chick." The slamming door punctuated his insult to Patti.

"I'm sorry, babe. He's a jerk. When his surgery is over I'm quitting the band."

The loft went quiet for a minute, and then Patti

came around the corner into the bedroom area. When she saw Deena, she screamed. Toby rushed to her side, just as Deena left the nest of blankets to find her clothes.

"Oh, Deena. Didn't know you were still here."

"Hungry?" Toby asked. They all ignored the fact that Deena didn't have any pants on.

"I could eat." Deena grabbed her jeans as Toby turned around and wheeled out of the room. She and Patti both dressed. Deena combed her hair and borrowed Patti's make up. They'd done this routine a million times, getting ready to go out or just down to The Pub. With one difference—then, they'd both been single and lonely.

"Ian's threatening me, Patti." She blended dots of concealer under her eyes. It was no fun at all to have a hangover in the middle of the day. She would never do that again.

Patti, trying on another shirt, didn't answer. Deena brushed loose powder over her face.

"He called me a fat chick."

"Bastard."

"Bacon's getting cold, ladies," Toby called from the kitchen.

"Mascara, and I'll be out." Deena tried to ignore the pounding in her head and the queasy feeling in her stomach.

"I need bigger clothes again." Patti's voice close to breaking.

Deena put the wand of mascara down. "Honey, what's up?"

"I *am* a fat chick." Patti cried really low so Toby couldn't hear.

Deena sat next to Patti on the bed. As per usual, she didn't know what to say. "Are you happy?" Lame, but the least she could do.

"Not right now, I'm not."

"But that's just because asshole Ian made you

feel bad. Most of the time, you're happy, right?"

Patti blew her nose. "I guess it's maybe 50/50."

"I bet is would be more like 90/10 if you found a band. What are you waiting for?"

Toby walked in. "What's wrong?"

"Ian," Deena answered for Patti.

"He's such an asshole. He stole your lyrics, Deena, and he's not getting away with it, no matter what. I'm sick of him putting Patti down." Toby hugged Patti.

Even hungry, third wheel Deena figured Patti and Toby would probably soothe each other better alone. Right after her sandwich, she'd leave to give them some alone time. "Let's eat. I'm starving."

"Easy for you to say." Patti's voice got loud. It had a mean edge Deena had never heard before. "You can eat bacon, potato chips, pasta, drink wine by the gallon, and you never gain a pound."

Deena stopped on her way to the kitchen and turned around. Patti's voice came over the bookshelves, but Deena couldn't see her face. She walked back to stand and face her friend.

"I hate that about you." Patti stared Deena down.

Deena, hardly believing her ears, turned away first. "Fine. Well, I'm going to go now."

"See what I mean? She just walks out on bacon like it's nothing." Patti directed her words at Toby, ignoring Deena completely.

Deena didn't say anything else. She opened the door and walked out, wondering what had just happened.

Chapter Twenty-Six

Ian woke to birds chirping outside his window. He listened, he always listened to sounds, finding melody in everyday things. Then he remembered that today his throat got slit. There was nowhere to put the fear that filled him. Nothing to do with the rage.

His phone rang.

He didn't bother with clothes. If Fat Patti spent the night, too fucking bad, she'd sucked it all before when she'd been thin. When she'd been his. He took his phone into the bathroom and listened to Cal's voice droning on about lawyers and the record company. He couldn't really hear him over the gush of piss hitting the water in the toilet bowl.

"Are you listening to me?"

"Not really."

"Well you better start…"

Ian stared at his neck in the bathroom mirror. What the hell was Cal bitching about now? "Dude I just woke up. It's not even six yet. What is up your ass?"

"I told you, Ian. Deena has a case. You lied. To me, to everyone. Those are her lyrics, and she's got the proof."

"Not for long. Oh and by the way, you're fired."

Ian packed a bag for the hospital. No sign of Toby or Pudge. Must have spent the night at her place. Driving down Main, he called Deena. No answer. Where would she be?

Minutes later, he pulled into Deena's driveway. No Miata. The house, the street, was still asleep.

The vacant house next door had a for sale sign on the lawn. He peeked in the garage. Deena's car wasn't there, either. He tugged on a pair of gloves and tried the back door. Locked. He pulled out a credit card, popped the lock without a problem. As two cats ran out, he let himself in.

He moved from the kitchen into the dining room and then the front room, the room with all the candles. The room he'd entered thinking he would ask Deena to marry him. The room he'd left in humiliated defeat. He went quickly into the hall, checked all the bedrooms. No one. Next he moved upstairs.

No one lurked up there either and no sign of the notebook. He came back down and made his selection from Deena's vast array of candles. Inside the kitchen, he set the silver candleholder on the sill. Cans of used paint were conveniently located in a kitchen corner, so he pried open a few with a butter knife, pulled a packet of matches from a drawer by the stove and lit the candle and watched as it caught on the linen curtain. Then, he pulled off the gloves and threw them into the fire. He didn't bother shutting the door on his way out. Just drove to the hospital and checked himself into pre-op.

****

"Dee Dee?" She could hardly hear her father over the sirens.

"Dad, are you at work?"

He didn't answer her question, instead asked where she was.

"Grocery store. Why? How did you know I wasn't home?" Her skin pricked with chills. Her body understood something her mind couldn't yet accept.

"When can you get home?"

"Is my house on fire?" She gave a little laugh.

"Not anymore."

Anxiety gripped her and she forced herself to

breathe. "I'll be right there." Deena left her grocery cart in the supermarket aisle.

She got into her car and spun out of the parking lot, pulling her phone from her purse. She clicked on to the last call. Her dad answered on the first ring. "How bad is it?" Deena choked back tears. She would not cry. She would not break down.

"Please stay calm, Dee Dee. Concentrate on driving. I'll stay on the line with you until you get here."

Deena flew past everyone on the road.

"Don't speed, honey. If you get pulled over, it will only delay you more."

She slowed to within five miles of the local limit. "Okay, I slowed down. And I'm calm. Now tell me my house hasn't burned to the ground."

"It's still standing."

"What happened?"

"The arson investigator is working on figuring that out right now."

"Arson?" *This is a joke. This is unreal.*

"Where are you?" he asked.

"Warren and South."

"Six streets to go."

"Dad, where are the cats?"

"They're fine. I found them out back and put them in their travel cages."

"So the garage is fine?" Relief welled inside her. At least the cats were safe. Her phone started beeping like it did when her battery was about to die, but that didn't matter, because she was home. "My God, what happened?"

"Candle in the kitchen started it."

"All the paint—"

"—Explains the accelerant." Her dad finished the sentence.

The fire truck was still in front of the house, but she stared at the charred, black ruin. Several neighbors gawked from their front porches, but she ignored everyone, and started back to the garage where the cats must be going crazy. They didn't like being crated.

Her dad hugged her, holding her back. "Thank God you weren't inside."

"Yeah, I didn't sleep much last night, so I decided to grocery shop. The cats needed litter."

She tried to pull away again, but her father wouldn't let her go. "The arson investigator needs to speak with you."

"I need to check on the cats." She pulled away and walked toward the back yard. She passed the gaping hole that had been the front picture window. Shards of glass covered the lawn. From the corner of her eye she saw black lumps. Jack's leather sofa. Her grandmother's hope chest. Myra's china cabinet. Everything in it. The stuff that made up their lives.

Her father followed her out to the garage.

"Granny's hope chest is gone." Deena stopped as the fire truck pulled away, resting her head on his shoulder for a minute. She wanted to cry, but she wasn't going to give in. "That was the only thing I had left of her."

"You'll always have her in your heart," her father said.

Deena walked into the back of the yard, stood staring at the patio door blown off the second floor. Twisted, blackened wrought iron clumped in a heap on the patch of scorched lawn.

"Nothing left inside to save."

At least her cats were okay. And Jack had his laptop with him and some clothes.

Derrida meowed as Deena let herself into the garage. Shadow just stared. She crouched and let them out of their cages. She pulled Shadow into her arms, petting Derrida. The cats stuck to her, meowing. "What are we gonna do?"

"After you talk to the arson investigator, you're going to pack them up and come to my house."

A guy in dress pants and a button-down shirt came into the garage. He wore thin gloves and carried an evidence bag in his hand. "May I speak to you now, Ms. Smith?"

"Yes, of course."

"We think the fire started with a burning candle left on the kitchen window sill. It blew a window and fell outside, which is why it's somewhat recognizable as the item used to start the fire." He held up the slightly melted, totally blackened object, stored in a plastic evidence bag.

"That's the silver candlestick holder Patti bought me for my birthday last year."

"It caught the curtains, caught a paint accelerant on the floor of the kitchen, and moved through the rooms. The initial blast of flame threw it into the yard."

"I've been painting."

"That would explain why the walls went up so quickly."

"But I didn't keep that candle holder in the kitchen."

"The fire started this morning at approximately six a.m. Where were you?"

"At the grocery store. I know it's absurdly early to shop, but I couldn't sleep so I took care of an errand. You can check the Hall Road Meijer. I left a cart with melting ice cream and forty pounds of cat litter not more than ten minutes ago."

He nodded. "Does anyone else have a key to your back door?"

"My boyfriend, but he's in New York on business." She needed Jack here now.

"Who would set fire to your house, Ms. Smith?"

Ian. Part of her couldn't believe he would do it. The other half knew without a doubt that he had.

Hadn't he threatened her yesterday?

"There is someone you can check out." She told the investigator the story of the notebook and how Ian had been acting lately. "I'm in the process of suing him, maybe he figured he could burn the evidence, but it's already with my lawyer." Deena gave the guy names, but since her cell phone was dead, she didn't have any phone numbers. Damn. Her charger had burned along with everything else.

"The police will check this out. Will we be able to reach you at your father's?"

"Yes, she'll be there," her father answered on her behalf.

****

"Maybe you should make a list."

Deena had come home to the house she'd grown up in. The house that never failed to give her the creeps. Today she sat on the same faded blue sofa her mom had chosen a lifetime ago. The only comfort she derived from being here was the fact that her cats were curled around her.

Her father continued, "For the insurance. You'll need things."

"My phone book's in here." She held up her dead phone. "My insurance policy burned with everything else."

Her father didn't answer. He found a pad of paper and a pen and brought it over to her. She took the paper and pen, but didn't write anything.

Her dad paced for a few minutes and then picked up the phone and dialed. He spoke into the receiver for a while, but she didn't know what he said. He was right there, in the same room with her, but he seemed to be underwater or something. When he hung up, he came and sat in his old recliner, facing her. "I just spoke to Neil Lumback."

Neil. Her insurance agent.

An old family friend.

Good.

She should try to resurrect her life from the ashes, but she didn't feel like it.

All she felt was numb.

Chapter Twenty-Seven

While Jack waited for Elliot to return with his paperwork, he checked his voice mail again. Three messages from Deena last night, when he'd been out celebrating his new job with the rest of the staff, but this morning, nothing.

He tried her cell. It went straight to voice mail. He hadn't even had the chance to tell her anything about the job before she'd hung up to take a call from Hensley.

Elliot returned with his contract. Jack read it over and signed.

"You should seriously think about moving to New York, man." Elliot shook his hand.

"I will," Jack said. *Not in a million years.*

"Beta post the first column tomorrow. We need everything ready to roll Monday morning at six sharp."

"Sure." Jack had already seen the website. It looked great. And writing his first "Letter From the Editor" wouldn't be a problem. Writing had never been the problem. Teaching writing to kids who could care less—that had been the problem.

In the cab on the way back to the hotel, he tried Deena again. Again, it went straight to voice mail. New York traffic snarled around him, citizens in tight packs moved to cross the street when the cab crawled to a stop. Opening the door, Jack handed the cab driver money. "I'll walk from here." He got out of the cab and walked, losing himself in the fast pace of the city. He spotted his hotel ahead.

He should get back there and start drafting that

column. But he hadn't eaten all day, so he turned on impulse into a diner that featured Greek food. Better than room service and a girlfriend who didn't answer her phone.

While waiting for his food, he called his parents to tell them he'd signed the contract. After congratulating him and asking when he'd be back in Michigan, his mom gave the phone to his father.

"Deena dropped off her notebook yesterday."

"Wow. I wonder how she got it."

"She didn't say, but Hensley's guilty as sin."

"Well. Good then."

"Son…" his dad sounded too serious for someone who'd just delivered good news. "There's something else."

"I'm listening."

"Her house burned down. Deena and the cats are fine, it's just the house. It's gone. I'm sorry."

Jack said something, he must have, because he wasn't talking to his dad anymore. The waiter brought his meal, but Jack couldn't eat. He paid the bill and walked back to the hotel. There, he sat at the desk in his room, trying to decide if he could work or not.

He couldn't. And yet he had a tight deadline. It was Friday afternoon, and he was the brand new editor of a website going live on Monday morning. He had to write something brilliant in two days or "Radical Tattler" lovers everywhere would click once and never come back.

He couldn't blow the job of his dreams. But for once, he didn't have words to spare. Instead, he checked flights home. Nothing was available until morning, which upset him, until he realized Deena would be staying with her dad, who probably had a listed landline. At least he could phone her.

He called and called, and Deena's father's phone rang and rang. The man didn't have voice mail,

Cynthia Harrison

apparently. Jack texted Deena about his flight times, hoping her phone hadn't burned in the fire.

To make the time pass until morning, he wrote. Or tried to—it all sounded like shit. He didn't care, he just spilled the contents of his head onto the page, telling himself these words wouldn't be the ones he posted on the site Monday morning, but at least he was no longer staring at a blank page.

His phone chirped. Not Deena's ring tone. He looked at the screen. Don.

"Just wanted you to know. Tell Deena her book made it through. We're offering her a contract. Well done, dude."

They chatted a bit about Jack's new job. Jack thanked Don again for the introduction and for having faith in him. He thought about it, but then didn't say anything about the fire at Deena's.

****

"Listen, kiddo. How's that list coming? I called Neil Lumback again. He'll be back in touch later today."

Deena handed the really short list she'd written to her dad.

- Jeans (6 pair)
- Boots (Doc Martens)
- Laptop (Dell)
- Pablo Neruda (*Twenty Love Poems and a Song of Despair*)

"It's a start." He handed the wholly inadequate list back to her.

"Sure, Dad."

"I've got to go to work. I've got a plumbing job in Bloomfield Hills that can't wait any longer."

"No problem. I'll wait for Neil's call back."

Deena tried to sound less depressed than she felt. It would be a relief when her dad left her alone. Then she could feel as bad as she wanted without making an effort to mask it. She sat curled up on the sofa until she heard his car back down the driveway and out into the street. The phone rang, but she didn't answer it. Instead, she walked to the window and pulled aside the sheers her mother had deemed elegant, but were now just dusty and sad. She watched her dad's truck taillights until he turned off their street and disappeared.

She didn't like coming home in the best of times, but under these circumstances it was almost unbearable. Her mother's invisible imprint mocked wherever she looked. How shabby her mother's things had become. Yet her father couldn't bear to part with any of it.

She let the curtain fall and Deena wandered into her childhood bedroom, into the walls full of posters: Leo and Kate in the Titanic pose, Oasis, John Rzeznik from Goo Goo Dolls. She picked up a snow globe she'd gotten for Christmas one year. She'd loved it at the time. Probably because she hadn't been allowed to love the collector dolls her mother bought her twice each year, one for her birthday and one for Christmas. She'd been allowed to open the dolls carefully, and to hold them once, before her mother put them away in the closet, still in their boxes. After her mother died, there were no more dolls. Her father gave her money for Christmas and told her to buy what she wanted. She shopped for herself online, and he never asked what she bought—books, makeup and clothes that were all far too adult for her. He didn't put up a tree, and they went to her grandparents' house for dinner. Grandma had a small tabletop tree, under which was a card with money inside for Deena.

Deena had gone away to college at eighteen, leaving everything behind but her make up.

She set the snow globe down, walked over to the closet. Her old clothes were still inside. Her father hadn't moved a thing. All her Madonna wannabe outfits, a couple pair of flared jeans, and several tight baby tees, even though her dad refused to let her get her navel pierced, which was the whole point of showing your belly button. Everything hung there like embarrassing reminders of who she'd once been. She hadn't taken these clothes to college, where she'd completely reinvented herself.

She looked up to the top of the closet. The dolls, all the Wendies and Cissies and Elises in their pink and white striped boxes, still sat on a high shelf.

When her mom died, her dad had mourned for years. Deena's feelings, then and now, were more complicated. She pulled one of the boxes down from the shelf, opened it, and took the doll out of it's pink tissue casket. The box fell to the floor as Deena smoothed the softly curled hair, rubbed the cheek of the painted face, straightened the black dress with it's white polka dots. She set the doll carefully on her bed and reached for another box, and then another.

The ringing phone wouldn't stop, so she left the dolls, a dozen of them, all over her bed.

Deena picked up the kitchen phone, cradling it to her ear with a raised shoulder.

"Deena, it's Neil Lumback. I went over to your house. Nothing official yet, but between you and me, it's going to be a complete rebuild. From the bottom up. The structure's too damaged to be repaired."

"Oh." She hugged Shadow tightly to her. The cat meowed and escaped. Deena sat down on the kitchen floor, still holding the phone.

"I'm sorry, hon. And don't worry, everything is covered. I'll need an itemized list of the contents as soon as you can work one up. You wouldn't happen to have a video in a safe deposit box, would you?"

"No." Then Deena remembered that the day Patti had helped her find the wrought iron, she'd first zoomed through the empty lower floor and the too-cluttered upstairs with her phone's video camera. "I think my best friend might have one." She hadn't seen Patti since the incident in the loft. She really should call her and tell her about the fire.

"Excellent. That will help jog your memory. In the meantime, your dad asked me to arrange for a condominium for you over in Cherry Hills."

He gave her the address of her temporary home, and told her to pick up the key any time at the clubhouse office. "It's furnished, complete with everything except your personal items."

Deena disconnected after he explained a few more things she didn't actually hear. Her dad was a sweetheart. He probably realized how urgently she wanted out of this house. She headed back into the bedroom to see what clothes she could salvage. On the bed, the cats played gleefully amid a mess of snarled dolls' hair. Derrida clawed a dress with his back legs while biting a head. Deena laughed and lcft them to it.

She went out to the living room and sat on the sofa. Why would Ian commit arson? Was he a complete psychopath? How could she have been fooled about him for so long? He'd loved her once. Or had he only said the words? And she, used to facsimiles of love, had believed him. She looked through her dad's thick public phone directory for Bill Karris's phone number.

She listened to the phone ring and ring. Strange for no one to be in the office on a Friday. No answering machine, either.

"Hello?" The voice sounded out of breath.

"Bill Karris, please. This is Deena Smith calling."

"Oh, Deena, hello. It's Melinda. Bill's at the office, dear."

It took Deena a minute to make sense of the words.

"Melinda! Sorry to bother you! I thought I *was*

calling the office."

"I just this minute got in from work. Bill won't be home for hours yet, but I'll give you the number." Melinda reeled off a phone number. Deena didn't write it down. The normal details of life slipped away. Nothing mattered anymore.

"Deena?"

"Still here. Thanks for the number." Why had she wanted to call Bill? She couldn't remember.

"We heard about the fire. Can I do anything to help?"

Deena pulled the kitchen phone cord tight, reaching for a chair. She snagged the back of a chair with her fingertips, pulled it over, and sat down.

"Deena, what is it, dear? Something I can help you with?"

"I think Ian, the guy who stole my lyrics, is the same person who burned my house down today."

Melinda's gasp strangely comforted Deena.

"The police say he didn't, because he was in surgery at the time, but they also say the fire was deliberately set. And he's the only one who would do that."

"Are you okay? Are you sure you don't need anything?"

Tears built up behind her throat. She hadn't cried yet. She had to get off the phone first. "I have to go, Melinda. Would you just tell Bill that Ian set the fire? I thought he should know. I'm pretty sure Ian thinks he burned the notebook, but I brought it to Bill's office yesterday."

"I'll tell him, dear. Where are you?"

"At my dad's." Deena gave her the phone number.

"Is your father with you?"

"No. He's on a job."

"I'd like to come over, if I may."

"That's really not necessary." Deena had to talk

around the growing thickness in her throat.

"It's almost dinner time. Let me take you out. I need to know you're okay."

Deena's eyes filled with tears. They started spilling down her cheeks. She brushed them aside, determined not to let any sobs escape until she'd hung up the phone.

"I'll be fine." But her voice shook. She hoped Melinda didn't notice.

She hung up the phone and let the sobs loose.

Chapter Twenty-Eight

When the doorbell rang, Deena looked up. It rang again, and then a third time. Finally, she got up to answer it. Melinda Karris stood on the stoop, a large shopping bag in each hand. She was dressed casually, in a matching yellow top and slacks. The toe nails peeking from her sandals were pearly pink, and her handbag matched the strappy little shoes. Deena's hand went to her hair, which she'd combed, maybe, at four or five this morning.

"Hello, sweetie." Melinda came inside, dropped the bags, and hugged Deena.

Deena worried about how she might smell. Paint fumes. Fire soot. Sweat. Tears. She needed a shower. Melinda must be disgusted. Deena tried to work up some sort of remorse about this, but she couldn't. She just didn't care that much.

The cats milled around, inspecting Melinda. "Hi, Derrida. Is this your new kitty friend?" Melinda bent at her knees to pet Shadow. Derrida butted Shadow away from Melinda's hand with his head.

"I brought you some clothes. They're not quite your style. And they'll be a little big. But maybe we can go shopping after dinner."

Deena, her eyes swollen and sore, looked at the bags sitting on the living room floor. She must have cried before. She couldn't remember. "I'll just be a minute." She took the clothes into her bedroom and upended the bags. Soft pastel colored shorts and tops spilled onto her bed, covering the dolls.

"This was your bedroom growing up?" Melinda stood in the doorway.

"Yes."

"Those dolls are worth a fortune."

"Are they?" Deena couldn't work any enthusiasm into her voice, but she was happy that Melinda didn't try to fix them up from the mess the cats had left them in.

Deena's stomach growled. "I'm really hungry." She realized that she hadn't eaten since yesterday. "I'll just pop in the shower."

The warm water felt good. At least her outside was clean. Her dad had neither blow dryer nor curling iron, so Deena pulled her wet hair into a ponytail. Melinda's clothes fit her a bit too loosely, but the material was soft and comforting against her skin.

Deena came into the living room, noticed both cats purring on either side of Melinda on the sofa. Melinda stood and picked up her purse. A car door slammed and a minute later Deena's dad came into the room.

"Hi, Dad."

"Hi, honey." The relief in his eyes made Deena feel ashamed for worrying him. She had to snap out of it.

"Hello," he said to Melinda.

"Dad this is Jack's mom, Melinda Karris. Melinda, this is my father, Bob Smith."

"Hi, Bob."

"Mrs. Karris."

"Melinda, please. I'm taking Deena to dinner, and then we're going to do some shopping."

"Oh, that's good." Bob Karris took a Lean Cuisine out of the freezer and popped it in the microwave. The house was so small that she could talk without raising her voice from the kitchen to the living room. Heck, the whole place would fit into the Karris's living room. Then she decided not to be ashamed. Melinda didn't seem to mind.

Deena kissed her dad and followed Melinda out the door.

"Your dad's house reminds me of the place where I grew up." Melinda steered the car with enviable calm into Main Street traffic. "Where would you like to eat?"

"I really need a new laptop. I'm job hunting, and its all done over the net these days. And a phone charger. Can we go somewhere close to the Apple store? P.F. Chang's?"

"Of course, dear." Melinda patted her hand. "Poor thing."

Over dinner, Melinda presented Deena with some information. "I called Bill while you were in the shower. He called the hospital and the fire department and got right back to me."

"Why?" Deena held her egg roll to her lips, afraid to take a bite. Hunger won out. She chewed.

"We wanted to get the times straight. I can't get it out of my head that Ian Hensley is the only person with a motive for torching your house. It's so clear to me, and Bill agrees. And we were right. Ian's surgery happened an hour after the fire."

"According to the police, he had pre-op before that."

"Yes, and unlike the police, we checked that, too. Ian was late for pre-op. He got there twenty minutes before his operation. He had time to set that fire."

Deena's stomach cramped. "He could have killed me, he could have killed Jack. The cats."

"He'll be questioned by the police now. Bill's been in contact with them. Ian Hensley won't walk away from this. Any of it." Melinda sipped her iced tea, then took a tiny cell phone from her purse and pushed a number on her speed dial. "Jack's cell."

A moment later, a hesitant smile crossed her face. "Jack, dear, am I catching you at a bad time?"

Deena watched Jack's mom. Someday, she

wanted to be a mother just like Melinda.

"I'm having dinner with Deena." Melinda listened, and Deena strained to hear Jack's voice.

"She's fine; she's right here." Melinda smiled at Deena across the table. "They're fine, too. All staying with her father. But here, let me put her on." She handed the phone to Deena.

"Jack, I'm sorry. All your stuff."

"Honey, I don't care about that! They're just things. Did you get my texts? What happened to your phone? I'm so glad you're okay."

"My phone needs a new charger."

"I'm taking the first flight out in the morning."

"What about your new job?"

"I never got a chance to explain. It's an online editorship. I can work from anywhere. Even Ash Creek."

She hesitated. "I'm moving into a temporary condo tomorrow." She chewed a ragged fingernail, glancing at Melinda, who was busy eating. She lowered her voice. "Are we still living together?"

"Yes. For sure." She heard him exhale.

They said goodbye, and Deena hung up the phone, handing it across the table to Melinda. The restaurant noise hummed around them. To all these people, it was just another day.

"You raised your son right." It's not that her dad had done a horrible job. He did the best he could. Everyone did the best they could. If they knew better, they'd do better.

****

When Deena got back to her dad's place, she realized he didn't have WiFi. He didn't even have cable. She called the condo number Neil had given her, and someone was still there. She said she'd hold the key for Deena if she could be there in an hour. And yes of course they had WiFi.

Hell, she could be there in twenty minutes. She

didn't have a lot to pack.

Her dad helped her crate the cats and brought out an ancient Samsonite suitcase for her meager wardrobe. In less than an hour she was at her new condo, plugging in her phone and booting up her new laptop.

No responses answered her job application blizzard. Several emails from Jack waited. A reminder of the interview time at TCC. She'd almost forgotten. Day after tomorrow. She deleted spam and almost did the same to forwarded email from Jack via a textbook publisher. The subject line "Writing Like a Rock Star Contract" intrigued her, so she clicked it open.

The body of the email was short and to the point. There was no message explaining anything from Jack at the top. *Great job! Everyone here loves your book. Contract attached. Best, Don Hastings.*

So weird. Wasn't Don Hastings the friend who helped Jack find an editorial position? She clicked on the attached contract. Lots of legal jargon jumbled the screen, but she deciphered the proposed, generous advance.

She almost emailed Mr. Hastings that he'd contacted the wrong person. But her name in the contract caught her eye: Deena Smith aka D. Smith. Together with the Rock Star title, she was sure that in some weird way, this contract was for her. For *MindSprings*. And Jack had mentioned wanting to send an edited version of her book out to his friend in New York, but she'd said no. She'd been very clear. Yet he'd apparently gone and done it anyway with a crappy exploitative new title.

Still staring at her screen, she grabbed her phone and dialed Jack. Who didn't deny for a minute what he had done.

"I thought you'd be happy."

"But why didn't you tell me? Why didn't you

listen when I said no? What else did you change besides the title?"

Jack explained that he hadn't wanted her to be disappointed if the book didn't clear the various editors and marketing people. "But, sweetheart, it got me my job! Don saw the original and my revised version and called *Radical Tattler* right after that. I won that job on the strength of edits on your book!"

Jack didn't seem to realize she was upset at all. He blathered on about his new job, but she'd stopped listening.

"What else did you change?" She cut into his tangent about the website start up.

"I'll send it to you."

Almost immediately, an email from Jack popped up in her mailbox. She opened it and scrolled through the document, feeling sick inside, right down to her soul. Jack had done the same thing Ian had. He'd taken her words and changed them into something they weren't meant to be. He used her lyrics and even a version of the Paris story she'd told him, written as an "Introduction." As if she'd written it, not told Jack the story in confidence. Betrayal sucked.

Worse he didn't have a clue that he'd done anything wrong. He had wanted an editing job and used her life to leverage one.

"I can't believe it." She turned away from the computer screen.

"Isn't it great?"

"No, Jack. It's not. You used me. You're more like Ian than I realized."

"What? No! He stole from you. Plagiarized. I gave you complete credit."

"Without my consent, which I would *not* have given." Deena had so wanted to start over as a teacher, to put the past behind her. Jack didn't understand her at all.

"If you come home tomorrow, please don't come here. You can pick up Derrida, but we're not living together any more." She hung up without waiting for a reply or saying goodbye.

It had been exactly this way, once before, in Paris, after Ian left her. Her head ached, and her mind fragmented. Her life, everything she'd slowly built after Paris was gone. Her home. Her best friend. Her job. Her boyfriend. Even her book seemed tainted now.

Shadow meowed, and Deena smiled. She still had him. That much was true. She had her cat and Sarah. But she wouldn't burden Sarah with this. She needed Patti now. Except Patti was pissed because Deena was a size ten. Plus it was two in the morning. Patti was probably asleep.

With her boyfriend.

Chapter Twenty-Nine

The next day Deena ignored Jack's phone calls. She texted him once, about picking up Derrida. He texted back that he was staying with his folks, he had a ton of work to do, and could she please keep Derrida until he went live with the website.

She didn't want to read about his job. She didn't care where he was staying. "Text, when you're ready to pick him up," she tapped into her phone.

Jack was so selfish. His new job came before his traumatized cat. She reflexively looked at Derrida and Shadow lounging together in a patch of sunshine. Okay so maybe the cat wasn't traumatized. Maybe she was projecting. This was exactly why she needed Patti. A voice of reason when she was falling apart.

She'd texted Patti about the fire and the video, but she hadn't heard back. Which made her want to fall apart, but really, she didn't have time. She had an interview tomorrow to prepare for. She needed to buy new interview clothes and get some food into this condo. She needed sleep. Last night she'd gotten little rest. Instead she'd replayed Jack's betrayal over and over.

She hadn't responded to Don Hastings' email yet, either. She'd wanted to tell him she was withdrawing the manuscript, but she was out of work, and the advance he'd offered was nice. She at least needed to consider it. Maybe he'd agree to change the book back to *MindSprings* when she explained that Jack had made the changes without her approval.

On her way to Nordstrom's and the grocery store, Deena stopped at Starbucks to order a double espresso. Straight.

The caffeine coursing through her veins helped Deena power through her day, as she filled in her pitiful wardrobe with beautiful clothes and stocked her kitchen with healthy food. Every time she started to think about everything she'd lost, she did a Patti-type affirmation. *I make my life anew.* She plucked out the negative thought, inserted the positive, and it actually helped, although she still missed Patti.

By the end of the day, Deena was so tired she slept a full nine hours before her alarm went off, signaling that she needed to get up and get going if she wanted to be on time for her interview at TCC.

****

Deena walked from the parking lot to B building at TCC. Everything was smaller than the university and prettier. There were no goose droppings to worry about and flowers bloomed in anchored planters everywhere. At the center of the small quad, a beautiful water fountain spurted up and then fell in sparkling drops into the pool.

Deena's insides erupted just like that spume of water, and she ducked into the first building she saw, searching for a bathroom. She found one and went into a stall, knelt on the cold tiled floor, and gave up the banana she'd had for breakfast.

Dizzy and disoriented, she took out a little disposable toothbrush and cleaned her teeth. Then she folded several paper towels together and ran them under cold water. She pressed the cool wet cloths to the back of her neck. She was starting to feel almost human again, but to get through this interview, she had to be super strong. She couldn't melt into a puddle of tears over Jack's betrayal.

She'd thought about whether she should

mention *MindSprings* or not, and she decided right then in the restroom that she wouldn't. It might throw her off her game. She peered closer in the mirror above the sink and repaired a bit of damage to her mascara.

Was it something she ate or was her body letting her know it was hurting? Her heart specifically hurt. She'd lost her anchor in the world. Everything had been stripped away. But she was still here, and her core was strong. She could do this. She would do this.

She went back outside and looked around for B building. When she found it, she marched with false cheer to the dean's office.

****

After she got home from her interview, someone knocked on the door. It didn't feel, would never feel, like home, but it was her door for now, so she went to answer.

Patti stood there holding a bottle of wine in one hand and a box of salt in the other. A long French baguette wrapped in cellophane stuck out of the purse slung over her shoulder. She thrust the salt and wine at Deena, pulled the bread out, looked around, and sat in on the snack bar that separated the living and kitchen areas. "Happy new house."

Deena was so grateful Patti had tracked her down, she hugged her. And Patti hugged her back. "I got your text. I thought you were kidding, so I drove by Shakespeare Street. You weren't kidding."

"Nope." Deena awkwardly broke the hug. The last time she'd seen Patti, they hadn't parted on good terms. "Thanks for these." She held up the salt and wine before setting them on the tiny dining table in the corner of the living room.

"Nice place." Patti looked around.

"It's small and impersonal, and the cats are disoriented from moving around so much. But

213

thanks."

"I sent the video to your insurance guy," Patti said. "I copied you. Do you have a laptop yet?"

"Yep. I'm pretty much all set for now."

"Where's Jack?"

Deena wanted to confide everything to her best friend, but she wasn't sure if they were still best friends. All her relationships seemed to have sharp edges these days. Ian, Patti, Jack.

"We broke up." Deena left it at that. Plain and simple.

Patti's jaw dropped as her butt hit the sofa.

"I'll open the wine." Deena went to find a corkscrew in her new kitchen.

"What the hell happened?" Patti accepted the glass of wine Deena handed her.

"Ian burned my house down." Deena could say it now without falling into a dark hole of despair.

"You're kidding, right?"

"Nope. He did it right before he went into surgery, to give himself an alibi." Deena gave Patti the condensed version of the last few days' events.

"That bastard. Did you hear that the tumor was benign?"

"No."

"Yeah."

They sat sipping their wine for a few minutes.

"I feel really bad about this, Deena."

"It's okay. I'm over it. At first I thought the world had ended. But it's weird, I really haven't missed much of my stuff. Maybe my copy of *Ariel*."

"Good old Sylvia Plath. Tell me how come you broke up with Jack."

Deena gave Patti the short version of the *MindSprings* fiasco, feeling so much better since being offered the job and having her friend back. All was not black. Just Jack. And her house.

"Crap." Patti seemed like she wanted to say

more about it, but then she changed gears. "Sorry about the other day. What I said."

"You sounded so bitter. What was that about?"

"I don't know where it came from. I just...I don't know." Patti twisted the rings on her fingers. "But I am sorry."

"It's okay. I know you've been going through some stuff with your weight. I don't really get it. I think you look great. But I'm sorry it bothers you. To me, you're the same person you always were. Just crankier."

They laughed and it was like nothing had ever come between them.

"I got a new job teaching creative writing."

"Wow. That's awesome. So will you still be able to use *MindSprings*?"

"No. I need to go to the bookstore and find something."

"Or, write another book."

Deena hadn't thought of that. She only had a vague idea of the curriculum she wanted to use. But if Don Hastings published one of her books, he might be willing to publish two. She really had to call him.

"Oh my God!"

"What?"

"That day at my apartment. When you were sleeping. Ian used my computer. I thought it was weird, when I logged on, that my history said I'd visited Arson.com."

"I heard him on the computer," Deena said. "You were in the shower, and Toby had gone in there to talk to you."

Patti pulled out her phone and called Toby. "Go to my apartment and find out exactly what was printed from Arson.com. Can you do that? Is it possible?"

Patti clicked her phone shut. "Toby's going to bring over a printout."

"Should I call Jack's dad?"

"Maybe, I don't know. Maybe we should wait until Toby gets here. I don't even know what was on that website."

Deena's phone beeped with a text message. Sarah wanted to know if she could stop by for a minute. She had a surprise.

Holding back a laugh, Deena typed in, "Sure, sweetie, come on over." Deena shut her phone. "I'm going to cut that bread. I've got some turkey slices and cheese. Looks like I'm getting more company."

By the time Deena had put a plate of cold cuts together, Toby showed up. Sarah and David arrived right behind him.

After everyone had gathered around the table, Deena broke the news. "Sweetie, I know you love Yellow Star, but Patti's got proof that Ian burned down my house," Deena told Sarah. "Your house," she told David, noticing that David and Sarah were holding hands.

Toby handed Deena several computer printouts about arson, while explaining what they were about to David and Sarah. "He was over at our house the day before the fire. And he used the computer. And this is what he accessed. I found it. This proves it; Ian set that fire."

Deena felt strange about contacting Bill Karris since she and Jack were no longer a couple. But he was still her lawyer, so she called him and after explaining what she'd found out, and asked if she could put him on speaker.

"Sure," Bill said. "Fingerprints could prove he used your computer, but not that he went to this site. Your friends could have gone to this site, Toby could have, even you could have done it." Bill didn't sound like he was accusing her. He sounded sad.

"Yeah, but why would we do that? He's the one with the motive. And now here's the proof."

"Circumstantial evidence. They'd never convict Ian on that."

"He shouldn't be allowed to get away with this," Toby said.

Deena looked at Sarah looking at Toby, starstruck.

"I'll call this in to the PD; they'll send computer techs to the loft."

"Won't that help?" Deena asked. She made herself a sandwich. She motioned for the others to do the same. She got out the milk and a liter of Coke.

"Only two percent of arson arrests lead to conviction." Bill's final piece of data fell into the room like a rock. After the call ended, they sat around the table, not talking, eating their sandwiches in silence.

"If we can't make this stick, we can at least leak it to the press. I know I've got that card Cheri Croft gave me somewhere in here." Deena dug through her purse. It was one of her few personal items not destroyed by the fire, and it gave her comfort to have it. "What was it you wanted to tell me, Sarah?"

"Only that David and I are engaged," Sarah stuck her hand out to show everyone her ring.

"Wow, congratulations, you two!" Deena got up and gave Sarah a hug and a kiss, then she hugged David.

"We thought about doing it right away, because of the baby, but, really, we don't want to rush things."

Deena remembered that a short time ago she and Jack had seemed to be heading in the same direction. She should have known it was too good to be true.

Chapter Thirty

Bill Karris met Deena in the reception room of his office, a busy room, full of secretaries talking on phones, tapping on keyboards, and running back and forth to the printer station. She'd brought Derrida in his carrier, and Bill motioned Deena and the howling-mad cat into his office. He opened the crate after shutting the door.

Deena put fresh litter in a disposable litter pan.

"I'm sorry about you and Jack."

Deena pointed toward Derrida, who was temporarily distracted by his new environment, and then the door. She scooted out and Bill followed.

"Get my son on the phone and tell him to pick up his cat," Bill said to his secretary. "And can you find a bowl of water?"

She just nodded, already picking up the phone as they walked into the conference room.

Ian was already in the conference room with a rep from the record label. Bill introduced Frank Evins, who shook her hand. His navy blue eyes looked right into hers, as if he wanted to see her soul. She shook off the fanciful thought. The color of his eyes made them so penetrating, but he didn't possess some supernatural power to see inside her soul. She stole another look at him after taking the seat Bill pulled out for her. He looked up, catching her gaze, and smiled.

"You completely misunderstood me, Dee." Ian's voice was still rough from surgery. The incision across his neck was purpled under black angry stitches. Everyone ignored the remark.

Bill's assistant knocked and entered, carrying her marble notebook and the Paris notebook. Bill inclined his head toward Evins, who held his hands out for both books.

"I don't know if you're aware that your client has been questioned by the police in an on-going arson investigation at my client's former home..." Bill explained before Ian cut in.

"They didn't charge me with anything, dude."

"It is our belief that your client attempted to burn down Ms. Smith's house in order to destroy the notebooks. They prove without a doubt that Deena Smith wrote most of the lyrics for Yellow Star's second album."

Mr. Evins looked at Ian and then back to Bill. "Any evidence on the fire?"

"Circumstantial."

"May I see it?"

Bill handed Evins copies of the arson documents Patti had retrieved from the computer. "Sworn deposition by Tobias Glent puts Mr. Hensley at the computer that first searched and downloaded these items the day before the fire."

"Hearsay."

"Compelling hearsay, coming from another band member, wouldn't you say?" Bill responded. Then he did a Power Point with a timeline of Ian's whereabouts the morning of the fire. He passed over a copy of the hospital sign-in.

"Nothing in those notebooks proves anything anyway." Ian was clearly unrepentant.

Deena stared at him in disgust. How could she have ever loved him? He was evil.

Ian gestured at the notebook. "She could have gone out and bought two notebooks and crossed stuff out and put my words in."

That did it—Deena's patience snapped. "You never had any words, Ian."

"How can you say that? I wrote *Army Girl* for you. Every word."

Bill Karris held up a hand to silence Ian.

Evins was looking closely at first one notebook and then the other.

Bill tapped the table in front of Evins. "If you'll flip to the back of the Paris notebook, that's the one with the French writing on the cover, you'll note a list of names and European capitals."

Evins did so, while Ian slumped further in his chair, muttering, "Fuck."

"Exactly." Deena smiled. If Ian wasn't going to go to jail for arson, at least everyone here knew exactly what he'd done.

"We have sworn depositions from several of the call girls listed. They were all happy to brag about servicing Ian Hensley during his European tour."

"Jesus, but you're a thorough little bitch." Ian eyed Deena.

"I'm just taking back what you stole from me." Deena stared right back at him.

"You always said the words were nothing, that anyone could do it. How would I know you'd get all crazy about this?"

It was as close to an admission of guilt as they were going to get. Mr. Evins closed the notebooks.

Deena shook her head. "I was wrong when I said that writing lyrics was nothing special."

"Any wanker can write lyrics." Ian words suggested he was still in a fighting mood.

"Except, apparently, you," Bill said.

Deena smiled.

"First of all," Evins said, "Ms. Smith, I want to say that the lyrics here are even better than those on Yellow Star's debut. And they're clearly the work of the same person. You're a very talented young woman."

Deena hadn't been called young in a long time—

one of the hazards of working with teenagers. Evins looked to be maybe five years older than her. She met his look, wondering what he would say next.

He opened his briefcase and retrieved a set of papers. "However, our contract with Yellow Star clearly states that the label has the authority to pull the plug on this project at any stage. And I'm sorry to inform you that Yellow Star's second record has been shelved. Permanently." He passed a copy of the contract with the pertinent small print circled in yellow highlighter to Ian. He gave another copy to Bill Karris, who passed it to Deena, who sat there, stunned.

She had been so sure that she'd be vindicated. Well, she had been. Just not in the way she'd expected. Not at all in the way she'd expected. A bitter pang for the money she wouldn't see passed through her body. A byline that would not be hers. She'd been counting on those external rewards more than she'd realized. But one look at Ian's face told her he suffered ten times more. This probably hurt him as much as jail.

The rest of the meeting wrapped up pretty quickly. Ian stormed out of the office, leaving the door wide open, spewing profanities for the benefit of the secretaries.

"Ian," Deena heard Cheri Croft call out, "how would you like to be on the cover of *Rolling Stone*?"

"Cheri baby! For real?"

Ian actually sounded happy for the attention. What an ego. After thanking Bill and Mr. Evins, Deena left the office while Ian was still occupied with Cheri.

On her way out, she noticed Bill's open office door. No sign of Derrida or his crate remained inside. Jack had picked him up while she was in the meeting.

Chapter Thirty-One

Patti and Deena walked Biff on the sunny sidewalks of downtown Ash Creek.

"What do you think of little Sarah getting engaged before us?" Patti asked. They'd spent an hour on the phone last night discussing what had gone down at the law firm yesterday.

"I'm happy for them." Deena was sweltering in the heat, feeling limp as an August daisy.

They stopped to let Biff pee on a tree. He did this about every ten feet, so the walk wasn't really going at any great clip.

"I brought something for you." Deena pulled a tissue wrapped package out of her purse. They sat down on a bench so Patti could open it. Biff sat beside them, accepting pats on the head from passing pedestrians as his due.

Patti ripped open the tissue paper. *Le Sens Intime* was stamped in gold on the rose-colored book cover. "A journal?" Patti asked, holding the book, looking puzzled. "Thanks, but..."

"It's not a journal. It's my Paris notebook." Deena put her finger on the gold stamped letters. "This translates as, *The Intimate Meaning.*"

Patti opened the book and turned the pages. She stopped to read one or two of the lyrics. "I don't get it. You had to fight so hard to get this back. Why give it to me?"

"Remember what you said—if I gave you some lyrics, you'd play your guitar again. Maybe even find a band. I know a bass player who's just lost his lead singer."

Patti sat there, not saying anything, looking through the lyrics. "These are good."

"Thanks."

"Sorry everything turned out so lousy. The band getting dropped by the label and all."

"It's okay." Deena shrugged. "It wasn't meant to be."

"Maybe there's a silver lining." Patti handed the notebook back to Deena. "I'm playing my guitar again. Toby wouldn't leave me alone for one minute after he found out I played. He bugs me night and day to jam with him. And Frank Evins told Toby he'd like to work with him again. Soon."

"So maybe you and Toby can do something with these?" Deena held the notebook out to her. "Evins liked them."

"We like them too, but we've already got the songs. Toby wrote the music, remember? We've even played a couple of them."

"But you don't have *my* songs. You have Ian's bastardized versions of them."

"That's true." Patti put her hand briefly over Deena's. "I'll take the notebook, but only so we can copy out the real words. Then you get it back."

"Okay. That'll work." Deena didn't think she'd ever write a song again, but at least she finally valued the ones she'd already written.

"I would never have picked up the guitar again, and Toby wouldn't have thought to nag me into actually playing with him and some of the other guys, if you hadn't kept at me about it. Thanks for that."

"You're welcome." Deena felt somehow a little flat. She wasn't connecting the dots somewhere, and she couldn't figure out where to even start.

"Did you talk to that publisher friend of Jack's yet?"

"No."

"Because you should do that. Today."

"I know."

"We do the same kind of thing." Patti got up from the bench and started walking toward The Pub. "That must be why we're friends. We both have talents we're too quick to give up on. We let our insecurities win. We let people like Ian squash our hopes and dreams like bugs."

Deena missed Jack, and she hated herself for it. But she'd been more confident when they were together. He had a way of making her feel better instead of worse about herself.

Patti gave her a sad smile. "For what it's worth, I really do think Jack was trying to do something nice for you. Just like when I wouldn't play my guitar, you pestered me until I did it. That's kind of the same thing he did." She stopped at the back gate of The Pub.

"Maybe you're right." Deena wasn't sure about anything anymore. It might be possible that Jack had been trying to help her...and himself along the way.

On her way home, Deena stopped at the bookstore. She sat for a long time looking at every book on creative writing she could find. Nothing was exactly what she had in mind. She bought a few of them anyway, because she'd need something when classes started again. Then she wandered over to the magazines. Right next to each other she saw copies of the new *Rolling Stone* with Ian's picture on the cover and *Radical Tattler* with Jack's "Letter From the Web Editor" inside. She'd already read it on the website, but she bought the copy anyway. After deliberating for a few minutes, she picked up *Rolling Stone* and added it to her pile of purchases as well.

When she got home, she took in the full effect of the picture of Ian. "The Rise and Fall of Yellow Star" slashed across his throat. His arms were open like

Christ on the cross. Cheri Croft's prominent byline appeared under his bare feet. All he needed were nails in his feet and palms. What an asshole. Deena felt a familiar stab of pain and comforted herself with the knowledge that she'd soon be back in the classroom.

She read the article and then called Don Hastings in New York. "I'm sorry it took me so long to get back to you."

"That's fine. Your agent kept me up to date on all that's happening in your life right now."

"My agent?"

"Jack."

"Well, that's not an official relationship." Deena cleared her throat. "In fact, that's what I wanted to ask you about."

Don Hastings waited silently.

"I um, well, I wonder if the original book, in its original form, with its original title, might be better without all of Jack's edits."

"You're kidding, right?"

Of course, she hadn't been, but she didn't have time to say so before he went on.

"Jack took a weak manuscript and gave it a strong hook. As D. Smith you've got what we call a platform. We would have passed on the manuscript without Jack's edits."

"Oh. I guess I never thought of it that way." Deena swallowed the disappointment, tried to keep it tamped down.

"Believe it. Without Jack there would be no book deal."

Wow. This guy was balls to the wall. Deena had to process what he said more than the way he said it, but right now, she needed to get on board with New York. "Okay, well, let me run this by you. I've got a new book in mind. One that focuses on creative writing. That's what I'm teaching now. And I have another entire notebook of song lyrics."

"I saw the story in *Rolling Stone*." Don said. "Great idea. Shoot me a proposal along with the signed copy of your contract for *Writing Like a Rock Star,* and I'll take a look."

Deena thanked him. She disconnected wondering what he'd meant by proposal, so she Googled it. Okay, ten pages, summarize, outline, chapter headings, sample chapter. Jack must have done all that.

For her.

She couldn't help it. She logged on to his magazine's website. Again.

****

Jack had never been inside a firehouse before. Of course he'd driven by them. But he was frankly amazed that they actually had a pole. Of course, Ash Creek's firehouse was old. And there were stairs as well. Stairs he climbed like he was marching to his doom.

"Hi, Jack." If Bob Smith was surprised to see him, he didn't show it. Jack was a bit surprised to find himself here. He hadn't planned on this visit when he got up this morning. It just sort of happened, the way things had started happening ever since he'd been going out with Deena, with no conscious plan, no checklist, no paper with a line drawn down the middle marking out the pros and cons.

"I wanted to tell you, sir." He was glad that they were alone in the large room that looked like an office, with a couple of computer stations, two phone lines, and a sofa along one wall. "I'm not sure you know. Deena and I broke up."

"Yes. I got the story."

Jack nodded. "I was trying to help her."

"I'm sure you were. I'm not the one you need to convince."

"She won't answer my calls. I was hoping you'd give me her address."

Jack had been in misery this entire week without Deena. Work had absorbed him at first, but always in the background was the sore spot in his chest. Sometimes it threatened to engulf his whole body.

Bob wrote out an address and handed it to Jack.

"Thank you, sir." Jack wasn't sure what he'd say when Deena answered her door, but maybe it would come to him in the moment.

He drove to her house thinking up and discarding opening lines. When she finally answered the door, he wanted to grab her and kiss her and never let her go.

Instead, he said simply, "I've missed you." He looked down at his shoes. "I know you lost your whole life in that fire, and I'm sorry. I'm sorry I didn't tell you about the book—honestly I thought it might not fly, and I didn't want to disappoint you."

He stood on her doorstep, waiting for any sign from her that he would be welcome.

Chapter Thirty-Two

Deena, despite ruling out any further romance with Jack, invited him in. He sat on the uncomfortable sofa that came with the condo, and she took the matching, equally uncomfortable chair across from him. "I want to thank you for all the work you did on my book. And to let you know that I am fine. I didn't lose my whole life in the fire." She wanted to be honest with him in a way that didn't hurt his feelings. "I still have my friends and family."

"You could still have me, if that appeals to you at all."

She shook her head. She forgave Jack. She understood why he'd kept his edits a secret. But there was more to the whole mess of their relationship. She remembered his inability to commit. To a city, to a job, to her. How he talked about wanting kids, but in a vague way, as if it were a million years down the road. He mentioned marriage and immediately took it back. He moved in with her, but said it was just temporary.

She'd been through too much in the last couple of weeks to let him back in to her heart.

"Well? I can see the wheels turning. Are you going to give me another chance?"

"Not as we were. We can be friends." She hated the way that sounded but it was all she had left to give.

"Why can't we just go back to the way things were?" Jack hadn't even looked around. His eyes never left hers. It made what she had to do more difficult.

"There were things about us I was unhappy with, way before I found out about the book."

"Like what?"

If he didn't know, she wasn't going to tell him. She recalled all too painfully the horror on his face in Home Depot when she thought she heard him say something about marriage and asked him if he was thinking of marrying her. His loud *no* had been adamant. Everyone in the paint section of the store probably heard.

"Could we just start slow? Go on a date?"

She did need a date to Sarah and David's wedding. They had decided to marry before the baby's birth after all. Patti would be there with Toby. Since it was a very small ceremony, Deena would be the only single lady. Even Myra had found a gentleman friend in Florida and was flying up with him next week for the ceremony.

Deena wanted to say yes to Jack, but not if it meant being stuck in the same passive-aggressive rut they'd grooved into before.

"Let's at least talk about it."

She looked around at her impersonal condo. Something about its lack of charm had made her stronger. It was like her house had closed itself to Jack, making it easier for her to do the same. "I really don't know what else to say. We tried. We failed. Still friends?"

"Yes, but if you could just give me a reason why we can't get back to being lovers." Jack leaned so hard toward her she thought he might get up from the couch and fall at her knees. That would be the day.

"I just think we're on different pages where relationships are concerned."

"But what does that mean? Specifically? Like, can you give me an example of one way we think differently about our loving each other?"

She thought about how to say what she meant without opening herself up to him again. She wasn't going to remind him of the Home Depot incident or any of the other ways he pulled her close only to push her away. He didn't get it. "I don't think you're ready to settle down."

"What does that even mean? I lived with you. You were the one kissing Ian in the newspaper for everyone to see."

"You promised you'd never bring that up. And he kissed me. I didn't kiss him back." She was getting tired of talking. She just wanted him to go.

He got up then, and she thought she'd get her wish. But instead of leaving, he paced the floor, his stare fastened on his feet, his hand rubbing his neck. "What did I do wrong?"

She got up too. If she opened the door, maybe he'd take a hint. "It's not about right or wrong. It's just a feeling I have from a lot of different things." She edged toward the door, twisted the knob.

He turned in his pacing, came over, and stood so close to her she smelled the scent of his skin. Soap and sweat and a sharp tinge of lime. "So there's nothing I can do or say to change your mind?"

"No." Her chest started to hurt. She didn't want anything not freely given. She felt like she had smoke in her lungs even though she had been nowhere near the fire that had burned down her house.

She opened the door a little wider and stepped back from him. "Good-bye Jack."

He walked out without another word, and she shut the door. She was safe inside the condo, but she still hurt. She probably would for awhile.

She looked around.

Everything was a shade of white. White as a marshmallow.

The walls, the rug on the wood floor, the furniture, the kitchen appliances and cupboards.

White and quiet.

Almost like a hospital.

This was a good place to heal.

Chapter Thirty-Three

Jack drove straight to his sister's house from Deena's. If he could remember exactly what she'd said, maybe Leslie could translate for him.

When he pulled into the driveway, he saw Tyler playing in his sandbox with a little girl who wasn't Jack's niece. Then he noticed his sister on the patio with the baby monitor on the table next to her.

"Hey." Leslie closed the book she'd been reading.

"Hi." He kissed his sister and waved at Tyler.

"We're making castles, Uncle Zak." Ty didn't move from his squatting position in the sand.

"Great."

"Have a seat. Dude, you look depressed. You want a beer?"

"No thanks."

"Okay, now I'm really worried. Spill."

So Jack told his sister as much of the conversation with Deena as he could remember. "What does she mean when she says we want different things?"

Leslie shook her head. "You told her you love her, right?"

He nodded.

"And she feels the same?"

"Correct."

"Good."

"How can that be good? She doesn't want to be with me anymore."

"With enough love, you can solve any problem."

"I don't think so."

Leslie patted his hand like he was a little boy.

Any minute she'd offer him a cookie. Which, come to think of it, wouldn't be an offer he'd refuse.

"Here's the deal, bro. You moved in with her. Who asked who?"

"Nobody asked. I did it while she was at a party. She didn't mind. It was just until I found out about the New York job."

"So you moved in without discussion and planned to maybe move back out if you got a better offer?"

"I told her she could come with me!"

"Okay. How did it go? Living together?"

"Good. Mostly good. Everyone has disagreements, right?" He couldn't get cookies off his mind. Ty liked Lorna Doones, and while Jack preferred to dunk them in melted chocolate, he'd take a few plain right about now.

"Give me one example."

"That's just what I asked Deena to do, but she wouldn't."

Leslie raised an eyebrow and waited for him to answer her question. There was the breakfast thing. That was nothing. Deena wouldn't break up with him because they had different morning personality styles. "There was the time her dad came over." He wasn't sure this qualified either. Deena hadn't seemed mad at him at the time. "He asked me my intentions toward his daughter."

"Yikes. Your response?"

"I didn't know what to say, so I didn't say anything. Deena kind of covered for me, and I went to get us all another beer."

"There's your mistake. Deena was not okay with you blanking her dad. She very likely was just as curious as her father about your intentions."

"Whoa. I had just moved in. I wasn't even sure I was going to stay."

"That's another problem. You probably made her

feel like she was a convenient and free hotel. With benefits."

"I told her I'd help with the house payment. And cleaning."

"You know you're a neat freak, right?"

Jack really wanted some cookies. He'd leave the crumbs all over his sister's patio table and see how she liked it.

"Listen, Jack, I love you, but you two—you have to work out compromises. She probably felt like you were calling her housekeeping skills into question."

"But…"

"No buts. You should have handled this stuff as it came up. Sounds like you let a few things build. What about kids?"

"Mommy, can me and Jenny have some cookies? And juice?" Tyler ran up to Leslie and rested his elbows on her knees. "Please?"

Leslie brought out juice and cookies, and Jack tried his best not to take more than his share. Ty and Jenny went to the glider on his swing set with their snack.

"Well?" his sister prompted when the kids were out of earshot.

Jack sighed. "We talked about kids. In a vague someday way. Not necessarily that we'd be parents together. I mean, we'd only been dating for like six weeks."

"Did you ever discuss your future as a couple? Did you ever window shop at the jewelry store downtown? Did she point out any particular style of ring? Did you ask her what she liked?"

"No. Like I said, we hadn't been dating long when I moved in."

"Here's the thing, Jack. Moving in was a major big deal. If you didn't want to think about the future, you had no business moving in with her."

"But why?"

"Because you aren't kids anymore. Even though you act like it sometimes."

Jack had crammed an entire cookie into his mouth. He stopped chewing for a minute he was so shocked. "But she lived with Ian."

"In her twenties. A woman in her thirties wants to know she is not wasting another decade of her life on a loser who will cheat on her, steal her songs, and so forth. She's got a biological clock, you know. We all do."

Jack took a sip of juice to wash down the dry cookie. "Are you sure?"

"Think about it."

He tried to, but it seemed to him like everything had been mostly fine. Deena was the one who wanted to break up when he moved. Okay, that was because Ian cheated when they were in different cities, but still. Why did women have to be such mysteries?

"So here's the deal. She doesn't feel secure in your relationship, she doesn't want to spend another decade with some guy who may or may not ask her to marry him. She's probably ready to be a mom. And not a single mom. She wants the whole picture."

"How do you know that?"

"Do you even listen to her songs? Has she told you that you have different ideas about relationships?"

He thought about those things. She did have a few songs that talked about wanting more than her man could give. But she'd written those songs about Ian. Jack shook his head. "She's D. Smith. She lived with a rock star. I think you're projecting your own story onto her."

"You asked my opinion, and I gave it. That's all I can do, bro." Leslie shrugged her shoulders just as the baby monitor came alive with a loud bawl from the nursery. Jack tensed, but after one sharp cry,

Ashley started babbling in baby language.

Leslie got up and grabbed the monitor. "I need to change her diaper. Want to stay for dinner?"

Jack ignored the invitation. He only wanted one thing—a way to get Deena back. "Are you sure she wants all of this?" He waved toward the kids on the glider and to the baby monitor.

"Yes."

"How do you know?" He got up to go, frustration filling his gut with bile.

"Hensley wanted her back. She didn't go. She chose you. You blew it. End of story."

"See you, Ty," Jack called. "'Bye, Jenny." He walked with Leslie to the side door.

"Not staying?"

"No. Just tell me how to fix it."

Leslie blew out a puff of air. Then she told him what to do.

Chapter Thirty-Four

Deena arranged the crown of flowers in Sarah's hair. "You look beautiful."

"Do you think David will like it?" Her long white dress fell in silky folds around her growing tummy.

"He will love it." It was true.

Someone knocked on the door. "Ready?" Myra asked, peeking inside.

Deena felt awful about Myra's house. Well, her house, but it was still the home Myra had raised her son in. And she'd entrusted her china and dining room table to Deena. Who then allowed a madman to burn it all up.

Deena had apologized to Myra the night before, but Myra made light of the fire. "I'm just glad you're safe, dear," was all she'd said. And Deena didn't want to put a damper on Sarah's big day by moping about her burned down house and broken heart.

She left Sarah and Myra and went to see if David was ready. The ceremony would take place outside in the garden of David's restaurant. Yes, there he was, and the minister too. David saw Deena and gave her the high-five sign. Showtime.

She told Myra they were ready, and the mother of the groom took her seat as Deena walked down the aisle, proceeded by David's three children, who were having fun pulling petals off their de-thorned roses and scattering them down the path to the arbor, where David waited for his radiant bride. Deena listened to every word of the ceremony. She'd heard those words so many times. To love. To honor. To cherish. They exchanged rings and kissed. Deena had been to dozens of weddings and the part where Sarah and David were pronounced husband and wife caused a little stab of complete happiness and envy, same as it always did, in her heart. After the ceremony, Deena went inside to check their table. Everything was ready.

"Am I too late?"

Deena looked up to see Jack standing there in a suit.

Just then, the rest of the party trooped inside.

"Oh, Jack, I'm so glad you could make it." Sarah lifted her arms high for a hug.

No. This could not be happening. But it was. Every time Deena thought she was doing better, getting over him, Jack showed up and threw her into a state of nervous sadness.

Jack shook David's hand, smiling so wide his face looked like it might break. Of course—he was skittish about marriage, even if it wasn't his own.

Deena sat down, and Jack pulled out the chair next to her. She scanned the table. Yes, an extra place had been set for Jack. She looked at Sarah, who only had eyes for David. Her gaze went to Patti, who rolled her eyes and shrugged.

Deena wouldn't say anything to spoil the celebration. She turned to Jack and smiled. "How are things going at the new job? The website looks good."

"You saw the website?"

"Of course I saw your website." She'd spent hours last night reading through the web content...again. Jack had done an awesome job. "Also, I signed the book contract. Now I have to write a proposal for a new one."

"Really? They want another book?"

"Yep. And I want to write one."

"Maybe I can help with the proposal."

"Yeah, I hear you're my agent."

Jack blushed.

The servers were bringing out baskets of fresh rolls and the first course. In between sips of carrot ginger soup, Jack said, "I wasn't...I ah...it's not like I'll take ten percent."

"No. You should. Is that what agents get?" Deena buttered a roll and tried to maintain her composure.

"It's mostly fifteen these days. But we could work out some type of trade that benefits both of us." He leaned in closer to her before a server set down plates of salad, causing him to back off. Thank the stars. She didn't like the way Jack was staring at her neck. She felt naked in her updo and strapless dress.

The meal was several courses long, and when it was over, Deena realized she hadn't tasted a bit of her food. Her champagne glass was empty, even though the only sip she recalled taking was during Myra's toast.

Sarah and David got up to cut a pretty cake, and as Deena turned in her chair to watch, Sarah threw her bouquet of roses right into Deena's lap. Then she winked at Jack.

The burn of a blush crept up from Deena's chest to her face. She wasn't the blushing type, but this was a bit much. She looked at Patti, hoping to convey by ESP how uncomfortable she was with Sarah's spontaneous gesture. Or was it? Sarah had invited Jack to a very small and private ceremony. She had planned this.

After cake, Sarah, David and the kids went off for a honeyandkidsmoon in Florida. Myra and her friend were on the same flight. Before she left, Myra had confided that she would be keeping an eye on the children, at least for a few nights, so Sarah and David could have their privacy.

Before Deena could say a word, Patti and Toby

were also in their car, also pulling out of the parking lot. Which left her alone. With Jack.

"I went by the house," he said quietly.

That surprised her. Why would he care about her half-built new house? She opened her car door and tossed the roses into the back seat. "Why?" She couldn't think of a neutral response, and it just popped out.

"I still care about you, even though you're over me."

She couldn't cope with this right now. She lowered herself down into her seat and put the key in the ignition. "I care about you, Jack. That's not it. We just want different things." She pulled her door shut and started her engine.

Jack whipped around to the passenger side, opened the door, and got in the car. "We need to talk."

Chapter Thirty-Five

Deena didn't seem like herself anymore, and it worried Jack. She'd become quiet, calm, and closed off. *What had happened to the firecracker in a red bra and thong?*

Deena lowered the windows and turned off her car. "I don't know what to say, Jack."

"Can we go somewhere? To the park?"

She looked down at her dress and then up at him. "No. I don't think so."

"Fine."

Deena didn't say anything. She used to talk *a lot,* but now she just looked straight ahead over her steering wheel, waiting for him to say something else.

"Are there things you want that I can't give you?" This had to be the most uncomfortable conversation he had ever endured. The only thing that made it bearable was that everyone, his sister, Sarah, even Patti when she heard about it, had been in favor of his plan. Well, Leslie's plan. He'd find out now if his sister had been right.

Deena wasn't answering him. But he had looked at the facts. David was out of the running for future partner of Deena, so was Ian. He was alone on the field. He had to make that advantage count before she found someone new. Or, was there someone else? Someone Sarah and Patti didn't know about? It seemed far-fetched but nothing surprised him anymore.

"Did you meet someone else?"

"No, it's not that."

Whew. Okay. Good. "Then what?" He was pushing her, but they had to talk this through. He missed her every morning, every afternoon, and every night. It drove him crazy because it kept getting worse instead of better. "You don't love me anymore?"

"I'll always love you."

The first positive thing she'd said to him in ages—his hopes rose.

"So then what's the problem?"

Instead of answering, she looked around the parking lot. "Where's your car?"

"I took a cab. You'll have to drive me home." Well, she didn't have to, but for his plan to succeed, she needed to want to. "Can we go downtown first?"

"What for?"

"I need to get some of Derrida's special food at the pet store."

She looked down at her stilettos. He looked too. Her legs were so smooth and tanned, and her silk dress had hiked way up her thighs. He had to get her back.

To his relief, she turned the car back on and started driving in the direction of downtown. "You know I spent my twenties with Ian. I wasted so much energy on that relationship. And I can't ever get those years back."

"My twenties weren't that great. I like the thirties better." After years of feeling confused and depressed about teaching, he'd finally found a career that suited him. And after years of cutting a wide swath through whatever female population in whichever town he happened to land in at any given time, he had found the right woman, too. He probably should have said that, but then he wouldn't be able to properly execute the plan.

She parked in front of the pet store. "I just think..." She hesitated but then eventually continued, "I can see myself going through my thirties and realizing I did the same thing with you."

Jack was speechless. Didn't she know he was nothing like Ian?

"I would never cheat on you," he finally sputtered. This wasn't going exactly the way he'd envisioned it when he put the plan together. He looked at her.

Her head was bent as if she were studying her dress.

He hoped she wasn't going to cry.

"I know." Her voice sounded sad.

Jack noticed a car waiting to pull into their spot. He waved them off. "Come with me into the store?" he asked.

"Why?"

"Don't you need anything for Shadow?"

"No."

"Well, just keep me company."

"I could use a coffee," she admitted.

The smell of the roses in the back seat was making Jack a little queasy. "Coffee shop's right across the street."

They got out of the car, and Jack drew a big gulp of sunshine and sweet air.

"I feel stupid, like I'm too dressed up."

"It's Sunday. People will think you were at church."

"I doubt it. More like an old maid at the junior prom."

Old maid! Leslie had been right. Deena's biological timer was ticking.

The walk sign flashed and they crossed to the coffee shop. "Isn't this nice?"

"I don't know," Deena replied. But he could feel her softening.

They ordered their coffees and snagged two velvet chairs by the window.

Jack was anxious to get back across the street and continue with his plan, but Deena had picked up an abandoned newspaper and was looking over the front page.

Chapter Thirty-Six

How Deena had let herself be talked into chauffeuring Jack on his errands, she had no idea. But now that she'd revived with a cup of coffee, maybe they could get this show on the road, and she could go home and change into a pair of shorts and a t-shirt.

Jack had bought a chocolate bar at the coffee shop and was tearing into it. She smiled despite herself. He'd had two slices of cake an hour ago, but whatever.

She marched up to the pet shop and opened the door. Jack came in behind her, crumpling the candy wrapper and shoving it into his suit pocket. Then he took a long time picking out the exact Fancy Feast meals Derrida preferred.

Deena stood at the door trying not to tap her foot. Finally Jack finished with his purchase and they went outside. Before she could move to her car, he pulled her next door. "Oh, look." He held onto her hand with the one that wasn't clutching a bag of cat food.

She peered in the window of the jewelry store. A blue sapphire necklace sparkled in the center of the display, surrounded by a scattering of diamond earrings and platinum sets of wedding and engagement rings.

"Which one do you like?"

Her eyes opened wider. What was this about? Anything? Or just Jack being Jack again? She took of her sunglasses and squinted into the dazzling display. "None of them, really."

Jack stiffened next to her. She realized they were still holding hands.

"Let's go inside."

"Why?" She'd been saying that a lot today, but this was weird.

"Just come in." He was already holding the door open, his bag of cat food cans clanging against the plate glass door.

It was a typical jewelry store. Two long rows of glassed cabinets with another shorter one at the far end of the store. A woman with a red dot in the middle of her forehead smiled at them. "Let me know if I can show you something in particular."

"She caught the bouquet," Jack said.

"What are we doing in here?" Deena whispered.

"I want to know what kind of ring you like."

"Why?"

"In case anyone ever wants to buy you a ring, then they would know what to get for you."

Deena felt light-headed. What was he doing? She checked his face. He was smiling but seemed dazed. She didn't want a repeat of the Home Depot denial, so she didn't ask if he was the *someone*. But really, what else could it be?

She looked at the rings in the display case to her right. She worked her way down the row of jewels, most of them sets of necklaces with matching earrings and sometimes, rings. Everything was silver or platinum. The gold must be on the other side. She glanced across the aisle.

"Anything in particular you're looking for?" The woman had come over to where Deena stood.

"Do you have rubies?"

The woman looked startled by the request. "A few. Are you looking for a ring? Earrings? A set?"

She came out from behind the glass cases and moved to the other side of the room and up a few cases. Deena went over to see the rubies. She had never owned a ring. Ever. Not even when all the girls in school started wearing them on every finger. She stuck to her bunches of rubber bracelets. She didn't think she'd ever been in a jewelry store before.

"You like rubies?" Jack asked.

"I don't know. I think so."

"Let us see the rings." He turned to Deena. "Do you like gold or silver?"

"Gold."

"We have this." The saleswoman showed an opal ring surrounded by tiny rubies. The rubies were almost pink in the sunlight. And the gold prongs that held the opal and rubies in place gleamed. The band was simple and beautiful. But wasn't there a thing about opals being unlucky? She'd heard that somewhere once.

Deena shook her head and peered into the case. "That one's nice." She pointed out a square cut ruby with a diamond on either side. The stone was a little large for her taste, but it was so pretty. Elegant and simple. The woman removed it from the case and took Deena's hand. Her left hand. Deena tried to pull her hand out of the woman's grip, but before she did, the ring slid on. It fit perfectly.

"You said she caught the bouquet," the saleswoman reminded Jack.

So that explained the left hand thing. Deena admired the ring, showing it to Jack. Then she took it off and handed it back to the saleswoman.

"Thank you," Jack hurried to follow as Deena turned and walked out of the store.

She had to catch her breath. She wanted every ring, bracelet, necklace, and earring set in the place. Wow. She hadn't expected to fall in love with jewelry at her age.

"I have a feeling this wasn't a good idea." She opened the car.

"Why not?"

"I could really learn to like that stuff."

"All of it? Or just the rubies?"

"All of it."

She got into the car. Jack opened his door, but instead of getting in, he lowered his face to look at her and said, "I think I'll stay downtown for awhile. You go on ahead."

Now Deena was really confused. Could this mean what she thought it did? Was Jack going to go back in that store and buy her a ruby ring and bring it to her condo and ask her to marry him? Or was she spinning dreams again?

"Okay."

He shut the door and stood on the pavement in front of the pet shop, waving good-bye.

Chapter Thirty-Seven

An hour later, Deena had taken down her hair and combed it out. She'd folded the dress to take to the cleaners and put on a pair of shorts. She walked around the condo, picking up notebooks and candles and her Kindle and stashing things neatly away.

She was waiting for Jack, and part of her was angry with herself for getting her hopes up. But what else could it be? Her phone beeped with a text.

"Meet me at the house," Jack wrote.

She called him. "What house?"

"Your house."

"Why?"

"It's a surprise." From the gleeful tone of Jack's voice, she could tell he thought he'd really put one over on her. But where Jack was concerned, she had learned to not get her hopes up too high. She could be reading this all wrong, but she didn't think so.

Ten minutes later, she pulled up at the half-constructed home on Shakespeare Street. The sad little garage, now construction crew's headquarters, was locked up tight. They didn't work on Sundays.

Jack's car was in the driveway, and he was out back by the rose bushes that had somehow come through the fire without trauma. They bloomed furiously, fat red and pink flowers that felt like velvet when Deena touched one of the petals.

"Your roses." Deena remembered when he'd planted them.

"I bought them for you."

"I remember." He was still in his suit. She checked his pockets for a tell-tale bulge, but before she could find any hint of a ring box, he was down on one knee.

The ring appeared in his hand, she didn't know where from because her eyes had flooded with tears.

"Deena, I love you. I want to marry you and start a family. I want to build a life together, right now. Please say you'll be my wife."

She couldn't speak, so she nodded yes. He took her hands and put the ring she had chosen on her finger. The right hand. "The woman at the store said you wear it on this hand until we're married."

He stood up again, brushing off his proposal knee. "Ring. House. Marriage. Children. That's the order." He was rushing the words, but he wanted to get them all out and all right. "If that's okay with you. It's just a rough outline. Not written in stone. I'm flexible."

"Since when?" She smiled to take away the sting from her words.

"Okay, so I'm not always Mr. Take It As It Comes. But I have ideas, and if you like them we can work on the order together. Also I should have more input on paint colors."

Instead of saying anything, she kissed him. He tasted like chocolate. Just like Jack.

A word about the author...

In her twenty-year career as an English teacher, Cynthia Harrison published a non-fiction title used in the popular creative writing courses she teaches. She has published more than a hundred reviews, articles, and short fiction in print journals, including *Romantic Times*, *Publishers Weekly*, and *Woman's World*.

The Paris Notebook is her first novel with The Wild Rose Press, Inc. and she has been posting about the path to publication at www.cynthiaharrison.com since 2002. Read her "Blog Behind the Book" for *The Paris Notebook* there.

Cindy loves to hear from readers. Email her anytime at:

cindy@cynthiaharrison.com